I0647167

The Trees of Medley Gardens

Ranjit Lal has written over thirty books for both adults and children. Some of his books include *The Crow Chronicles, The Life and Times of Altu-Faltu, Bossman and the Kala Shaitan, Birds from my Window.* He has been a winner of the Crossword Best Children's Book Award for *Faces in the Water* and *Our Nana was a Nutcase.*

The Trees of Medley Gardens

RANJIT LAL

RED TURTLE
RUPA

Published in Red Turtle by
Rupa Publications India Pvt. Ltd. 2017
7/16, Ansari Road, Daryaganj
New Delhi 110002

Sales Centres:

Allahabad Bengaluru Chennai
Hyderabad Jaipur Kathmandu
Kolkata Mumbai

ISBN: 978-81-291-XXXX-X

First impression 2017

10 9 8 7 6 5 4 3 2 1

For my mother's friend, Shirin Kamaljit Singh, who loves and nurtures every green plant, and my doctor Sudhir Oswal who opened my eyes to trees.

1

'Vish, sweetheart, do me a favour, just go and check where is your crazy little sister.'

I had just entered the kitchen of our brand new farmhouse, where Mom was busy putting cups and saucers and other kitchen stuff on the shelves, helped by Amma.

'Mom, Tadpole must be somewhere around!' I opened the fridge and eyed a bowl full of condensed milk and looked around for a spoon.

'Get your head out of the fridge, Vish, and go find her! I yelled at her some time back and she just took off with the dogs.'

'What did she do this time?' I grinned.

'She was painting a forest on the walls of her bedroom, just imagine, she made such a mess,' Mom sounded exasperated. 'Now go look for her and tell her she has to drink her milk.'

Hah! Moms! As if Tadpole would come running for that. By the way, I'm Vishwajit, nearly sixteen years old and a pretty serious (but not geeky and I don't wear glasses), disciplined and responsible sort of guy. I wear my hair short and neat and have (according to Mom) lovely laughter lines crinkling up my face. Also dark eyes, straight ('noble') nose and slightly jug ears. I'm of average height for my age and don't work out in gyms (ever since one of the machines suddenly went berserk and nearly yanked off my legs) in spite of which I have seen girls looking at my shoulders and arms and abs during PE and swimming class at school. I don't do drugs, can't smoke because I start coughing and have only sipped beer occasionally. So pretty boring, you might say, but that's your problem. As for girls, well more about that later. I love the outdoors and hiking and trekking and also sitting in front of a computer having my mind zapped! Academically, I'm amongst the top five in class. Mom keeps saying that I have to set an 'example' for Tadpole to follow, because 'you know she worships the ground you step on'—though sometimes I think she just says that to flatter me and so that I don't go off the rails. All in all, I am a pretty sorted sort of guy, I would think.

Tadpole's my kid sister; she's eleven, pretends to be very solemn (like I am) and innocent, with her neatly cut bangs and bug eyes, but boy does she have a sharp little tongue in that head of hers. And yes, she's a little wacko—you'll see. Her real name is Sameeha, but everyone calls her Tadpole on account of her once emptying a jam jar full of tadpoles into her bath. (Somehow we found them swimming in our glasses of water at dinner time too—she said she was keeping them there 'for a little while only'!)

Anyway, we've just shifted into this brand new farmhouse, and we are surrounded by Wild West-like country—they call such places the boondocks, I believe. You have to get off the main road, bump down a semi-kuchha track for thirty-five minutes and then after all the swanky 'farmhouses' peter out, wind through these deep rocky ravines and small, silent lakes where Dad said quarrying had once taken place. Then you come to this culvert over another ravine crawling with ferocious thorn bushes and thorny trees that scratch at the car windows like fingernails on a blackboard. Finally you'll pass a long, long stone wall, with crenellations on the top like it was a fort, and with a big rusty black gate that says, 'Medley Gardens, Keep Out'. Beyond that is our brand new, completely circular farmhouse (called, naturally

'The Circuit House'—that's Dad's sense of humour, haha!).

Dad and Mom always wanted to live in a farmhouse (in the boondocks) and when Dad's business (he's a computer geek) suddenly did very well and he made gazillions, he just sold it all to a big IT company and designed and built this place. Good for Dad and Mom maybe, but not so good for me and Tadpole: our nearest neighbours are eight kilometres away and we don't even know them. Mom and Dad keep saying that now we have plenty of space to run around in, but it's a bit silly running around all by yourself. They're now busy planning to put down vegetable patches and planting fruit trees (there are a few scraggly thorny trees in the compound already) and grow wheat and corn and dal and stuff—but all that will take ages and it's just too boring.

As for 'Medley Gardens' next door, Mom said (vaguely) that it was a summer palace or retreat for some Indian sultans or Brit burra-sahibs during the Raj days and probably even before that. No one lives there anymore. It's a long low two-storey building with two arms at either end and what Mom called, *chattris* on the roof—they do look like umbrellas. The building is made of sandstone (Mom says), and has a big portico and driveway, overlooking this large unkempt brown lawn full of marble statues of naked ladies with broken arms and legs. The garden is divided into quarters by paths bordered by what must have been flower beds at one time. Only a couple of large flower beds of roses near the portico seem to be looked after and tended.

At one end of the grounds—the northern end according to my compass—on a small hill, there's what looks like a pretty large and very dense forest, full of huge old trees and bushes. It looks like an interesting place to explore. A very old baba and his wife totter around the house and garden—Mom says they're the caretakers, though Amma says darkly they're probably ghosts (just to frighten Tadpole) who have lived here for hundreds of years. The old woman has just one brown tooth sticking out of her mouth.

To the south side of our farm is more boulder-strewn countryside full of thorny bushes and small trees that look like acacias. Craggy mountains rise further away; pretty desolate country, I tell you.

Well, I knew where Tadpole had probably gone with the dogs. Her bedroom (we have our own separate ones!) on the first floor overlooks the boundary wall of Medley Gardens and in the three days that we've been here, I have caught her staring at the place through my binoculars—and especially at the forest—several times.

'Okay, I'll get her!' I now said and set off. And then, at the front door, took a stout walking stick along just in case. I knew there was a small broken gate (to allow people through) alongside the big main gate of Medley Gardens, which was easy to get through. I was a little scared, because the sign said 'Keep Out'. These things never bothered Tadpole; sometimes she could be recklessly fearless. But then she had four dogs with her—Dufus and Dorky were massive German Shepherds and the other two (Genius and HighQ—again Dad's sense of humour, I tell you!) pie dogs. All of them would die for Tadpole (and me I hoped).

Crisscrossed barbed wire blocked the broken small gate, but there were big enough gaps to get through. A path ran to the right and left and the main gravel driveway ran straight ahead towards the palace. I looked around warily and took the left hand path because it led towards the 'forest'. A whispery breeze blew through the casuarina trees along the wall sounding as if they were telling each other secrets about me, and I fixed my eye on the dusty path. Hah! Dog paw prints—plenty of them!

And small sneaker prints too! I was on the right track. But then they suddenly disappeared. I went back till they appeared again and then realized that Tadpole and the dogs had cut across to the east. I stepped off the path and headed that way. To my left, some distance away at the base of the hill, was a huge tree with glittering leaves—I think a peepal—and just beyond that slightly to its right on top of the hillock, what I first thought was a small forest. Then I realized it was the most gigantic banyan tree I had ever seen. It probably covered half the size of a football field and was supported by these massive prop-roots like pillars of a flyover. Straight ahead of me, shrouded by reeds and tall, feathery grasses was a large pond or small lake. It felt a bit eerie, as the lake lay under a shawl of silvery-blue mist, because it was now early evening in November. There was a small island in the middle of the lake out of which sprouted a group of palm trees, surrounded by thorny bushes. Then a movement caught my eye near the massive banyan tree. I climbed up on a large tussock. I couldn't believe my eyes!

Standing in front of the banyan tree's 'forest', calf-deep in mud, was Tadpole, her arms extended on either side of her. She was looking at the tree, her jaw sticking out. Her sneakers were next to her, the socks neatly tucked into them. The four dogs were lying quietly around her. I think Dufus had just got up and waved his big tail around, which was the movement I had noticed.

'Tadpole, what the heck are you doing?' I yelled, rushing up to her. The four dogs leapt up and raced towards me, barking joyfully. Tadpole started and nearly fell over but then regained her balance and turned her head around as much as she could.

'None of your business, go home!'

'Well you have to come home, Mom's calling you!'

'Don't want to come!'

'Okay, I'll fetch her then.'

She turned and I saw she had been crying. 'No, Bhaiyya please...' She gulped and pointed towards the huge banyan tree.

'I had a fight with him! He's a bully!'

'You had a fight with a *tree*?'

'Uh-huh.'

I rolled my eyes. 'So what happened?'

'I was mad at Mom because she yelled at me for painting, so I came here and kicked his legs.'

'Legs? Whose legs?'

'His. He has so many—he's so big and old he needs at least a hundred legs to stand on otherwise he'd fall down.'

'Oh you mean the prop-roots.' The tree certainly had several trunk-like prop-roots.

'Whatever. Well I kicked one, or maybe two or three...'

'So?'

'So he said "Cut it out, go pick on something your own size. Like those evil Oleanders!"'

'So then?'

'I kicked him again and said, "All you do is to stand in one place with your feet in the mud all the time—hah! What do you know?" And then he said, "Well look at me now: 30 metres tall, and can shade 2,500 people, let's see you do that and...did you know one of my ancestors provided shade for Alexander the Great and his famous horse Bucephalus and his army of 7000 men? And do you know who my father was? The famous Jogi Mahal banyan tree in Ranthambore National Park; he's the second-largest tree in India and over 600 years old, so there! My grandmother is the great Begum Rajmahal Banyan in Rajbagh National Park and is nearly 700 years old! Match that! And by the way, I'm the National Tree of India so show some respect, little girl! Jai Hind!"'

I nodded. 'Sure, sure, anyway Tadpole you had better come home now!'

She didn't budge and just went on (once she starts talking...) 'So I said, "Big deal, you still stay in one place with all your hundreds of feet in the mud and do nothing except talk!"'

'"Okay," he said, "So you try it and see what happens!"'

Oh-oh—the penny dropped now. 'So you buried your feet and legs in the mud and put out your arms hoping to become like a tree?' I could barely stifle my snort of laughter.

'Bhaiyya, you're making fun of me. I'll tell Mom!'

'And you're talking to trees! Any leaves or roots sprouted as yet?' I walked up to her and examined her carefully. 'Um...just some soil behind the ears but no...maybe if you drink your milk. Now let's go, Tadpole!'

'Go easy on her beta! And Baby, you'd better go with him. You can stand here forever and nothing will happen. I'm sorry if I upset you sweetie—didn't mean to! I'm just a little tetchy these days, can happen when you're 250 years old...' The voice was gruff but sympathetic.

'Who said that?'

Tadpole looked at me triumphantly. 'He did,' she said, pointing towards the banyan tree. And now the breeze whispering through the leaves tinkled with the high-pitched, silvery voices of giggly girls. 'Oh yes he did, darling!'

'Oh hell, Amma was right, this place is haunted, let's get out!' I grabbed Tadpole and yanked her out of her mud-hole. 'Come on, let's get out of here!'

'Hey, hey, easy does it beta! Didn't mean to scare you. By the way, I'm Ustad Big Ban and those lovely ladies are the Princesses

Ficki, Bo and Peepli. So pleased to meet you, children!'

'Wha…what?'

I got a grip on myself and started walking around the huge tree, peering through the trunks and looking up into the branches in case any smart aleck was hiding up there. There wasn't anyone. You could hardly see the main tree trunk it was so thickly surrounded by satellite roots that had embedded themselves in the ground around it; some of them even grew horizontally so you could actually pass under them like under an arch. But I saw no one and even the dogs weren't behaving as if there were strangers around.

Then a chorus of girls spoke tartly from a little distance away, their voices blowing over from where a copse of Neem trees stood. 'Children, dears, don't go near those monsters; they'll twine their roots around your throat and crrrck or insert them into your ears and nose and slurp up all your brains and then call themselves the trees of knowledge! They're anaconda trees! Stranglers!'

'Don't take any notice of them,' the gruff voice—well 'Big Ban'—said. 'A bird has to drop our seeds on your head and then if you wait and wait and if you shampoo every day…no chance, nothing will sprout.' He chuckled. 'But with some of these other guys—they never wash—so our seeds stick, put down roots and then…ah… then we take them to our bosom and embrace them. And they complain!'

'Bhaiyya, did you hear him? He said bosom!'

'Okay, okay, some other time, come on Tads let's go!' Was the fellow really about to lasso us with his dangling aerial roots or something?

'Do tell your dogs not to raise their legs against our trunks. It's very rude!'

'Guys, come on!' I whistled to the dogs. 'Sorry, but it's a

canine thing.' (I could have said, 'doggie' but wanted to make an impression!)

What was the matter with me? Now *I* was talking to a tree and worse, wanting to impress it!

'Bye, come again soon! You must meet everyone here and we'll show you things and tell you stories and have a good time! We know plenty; we've been here a long time.'

'With our feet in the mud...haha!' That was 'Princess Ficki'.

'Sorry, and don't mind those hypochondriac Neems,' Princess Bo added, 'They're always whining!'

'Bye kids, take care!' Princess Peepli fluttered her heart-shaped leaves at us.

It seemed like the whole forest was talking and waving to us.

'Yeah, yeah, sure! Thanks! Bye!'

I closely questioned Tadpole about the incident later that night.

'So for how long have you been...er...talking to those trees?' I asked her.

She shrugged. 'Well today was the first time, but we sort of fought. But they'd been waving to me since the day we got here—you know, asking me to come over.'

'Was that what you were painting?'

'Uh-uh, but Mom got mad.'

'Of course she would. The house is brand new and freshly painted. Did you get scared when that banyan fellow first spoke to you?'

She looked at me with wide eyes. 'Scared? No, why? Even the dogs weren't scared.'

'Because trees don't speak...they don't talk!'

'Well these do. You heard them and you spoke to them, too!'

'There must be some ventriloquist hiding nearby. Whatever,

we have to unravel the mystery.' Again, she only shrugged.

I grinned. 'So you seriously thought you could become a tree by putting your feet in the mud and sticking out your arms?'

'Well, if they can... My arms were my branches and my fingers were leaves. But my feet and toes got so cold and icky!'

She looked at me. 'Vish bhaiyya, can we go there again tomorrow and make friends properly? You know, maybe we can take them something—especially that Big Ban fellow who I kicked, just to make up. What do trees like?'

'Mud and manure I guess,' I said grinning. 'It'll be difficult to gift wrap those!'

'We'll find some *gobar* and take it for him.'

'You do it, you kicked him!'

2

The next day was Saturday and Mom and Dad had to drive off to some nursery to buy plants. Tadpole's eyes gleamed.

'Bhaiyya, we can go and make friends with those trees some more and talk to them!'

I was already wondering if that had really happened at all or was it all part of my (and Tadpole's very fertile) imagination. Peculiar things happened to you in the boondocks—everyone knew that.

'Okay, we'll go.' Whatever, it would be interesting to explore the place.

Of course we took the dogs—they were our SPG cover. No one dared come close to us when they saw Dufus and Dorky though I think the other two were more ferocious and protective of us.

We snuck through the gate easily and approached the trees.

'Good morning sweetie, good morning beta!' The big old Banyan, or Big Ban, sounded less grumpy this morning. 'It's a lovely morning, isn't it? What brings you to this sacred grove this morning? How may I be of service to you? What wish of yours may I fulfil? I am the wish-fulfilling tree after all.'

He was right about it being a lovely morning; it was sunny and cool and breezy.

'You're a wish-fulfilling tree?' Tadpole perked up. 'I have a wish. Do my homework for me!'

'Don't waste your wishes on silly things like homework! What about wanting to meet a handsome prince? Most little girls would wish that.'

'Ugh!' Tadpole rolled her eyes. 'Okay, then how about showing me the question paper of the arithmetic test we have on Monday?'

Big Ban's leaves shivered. Was he laughing?

'You want to bury your legs in the mud and stick out your arms to see what happens again?'

'Bhai-jaan, stop teasing her!' the Peepal Princesses chimed simultaneously.

Tadpole grinned. 'Actually no,' she said sweetly, 'you see, if I do I might get stuck in one place all my life like you and I don't want that.'

'She got you, Bhai-jaan!'

'Smart kid!'

'Touché!'

Then one of the princesses—I think it was Princess Bo— whispered in my ear. 'Beta, you know he'd love it if you call him Ustadji…'

'Ustadji?'

'Yes, on account of him being wish-fulfilling and the tree of knowledge and all that.'

'Oh.' Man, how do you address a tree as Ustad?

Sweet enticing voices wafted over from the lake. 'Come here Baby, look at our lovely yellow flowers, like trumpets they are, you can suck them for nectar, something so sweet you've never tasted before! And look at our shiny green apples lying all over the ground… Do bite into one darling…'

'Hsst! Don't you dare tempt them, you evil witches!' The Peepal Princesses hissed. 'Don't take any notice of them darling—

they just like giving people heart attacks. They're the notorious Oleander Siblings.'

What was going on? Tadpole didn't seem bothered.

'So Mr Big Ban, what are you going to do today?' she asked innocently. 'Visiting friends and relatives? Or going shopping? You know there are some cool new malls on the main road.' I was supposed to call him 'Ustadji' and the kid was cheekily pulling his leg, legs, roots...whatever!

Big Ban Ustadji made a creaking sound. 'I'm a little stiff this morning, so I don't think I'll really be going to any place. Besides I make and cook my own food...don't really need to go shopping.'

'How boring! But here, see what we got for you! Fresh *gobar*!'

Tadpole opened the biscuit tin she had filled with dung early that morning, and tied up with a red hair ribbon. 'This is for you, because we were...rude to you yesterday.'

'Thank you, sweetheart. Just spread it around those strapping young prop-roots there—they're always hungry and need the nourishment! Ah...yes, so sweet and full of natural goodness— they're already feeling stronger.'

'Dorky, Dufus and you other two get your faces out of that— it's not for you!' I shooed the dogs away; they had stuffed their faces into the dung. 'Sorry but they like it too,' I said apologetically.

'All sensible creatures do. Would you like to partake of a mouthful?'

'No...no thanks...'

'It's delicious! Seems genuinely organic.'

'Did you buy it at the mall or supermarket darling?' Princess Ficki asked. 'Was it on sale? Is it imported?'

'Or did you get it from one of those organic, health-food boutique shops? Is it designer dung?' Princess Peepli chimed in. 'Must have cost a bomb!'

'No, we... er...picked it up from the road outside the farmhouse. Some buffaloes had just passed by, so it's very fresh.'

I had serious matters to talk about. I cleared my throat. 'Mr Ban—er Ustadji, how is it that er...we can talk...I mean it's not usual. Trees normally don't talk.'

'Ah but we do!' I think nearly all the trees around us spoke together and I looked around taken aback. They went on: 'We can't help it if most of you don't know how to listen. We're talking all the time.'

'Of course some of us are *complaining* all the time and think they are talking!' That again from one of the Peepal Princesses and I heard a sniff of outrage from the Neems' copse.

'Well beta, we do communicate—it's a matter of wavelength I think. If you can pick it up then you can hear us. We, alas, hear you all the time and boy does your species make a lot of noise and talk nonsense all the time!'

'Human beings are the most intelligent species in the world so we have a lot to talk about.'

'Intelligent? Mahashay ji, really! Do you believe that? Did you know that the vast majority of literate Americans said that they would shoot a *Homo sapiens* if it walked through their front door? And most people think that Acetyl salicylic acid is a psychedelic drug that can get you jailed for life if you consumed or sold it?'

'I'm sure that drug is a bad substance!'

'Exactly my point! By the way Acetyl salicylic acid is aspirin, which incidentally comes from the willow tree.'

'Oh,' I said mortified. 'Ustadji you said something about a "sacred grove". What did you mean by that?'

'Ah, yes, you see this whole area around the lake? It forms a sacred grove—no one is allowed to pick our branches or leaves or anything from here. It's been forbidden for hundreds of years and the Babaji makes sure the custom is obeyed. There's a large patch of forest behind the palace, which is not sacred and from where he allows villagers to pick up twigs and leaves and even lop branches. But enough of this: I think you need to meet some of the rest of us here in Medley Gardens. Mithoorani, where are you?'

A large green parakeet with maroon shoulder patches poked its head out of a hole in one of Big Ban's trunks.

'What is it, Ustadji?' she asked irritably. 'It's Saturday morning!'

'Be a pet and show these sweet children around the garden. Introduce them to all the others. They're new out here!'

'Do I have to?'

'They've only just moved in next door and are sweet; they might bring sunflower seeds for you next time. Show them around, will you?'

'Oh, okay!'

Tadpole's eyes widened happily. 'Come and sit on my shoulder,' she invited.

'Oh sure! The things I have to do!' The parakeet whirred down on to Tadpole's shoulder and affectionately nuzzled her ear. 'You big baby, you!' she said in a deep husky voice, 'But you better get those sunflower seeds next time.'

Tadpole's eyes shone.

'Let's go!' she said gaily, 'which way?'

By now, several other birds had flown up—mynas and a group of untidy looking babblers that were passing what sounded like very rude comments, and a couple of hoodlum looking crows (I put my mobile deep into my pocket), and some bulbuls. They fluttered around us excitedly as the parakeet indicated that we start walking eastwards.

'We'll do a *parikrama* of the lake, and I'll introduce you to some of the trees there. You can't possibly meet everyone and anyway you'll forget their names,' she said.

'Wow, this is like being a VIP!' Tadpole said, looking at all the birds fluttering around. Some squirrels had come down from the trees too, and were scooting up and down excitedly much to the joy of the dogs.

'Well, you've met Princess Peepli,' Mithoorani said, indicating the Peepal tree immediately to Big Ban's left, 'and the other two, Princess Bo and Ficki—on the other side. Beyond her are the DDT Dozen.' I looked ahead where a dozen lovely Neem trees stood, lush and green. They were enormous.

'How long have they been here for?' I asked and went red, realizing I was now talking to a parakeet. Tadpole beamed.

'Um...ten...years...'

'My dear, you do flatter us but we've been here more than eighty years, in the time of your grandparents.' That was one of the Neems.

'We've been disinfecting, fumigating, pest-controlling and medicating this place ever since.'

'Which is why we call them the DDT Dozen!' the parakeet chuckled and nibbled Tadpole's ear.

'We're not DDT, thank you very much!' the Neem trees shrilled together. 'How dare you insult us? We're high class organic pharmaceutical trees and human beings are fighting over us!'

'Human beings will start a world war over cockroach poop,' Mithoorani responded tartly. 'So it's no big deal!'

'Don't worry, I think you're nice and beautiful pharma-whatever it is,' Tadpole said. 'I use you as toothpaste and the dentist says my teeth are very white and straight and strong!'

The Neem trees really were huge and had lovely feathery leaves arranged in circular whorls that seemed to swirl around in the breeze.

A myna flew down to Tadpole's other shoulder and ruffled his crest Mohawk style.

'Yo Chicklet, the name's Gingianus! You're a cutie! Call me Gingi!'

'Yeah that means brown bottom!' Mithoorani cackled. 'And he thinks he's going places!'

'Now let me tell you about this place! These Neem dames, good when you're sick or something weird is eating your innards or there are too many mosquitoes or you have bad breath and have to kiss someone. But beyond them are the luscious Mangoes—see that dense dark copse up ahead? Scores of Mango trees, producing scores of mangoes each: how many mangoes will that be?'

'I didn't come here to do Arithmetic!' Tadpole told him tartly.

'Gotcha! Scores and scores and scores of mangoes, of course!'

We walked beyond the Neems past some thorny scrub bushes, towards the copse of Mango trees. They were short and stocky and dense and their shade was dark and just a little too cool at this time of the year. But they were invitingly climbable. In summer they would be the perfect retreat.

'Oh no young man, don't even think of it!'

'Eh? What?'

'You're all the same. Come April-May and you aim catapults at us and then later swarm all over us like a mob of monkeys.'

'Yes,' Mithoorani said dolefully. 'Sometimes little boys can be very destructive.'

'Look who's talking!' Gingianus grinned. He rolled his eyes wildly and his little crest stood up absurdly. 'See what happens in February! She'll call all her appalling relatives from miles around— five hundred of them or more—and they descend on those poor things and strip their flowers. And then when the mangoes somehow manage to emerge in May, what a racket they make!'

'And worse, they don't even eat the mangoes properly,' one of the trees said, with a sob in her voice. 'A peck here, a bite there, discard this, drop that...disgusting! Like they're at this free-for-all, eat-all-you can buffet instead of at the altar of fine dining. People around the world are starving for lack of good mangoes and they go and waste...'

'You should always finish what's on your plate,' Tadpole told Mithoorani severely. 'It's bad to waste.'

'Oh no, we don't waste sweetie, we just taste so others can have a go if we approve. If it's good we let them know. Taste not waste not taste not waste not, that's our motto!'

'Oh god, now she'll go on for the rest of the morning. Come on, let's move ahead.'

I still had to pinch myself from time to time to believe this was all actually happening. We were being shown around, and introduced to trees by a parakeet and a myna that were perched on my sister's shoulders. The dogs seemed completely happy and fine with the situation.

Then I stiffened. On the breeze I distinctly heard an evil whispery, feathery chanting...

'Oooohhhhh, and we're the evil Julifloraa and we're gonna snag yaa! Oh, we're the evil Julifloraa and we're gonna stab yaa! Oh we're the evil Julifloraa and we're coming to grab yaa... Oooohhhhh!'

Cold prickles of sweat trickled down my spine and I glanced at Tadpole. She'd gone pale suddenly and clutched my hand.

'Bhaiyya,' she said plaintively, 'do you hear them?'

I nodded.

'Hey you stupid Julies, cut that out!' Ginganus flew up and squawked loudly. 'Is that any way to welcome guests?' He landed back on Tadpole's shoulder. 'Baby, watch where you put your feet—you see these little brutes here—hardly months old and armed to the teeth.'

We were walking through a little patch full of half-bush, half-tree like foliage with feathery leaves and fearsome spiked thorns sticking out perpendicularly from their branches. They were growing so densely we had to almost bash our way through them to get ahead.

'Hey, I've seen these guys before,' I said, 'the countryside outside is full of them!'

'Foreigners!' snorted Gingianus, 'Colonials from South America!'

'Aliens!' Mithoorani added darkly. She rolled her eyes. 'But what to do—their seeds taste divine!'

'Botanists call them *Prosopis juliflora*. We like to call them Julie Jerks!'

'A.k.a vilayati keekar!'

'Everyone thinks they're Acacias and they invade every place they can...'

'They've taken over nearly the whole of Delhi and the Ridge.'

'And have been trying to creep into Medley Gardens forever.'

'But but...ouch!' I'd stepped on a twig and felt the spike go right through my shoe into my heel.

'You there, behave or I'll call the gang and we'll strip all your seeds!' Mithoorani yelled at the saplings as I took off my shoe and stared at the two inch thorn sticking out of its sole.

'How dare you leave your barbs lying around carelessly for anyone to step on?' Gingi was really furious.

'So what are you going to do about it?' the Julies jeered, and added sweetly, Sorry, until the next time...but do check where you plant those huge feet of yours.'

I looked balefully at the bead of blood welling out of my

heel. Tadpole gripped my hand.

'Your shoe got a puncture!' she pointed out.

'And so did my heel! Come on Tads, let's get out of here.'

'Good idea!' both Mithoorani and Gingianus chimed. 'Ask Ustad about them—he knows everything about them.'

We left the thorny patch and went south. Just ahead were six ramrod straight trees, armed with fearsome pointed conical studs on their trunks and outspreading branches. Right behind them was perhaps the tallest tree in Medley Gardens. It towered above everything else. Its trunk was buttressed and its branches spread widely in the biggest embrace you'd ever seen. Occasionally a big leaf would drop lazily. From a hollow some way up its main trunk, a pair of small brown owls peered at us out of golden eyes and bobbed their heads.

'Be respectful,' Mithoorani said her voice hushed. 'That's His Royal Highness Semal Raja, Kapok Maharaj, Shahenshah Shalmali Shamboji Cebia the VIIIth—the King of the Forest!'

'He throws the most fabulous party every March-April!' Gingianus rolled his eyes. 'Man-oh-man every bird who's any bird is here. Not to mention animals and insects...and gatecrashers! There is unlimited food and drink!'

Mithoorani lowered her voice even more. 'But such a tragedy too...at that time of celebration and song and dance and eating and drinking and unbridled joy and carnival...' she rolled her eyes and made a throat cutting gesture with her claws. 'Crrrk!'

'Are those other trees his bodyguards?' Tadpole asked.

'No, Semal Raja doesn't need bodyguards. Those other fellows are his crown princes—they're still very young so need to be protected, that's why they're wearing those studs.' She lowered her voice to a whisper: 'You never heard this from me but they're all adopted. They're not his real sons, they were planted here. His real children live far, faraway.'

I stared mesmerized at the armoured tree trunks; they were like the hide of some ancient dinosaur. Gingianus chuckled.

'If any monkey tries slithering down them he'll end up with a cheese-grater bottom!'

'We stared at the magnificent tree.

'What tragedy?' I asked curiously. 'You just mentioned a tragedy...'

'You'd better ask Ustadji,' Mithoorani said. 'He'll tell you.'

'Do we have to curtsey before him?' Tadpole asked, gazing upwards in awe. 'He's so awesome!'

I shook my head. 'We bow before no one, Tadpole. We're human beings.'

'Good morning, children!' the Semal said in a rich deep voice. 'I'm His Royal Highness and Ultimate Exalted Majesty Raja Bombaxji Kapok Maharaj, Shahenshah Shalmali Shambolji Cebia the VIIIth!' That was followed by a throaty chuckle. 'But you can call me RSC!'

'That's for Red Silk Cotton,' Mithoorani whispered knowingly.

'You mean he wears red silk cotton underpants?' Tadpole asked her eyes huge.

'Tadpole, shh!'

'Sorry kids, I'm a bit busy in this season, so can't entertain you just yet.'

'Sire, you have begun preparing for the Grand Open House Opera already?' Gingianus asked respectfully, bobbing his head several times.

'Yes Gingi—I have to move stuff from the leaves into storage, so the leaves can drop and then gear up for the preparations for March-April. By the way, kids, you're cordially invited to Raja Bombaxji Kapok Maharaj, Shahenshah Shalmali Shambolji Cebia the VIIIth's Grand Annual Open House Opera! From around the end of March to the middle of April! RSVP! Any day and everyday!'

'We'd be glad to attend,' I said, not realizing I'd just accepted an invitation to what sounded suspiciously like a wild party thrown by a tree.

'Is it fancy dress?' Tadpole asked, her eyes big.

'You can come dressed or undressed any way you want!'

His 'princes', the Six Stalwarts as I called them in my mind, just stood stiffly to attention as we left.

We walked westwards now, to south of the lake and passed a column of tall silver-barked trees with silvery-green leaves. Even I knew what they were.

'Eucalyptus, right?' I asked Mithoorani.

'More firangs like those vilayati keekar!' Gingianus snorted. 'They think they're tall and fair and handsome but do they have a drinking problem or what! All they do is drink up all the water.'

'Hiya there kiddos! Don't take any notice of 'em whiners. But do we miss the cockatoos and koalas! Good dai maites!'

'The fools think they're still in Australia,' Mihtoorani snorted.

'They smell nice,' Tadpole said, crushing a fallen leaf. 'Like those cough lozenges Mama gave us.'

'And who are these guys?' I asked as we passed by a bunch of medium-sized trees with delicate feathery leaves.

'They're the El Jacos, jacarandas. You hardly notice them for most of the year till they flower in March and April. Lovely lilac coloured bell-shaped blossoms they have. And they scatter them all over the ground. It looks very pretty.'

'Yes, and we have so much more class than those local Laburnum show-offs!' one of the nondescript trees suddenly said, making us jump.

'Over-dressed béhenjis!'

'Dripping with cheap costume jewelry.'

'Can you imagine, being called Aunty Amaltas!'

'So where are you from?' I asked.

'Brazil, South America, but we love it here too...'

Indignant tree voices wafted over from some distance ahead.

'Don't listen to them, they're just the Jealous Jacos!'

'That's what we call them—Jealous Jacos. They're jealous of our beauty!'

The tree voices went on: 'Kids, come here, sit down and listen. Imagine, it's May, it's blazing hot, you're in a frizzled up jungle, everything's brown and dusty and thorny, there's grit in your mouths and dust in your eyes, you turn a corner and what do you see? One of us in full bloom, golden tassels dripping from every last branch set against a piercing blue sky. You forget the heat and dust, the thirst and tiredness and the fact that you're lost probably forever and will soon be eaten by wolves and jackals— because you know you've glimpsed heaven! Us! Me!'

They certainly weren't looking terrific right now, so I shrugged.

'Sure, sure! Nice meeting you!'

We had by now more or less joined up with the entrance path—done a whole circle of the lake. I pointed to the wall.

'Casuarinas right?'

Gingi nodded. 'Right. They miss the beach and sea so much that they still make sounds like the surf when the breeze blows through them. There are a lot more trees in the patch of forest behind the palace but maybe we'll meet them another time.' Tadpole had slowed down and I knew she was tired, so I nodded.

'Come on Tads, we'll say bye to Ustadji and go home. Thanks

Mithoorani and Gingianus for showing us around and introducing us.'

We went back to Big Ban, who was waving his aerial roots genially to and fro in the breeze like a friendly elephant swinging its trunk.

'Thanks Ustadji, we met many interesting trees.'

'And Bhaiyya's foot got poked by a thorn,' Tadpole complained. 'Otherwise they were very friendly.'

'The Julies have broached the boundary wall at the northeast corner,' Gingianus reported to Ustadji. 'They've got saplings sprouting everywhere. The Mangoes are pretty worried.'

'And soon we're going to come swarming over this wall and take over Medley Gardens completely! It'll soon be a paradise of thorns.' The horrible whisper wafted over the wall like a chilling breeze.

'Don't mind them dears. They were brought over from Mexico—sometimes I despair of the human species; they do such asinine things.'

'Oh Ustadji you forget, we overran the biggest grasslands in Asia, so you think Medley Gardens will be a problem for us?'

'You're just thugs! You'll never take over Medley Gardens.'

And then, unexpectedly, the Neems piped up.

'Oh and now Ustadji is suddenly all saintly and good and calling other trees thugs.'

'What's their problem, Ustadji?' I asked Big Ban. 'Why are they always on your case?'

'No reason....well not anymore....a long, long time ago maybe....something might have happened...my oldest, innermost prop-roots may know, though they're so old they do tend to forget...but these Neems hold their grudges far too long.'

'Don't you listen to him, you come here and we'll tell you. Such a terrible tale too!'

Tadpole was staring up at Ustadji. She suddenly shook her head.

'I still don't understand. Don't you get bored just standing there with your feet in the mud your whole, entire life? I get bored just looking at you standing there doing nothing!'

'Baby, you come again and I'll tell you a story. You see, if it weren't for us, you wouldn't be you, the world wouldn't be the world as it is, you wouldn't be able to read or write or do arithmetic, or cure cancer or heart trouble or headaches, body-aches, kidney stones, liver failure...'

'Oh God, he's got started again!' Princess Bo groaned. 'Now he'll go on all morning! Baby you come to me and I'll tell you a proper story. How Eternal Wisdom was found in the shade of my very own ancestor and...'

'Baby, sweet nectar-filled flowers, glossy green apples, come and try them, come and try them...just one bite!' The breeze was blowing from the lake again, where the Oleanders were.

'Ah!' Gingianus snorted, 'sorry, we never formally introduced you to the Oleander Siblings. They're not even proper trees, but look green and slinky all the time. Their milk and the so-called apples are deadly. They gave a stupid buffalo a heart attack once. Just keep away from them! Even goats do!'

'Okay bye and thanks, we'll come again,' I took Tadpole's hand and we headed out. The dogs were playing the fool with some squirrels around Ustadji and the Peepal Princesses. They started following us as soon as they realized they'd been left alone.

That night before going to bed, Tadpole came into my room. I was playing some computer game (and losing) and looked up.

'What?'

'Bhaiyya, you know that Ustadji fellow said that if it wasn't for them we wouldn't be here and if they were to disappear so would we...'

'He was probably just showing off.'

'I know but...'

'Well we can go back tomorrow and ask him.' I grinned. 'I bet he wouldn't expect that! Let's see what fancy cock and bull story he makes up!'

'Bhaiyya, we're talking to *trees*! You do realize that!'

'Sure kid, no reason why we shouldn't talk to them like we talk to anyone else.'

'I guess!' she smiled. She reached up and kissed my cheek.

'Goodnight!'

'Night, Tads!'

She left and I went and stood at the window and looked towards Medley Gardens. I could see the tall phalanx of the eucalyptus trees glimmer silvery in the moonlight. To their right, stood HRH Shahenshah Bombaxji Kapok Maharaj Whatever the VIIIth towering into the night sky. And there on the hillock at the back I could see the dark brooding sprawl of Big Ban... Ustadji.

The Tree of Knowledge, he'd boasted he was. How much did he really know? Well, we'd find out wouldn't we? Tadpole was an expert at asking question after question till it felt like Chinese torture.

Then I stiffened. The window had been left open. A gentle whisper wafted through.

'*And we're coming to get yaa! We're coming to get yaa!*'

The Julies again...

I shut the window and went to bed.

3

'So how do you kids like it here?' Mom asked us at breakfast the next morning, which was Sunday. 'Not too lonely for you? Made any friends?' That was a silly question considering our nearest neighbours were eight kilometres away and we didn't know them anyway.

'A few,' Tadpole said, 'some of them are quite nice.'

Mom realized she'd made a boo-boo (I think they call it faux-pas in French.)

'Well yes, if you like you can call your school friends over, once we're a little more settled.' She looked at me and smiled. 'You could invite Zafia over, she'd love it I'm sure!' Zafia was a school friend I was rather keen on, and Mom knew her mother well.

'It's okay Mom, we're cool.'

Zafia was sure to flip if she knew we had been talking to trees.

Tadpole was at the window staring at Medley Gardens.

'What's up? You want to stand in the mud again?' I asked. She shook her head. 'No, but it's just so sad! They're standing there all the time! They go nowhere, they see nothing, but what's around them, they can't go to the malls or parks.'

'Well, they are the park, you could say...'

'You know what I mean! They must be bored out of their minds.'

'They don't seem to be. They're probably used to it. I mean if you've been in the same place for over 250 years, you won't want

27

to move. As Ustadji said, you'd probably be too stiff.'

'I'll take my picture books and computer and show them places and shops. You can take your laptop too. If they know what they're missing...'

'It won't be such a good idea if they all suddenly decide to up roots and see the world,' I grinned. 'Can you imagine the traffic jams they'll cause?'

'Yes, but it'll be fun...'

We went across to Medley Gardens again later that morning, with the dogs. They greeted the trees like old friends, barking and wagging their tails and needless to say, did raise their legs against the trunks.

'Cut it out you guys!' I yelled hotly.

'It's all right beta,' Ustadji said benignly, 'it's a canine thing.'

Tadpole was trying to worm herself through all the prop-roots, right into the middle of Ustadji. The roots were so thickly plaited they were virtually impenetrable.

'That's far enough, you'll get lost and stuck!' Ustadji suddenly said a little gruffly. 'Don't try to go any deeper.'

'I want to go right into the middle—where your main trunk is...'

'It's too dense, and that's where my oldest memories live. Besides I think Ms Fang is still in residence.'

'Ms Fang? Who's she?'

'A cobra. Rather quick-tempered.'

That got Tadpole out pretty fast, what with me pulling her out too.

The dogs started darting around the various outer trunks, barking and soon we had quite a game on, chasing them.

'That's better!' Ustadji said back in his benign mode.

'Your oldest memories live there? What do you mean by that?' I asked.

'Well, the prop-roots that grew first naturally have the longest and oldest memories—they have seen some history, I can tell you! The younger ones on the outside know less because they've been around for less time and frankly couldn't care less.'

'So every prop-root has its own memory?'

'You could say that. And then of course, there's the central processing unit which is what allows me to talk to you as a single tree in a single voice...'

'Oh wow!'

'So you must know so much,' Tadpole said. 'You're like a Google or Wikipedia tree.'

'The Tree of Knowledge, yes,' Ustadji admitted modestly.

At that moment, the Neems whispered malevolently. 'Do you want to know the *real* reason why Ustadji did not want you to go where his oldest memories are stored? Come sit with us, we'll tell you!'

But we were breathless and sat down instead in Ustadji's deep cool shade for a break. Tadpole took a deep breath. I held mine. Inquisitive question coming up, I knew it.

'Big Ban Ustadji, yesterday you said that if it wasn't for you we wouldn't be here and if you all were to disappear we would too. What did you mean by that? I mean, we're cutting you trees down all the time and nothing's happened to us. We're still here.'

'Seven billion strong,' I added smugly.

Ustadji's leaves fluttered.

'Ah let me tell you a story...'

'Oh God there he goes again.' That was Princess Bo. 'Blah-blah-blah...'

Tadpole made a face, caught hold of one of Ustadji's dangling roots and began swinging.

'Bhaiyya, come on—swing on that other one—we can be like Tarzan and Jane! It's fun.'

'Er…can I?' I asked Ustadji half-embarrassed. 'It doesn't hurt, does it? Like someone's pulling your hair or something?'

'Not at all, swing on as high as you can. Then try and climb up! After all that's how it all began.'

'What began?' Tadpole asked, her face red with pleasure as she whizzed back and forth. 'Whee, this is so cool!'

'How if it wasn't for us, you wouldn't exist as you do…'

'What do you mean?'

'Well millions and millions of years ago there were creatures that lived in and on us.'

'Monkeys?'

'Well, let's say very primitive monkeys. Anyway, to get around and escape from predators they needed to swing on our branches and jump from one branch or tree to another and for that they developed strong arms and hands and legs that could grip.'

'Like ours?'

'Yes, but more hairy I suppose. Anyway, but they also needed to be able to judge how far to jump, and which branch to aim for and so forth. For that, what do you think they needed?'

'Good eyes?'

'And what else?'

'I don't know…'

'Okay, see if you can let go of the root you're swinging from and catch hold of that other one dangling near you without touching the ground with your feet. Think you can do it?'

'Whee, you mean jump like a trapeze acrobat?'

'Yes.'

'Tadpole, be careful!'

She stuck her tongue out at me and looked at the root next to the one she was swinging on. At the top of her swing, she suddenly released her grip and flew towards the other one and grabbed at it. She caught it and clung to it and began swinging.

'I did it, I did it, I did it!' she yelled.

'You're nuts!'

'Well done! Well can you now tell me what else you used apart from your eyes?'

'My hands…'

'Of course, but who told your hands when to let go and when to grab the next root?'

'My brain!'

'Exactly! So millions of years ago as those monkeys or whatever swung around in the trees, their brains too grew in order to make them do daring things like that. So a sort of race began between the brains and the hands. It's like…'

'Like when you put more software into your computer so you can do more things with it?' I asked.

'Ah yes, sort of. Say the brains would tell the hands, "can you grip the branch and twirl upside down" and the hands would try and try and try and finally succeed and tell the brains "okay been there, done that, now what new challenge can you throw at us, hah!" and the brains would have to think and think and think and in doing so got bigger and bigger and cleverer and cleverer.'

'So then what happened?'

'So then the monkeys' brains grew big and they became very dexterous with their hands as both raced to get the better of each other.'

'So?'

'Well then the weather began changing. It got very dry.'

'You mean you had climate change back then too?'

'Yes. It became hotter and drier and we trees decided to migrate to cooler places.'

'How can trees migrate? You're stuck in the mud all your lives.'

'Well over a period of millions of years…it's like this…I can't maybe migrate, but my children sort of can. If they are born elsewhere where the weather is better they grow well. For example, if the weather got better in the north all the seeds that were put down in the north would live and all the other ones would maybe not. So as a group and family we'd be migrating northwards gradually.'

'In slow motion!' Tadpole intoned, with a giggle.

'Whatever! Anyway, then you "monkeys" were left stranded on the ground because the trees had gradually disappeared and you looked around for something to do. There were no trees to climb, only grasses and shrubs and bushes…but thanks to us, you had these wonderful, clever hands that could do anything and those big brains. You started standing up and walking on two legs: You could see better over the grasses and thickets that way too and keep a lookout for saber toothed tigers. Then your brains said, "better make these smart aleck hands do something useful now that they're not needed to climb trees", and you started making tools and other things with your now idle hands. You know, pigs and elephants are very clever too, but they don't have hands, so they can't do much with their cleverness. I mean a trunk is good but not as good as a hand.'

'But elephants can knock down trees.'

'Ungrateful, greedy wretches, aren't they? They just strip our bark, eat our leaves, break our branches and tip us over. We don't like them very much. Or giraffes, or cattle, or well you kids are okay maybe but your kind hasn't been very good to us either, especially after all we've done for you.'

'So you helped us get nimble hands and develop our brains… what else?'

'Fire and wood! Think of where you'd be without those.'

'What?'

'Yes, our wood was one of the best fuels—and renewable too! You still use it for cooking and heating and building. You built ships and houses out of wood—and still do. So you had warmth and shelter and delicious cooked food and could travel. If you hadn't built ships you would not have explored the world and discovered and conquered other countries and set up empires and become rich.'

'And Alexander and Bucephalus would have got all hot and bothered because they would not have found any shade to camp under,' Tadpole suddenly piped up.

'Exactly! And you made moulds out of wood, which you used to make metal objects with. I mean without us you would have been wriggling worms still! Besides, we make oxygen, not to mention clouds and rainfall.'

'Bhai-jaan you forgot to tell about us and paper and everything,' Princess Peepli suddenly piped up unexpectedly.

'Ah yes, you know paper is made out of wood?'

'Ustadji of course. I'm not that dumb!'

'And what do you use paper for?'

'Ustadji, stop teasing me! For reading and writing of course!'

'So if it hadn't been for us you wouldn't be able to read or write or have money.'

'Or have to go to school…'

'Baby, you wouldn't have any knowledge or education or Ph.D. degrees!'

'But just common sense?'

I warned you, my kid sister was a smarty pants.

'No books, no newspapers, no magazines...'

'But we have Kindles now, and everything's on the Net and there's TV 24×7!'

'But you wouldn't have had those if you hadn't had paper and wood in the first place!'

'But you still stay in one place all your life...'

'Maybe we do, but we have travelled in our time—when we were seeds! I journeyed far from my mother's home in Bargadpur village, travelling by Hornbill Airways. But seeds of other trees can fly by themselves—we invented gliders and helicopters and parachutes much before you could even talk properly let alone think. Some of us sailed the oceans and seas, some of us use couriers like animals and humans to take our seeds around. So we've done our travelling! Besides, you should be thankful that we can't travel as full grown trees! Can you imagine what might happen if we suddenly started marching around or flying? Just imagine a flying banyan tree and the havoc it would cause with Air Traffic Control!'

'Nah, but you can't!'

'Now let me ask you: do you like forests?'

Tadpole nodded. 'Yes, I do...we went to Corbett once and saw a tiger! And Papa says we might be going to Rajbagh soon!'

'Right, but why is a forest a forest?'

'Because it has tigers and elephants and leopards and monkeys and rhinos...'

'And?'

Tadpole stopped swinging. 'Okay, okay... I get it. Trees...'

'Correct. No trees, no forest, no forest, no wild animals or birds...'

A couple of big shabby grey birds with down-curved beaks suddenly flew up—they were rather like creatures you'd meet in

Jurassic park and squealed delightedly.

'Ustadji, have you got a new batch of figs ready for dispatch?'

'Sure…check out Sector 44, Pocket IV, Branches 23-29. Help yourselves dears. And do meet my new human friends….um… kids, these are Honey and Billy—they're grey hornbills and have a nest hole in Trunk 36, 3rd Floor. Honey and Billy, tell me how are my kids and grandkids doing?'

'All well!'

'You have kids and grandkids?' Tadpole was incredulous. So was I.

'All over Delhi, my dear and far beyond, in the forests of Bandhavgarh and Ranthambore and Corbett and Rajbagh. Honey and Billy and their friends eat our sweet figs and scatter the seeds far and wide.'

'And drop them on the heads of other trees,' the DDT Dozen suddenly chimed in bitterly. 'Let's not get into that right now,' Ustadji said hastily.

'He thinks he's the only one that's got kids. Our kids and relatives are famous too—so many of them line the roads of New Delhi, others are in Rashtrapati Bhavan—the President meets them everyday. Some say he cleans his teeth with our twigs!'

'You guys are so bitter that even flies and mosquitoes keep well away from you!'

'If we didn't, then this sweet little girl and her brother here would be covered with flies and mosquitoes and crawling with maggots and so would you, so there!'

'Don't mind them dear, they're always bickering,' Princess Bo suddenly said to Tadpole, who was looking a little flustered. 'You come here and climb into my lap…I'll fan your cheek with a little fresh breeze.'

'Hah—as if she's any better!' one of the Neems snorted. 'Some stupid bird dropped one of her seeds on one of the Palace's chattris and now the upstart has a grip on it, cracking apart the masonry. Give her a few years and she'll be sprawling all over the palace. Talk about a palace coup!'

I decided to change the topic. There was something I had been wanting to ask ever since Ustadji had said he was 250 years old. 'Er...Ustadji, what was it like when you were born?'

'I don't recall offhand much about the very early days. I'll have to tap my innermost prop-roots and query them, though they can be pretty unreliable and forgetful too. Wait a bit.'

We sat quietly for a while, waiting, while the Neems muttered away. Then Ustadji spoke again. 'Ah yes, one of the oldest folders has just opened—this takes me back all those years! Apparently there was nothing much here... It had been a barren rocky wasteland except for the lake, which was surrounded by high feathery grasses. The palace was there of course, along with its beautiful gardens. I faintly remember when I was a very young sapling, the whole area was being dug up and trees were planted for the sacred grove by the fakir-baba who lived here at the time. The Sultan who built the palace had close connections with the great Mogul no less and had accumulated a vast treasure. But he had to flee when the empire collapsed. There was a lot of turmoil and fighting. Some birds told us that soldiers who died were buried here. That is why the fakir-baba declared it to be a sacred grove—so no one would disturb the graves. I grew along with the other trees. I watched the Neems grow up as well as the mango orchard and have seen Kapok Maharaj grow from a mere skinny sapling. Several have died and been replaced to ensure the area is always green and forested. The Princesses were planted here to keep me company.'

Tadpole and I listened openmouthed, and tried to imagine what Medley Gardens might have looked like then.

'When were the Oleanders born?' Tadpole asked. 'And how did the Julies get here?'

'Oh, the Oleanders came much later, and the Julies just barged in. The birds say there is a legend connected to the lake: when the palace was virtually new, the Sultan fell in love with a beautiful Rajput princess. To express his love—and demonstrate his power and wealth, he covered the lake—which was much bigger than it is now—with 25,000 massive lily pads. These he heaped high with diamonds as big as pineapples, rubies the size of pomegranates, emeralds as large as langda mangoes, sapphires and pearls and gold sovereigns and set them afloat on the water. In the middle of this fabulous flotilla, he and the princess floated on their own lily pad as he wooed her in the moonlight, while minstrels played music on the lakeshore.'

'Oh wow! But what happened to the treasure? Did the lily pads sink under their weight?'

'No one knows,' Ustadji replied. 'That's why it became a legend. Apparently, the treasure just vanished—probably the sultan and his sons took it with them when they fled after the empire collapsed.'

'What happened then?'

'I hardly know myself! There were years and years of confusion and turmoil and famine. I had to send down roots very deep to reach water. The palace was overrun by several local chieftains who used it as a place of pleasure and retreat. They fought and killed each other. Then, around 160 years ago—I was a pretty substantial tree by then—the English goras took over the palace. They too used it as a palace of Pleasure. In the sultans' time it was called the Dilkhush Mahal but the goras changed that to "Medley Gardens". Every evening horsedrawn carriages used to draw up and the Englishmen with their lady friends used to walk here and take the air or ride out into the country on elephant back to hunt tigers and wild boar.'

'There were tigers and wild boar here?' Tadpole's eyes widened.

'Yes, even maybe just seventy-five years ago. And also many generations of cobras and hundreds of birds…as for insects, there have been millions.'

'Now he's behaving like he's the only tree in the world!' the DDT Didis snorted.

'Yes,' Princess Bo said in a strange voice. 'He's not telling you how terribly moody and irritable he was back then, before we were planted to give him company. Trees can get lonely too, you know.'

'What happened after the goras took over?'

'One of their leaders surveyed the place and then just took over the palace. He used it as a holiday home or weekend retreat and he renamed it "Medley Gardens". To his credit, he too didn't touch any of the trees in the sacred grove, so we all grew safely. He even let the forest behind the palace alone—he and his friends went hunting there. Then he went away and his son and his wife lived here for many years. But then they too left, and sold the palace to a clever soldier of fortune who had married a local woman and caused quite a scandal. They had two daughters who settled in Canada, which is why it's so neglected. But look at me, 250 years old, hale and hearty—don't you think I'm truly magnificent?'

'Here we go again!' chimed the Neems. 'Toot, toot! Ustadji needs a mirror! By the way our ancestors have also lived here for many, many years.'

'Oh, you Neems can't let it go, can you?' Princess Ficki snapped.

'Yeah, get over it!' Princess Bo said.

I'd heard enough for one morning. Besides I didn't want to get caught in between whatever quarrel the trees might have with each other.

'Come on Tadpole, let's say hi to the others and then go home.'

'See you guys,' Tadpole said, unfazed and took my hand.

We walked into the cool mango grove, watching our step as we weaved our way through the grasping Julies.

'Hello sweethearts…' they whispered in an eerie sort of way.

'Take no notice,' I told Tadpole, clutching her little hand. 'They're just trying to scare us.'

'I'm not scared.' And then we were in the dim cool shade of the Mangoes. With their low spreading branches they looked easy to climb and…well we couldn't resist it.

'Okay, don't have a cow, we promise not to pluck or pick anything,' I said, as I dusted my hands and hoisted myself up. Tadpole had already scuttled up like a monkey. The trees just murmured in the breeze so I guess it was okay. We sat side by side on a thick branch, not too high up. The dogs circled the tree, barked a few times and settled down.

'Second Folic Infantry Battalion, halt! Mark time!'

'What?' I looked around surprised, sure that our tree had said those words.

'Bhaiyya, look—those ants near your leg.'

I glanced down. Right next to my thigh a column of marching ants had halted, and I presumed were marking time.

'Company about turn! Hup two three four!' They turned around and off they went.

'They were red ants—they would have marched inside your shorts and…' Tadpole giggled. 'You better say thank you to the tree and to them.'

'Er…thanks,' I said. Marching columns of ants were known not to stop for anything.

There came a sudden squawking and a flock of parakeets swirled into the tree all shrieking excitedly.

'Take cover! Take cover! Western disturbance heading our way! ETA 25 minutes. Take cover, take cover!'

'What? ETA?'

'Estimated Time of Arrival!'

With a whirr, Mithroorani landed on Tadpole's shoulder and nibbled her ear affectionately. 'Hi baby, I missed you, but you better go home now. There's a storm on its way. A flock just got caught about 20 kilometres south of us—they had to dive down and take cover without warning. One or two of that flock are apparently missing. It's a big wind coming!'

It was a bit prickly—not hot, but uncomfortable nonetheless.

'Come on Tadpole, let's go.'

'But we haven't said hello to all the others.'

'We'll do that later. They're not going anywhere.'

She gave me a wry grin. 'Yeah you betcha!'

We scrambled down and set off homewards. Already the trees were rustling excitedly as sudden rushes of wind coursed though them. They seemed to be enjoying themselves. Dead leaves chased each other in whirling, mad circles. The Julies tried to ensnare us as usual—I think they were collaborating with the wind—which would buffet and shove us towards them. The sky was ivory-yellow and darkening with each passing moment. Heart-shaped leaves swirled down from the branches of the Peepul Princesses. One of the DDT Dozen creaked and groaned.

We reached home just as the storm hit. From the windows we watched the trees in Medley Gardens sway madly in the wind.

'I hope they'll be all right,' Tadpole said suddenly. 'Storms push trees over…'

'They're pretty strong,' I said, hoping it was true. 'They must have been through many storms in the past.'

'I guess.' She looked at her hands. 'Hands and brains, Ustadji said. They gave us hands and brains…how can we ever thank them for that?'

4

$\mathcal{T}$here was school the next day, so we couldn't go to Medley Gardens in the morning. Mom dropped us off at the bus-stop on the main road in the car. Several kids were dropped here by their parents and we all waited under a huge, shady tree, which both Tadpole and I just had to ignore (you can imagine what would happen if we tried talking to it in front of everyone). In the bus, Tadpole and I sat separately, with our own groups of friends. I'd given her strict orders not to tell any of her friends about our strange experiences at Medley Gardens—we would be thought of as crackpots and there would be no end to the teasing and ragging.

I glanced at Tadpole across the aisle and up ahead. She was looking quite thoughtful, which was a danger sign. Tadpole rarely kept her thoughts to herself. As we got off the bus she walked beside me.

'Bhaiyya, do you think the trees in the playground and sports-fields here will talk to us also?' she asked.

'Tadpole, whatever you do, don't start talking to them!' I hissed. 'The kids will think you're nuts and so will the teachers! You know what they're like.'

'Yes,' Tadpole said, 'like what Ustadji told us, we talk a lot of rubbish and hardly listen to any sense...'

'So keep quiet.'

'I'll try,' she said, gave me a small smile and ran off.

Our school compound had a lot of trees growing along its perimeter. Some were old some were very young and recently planted. I could (thanks to Medley Gardens) recognize neem, peepal and semul amongst them. There were others too, which I hadn't met and didn't know. There was one huge semul growing just outside the Principal's office. It soared up as high as the building. At lunch I went looking for Tadpole. I had a sneaking suspicion that she would be up to mischief. And I was right.

I asked her friends where she was. They said she had gone off to the bathroom ten minutes ago. That was rubbish. Tadpole hated the school toilets and wouldn't spend ten minutes there. I set off towards the trees along the boundary wall and then began walking alongside them, looking for her. And there alongside the rear wall, I found her. She was standing under a big old neem tree, looking up at it her mouth open in surprise.

'Hello dear, you must be Baby from Medley Gardens,' the old Neem suddenly said. Tadpole jumped and looked up at the tree and then around. I quickly dodged behind another tree.

'Um…hello, are you talking to me, please?' she asked cautiously. 'No, I'm Sameeha, but you can call me Tadpole.'

'Yes dear, I'm talking to you. You are from Medley Gardens, aren't you? All the trees there call you Baby, don't they?'

'Yes, I live next door to Medley Gardens. But how did you know I could…er…talk to trees?'

'Oh dear, news spreads pretty fast you know. You think those mynas and parakeets can keep their mouths shut for ten seconds? I think all the trees in Delhi and far beyond probably know that you can talk to us! Nothing to be ashamed of darling—except don't try and get too friendly with those snooty banyans and peepals.'

I walked up to Tadpole. She turned defensively, 'Bhaiyya, I

promise I didn't say anything—she just started talking to me, what can I do?'

'I know, I heard her! But you shouldn't have come here.'

She put her hands on her hips. 'Bhaiyya, you heard what she said? That by now probably all the trees in Delhi know that we can talk to them—so how are we going to avoid them all, eh? They're everywhere. They'll be talking to us all the time!'

'Well, keep it down and don't make it obvious!'

She looked up at the tree and went on, 'Sorry—this is Vishwajit my brother—he thinks if people know we talk to trees they'll think we're nuts.'

'That's their problem then, don't you think, for being so stupid,' the Neem said calmly. 'Besides, there are people who actually hug us too, so there! Anyway now tell me how are the DDT behenjis doing? I keep asking those mynas and parakeets, but they have the attention span of fleas!'

'They're good.'

'Still whining and whingeing about Ustadji and his Peepal girlfriends?'

'Yeah,' I grinned. 'You know how they are.'

'Well, they do have a point, you know.'

'Which is?' I asked, dying to get to the bottom of this mystery.

Tadpole grabbed my hand. 'Bhaiyya,' she whispered fiercely, 'Now *you're* talking to her! Besides, Ms Hawakhanewalli is coming this way.' Ms Hawakhanewalli was a PE instructor probably deputed to do guard duty during lunch break. She was striding towards us, her expression hostile.

'Why are you loafing around here?'

'Ma'am, we're just admiring this neem tree. It's so pretty, don't you think?' Tadpole said innocently. 'Look at its leaves like those fans you get at fairs…'

'Eh? What are you talking about?'

'Ma'am, did you know the neem tree is famous for keeping insects away?'

Ms Hawakhanewalli was tall and imposing and glared down at us trying to make sense of what we were saying.

'What mischief are you up to here? I didn't ask for a lecture on neem trees! Turn out your pockets!'

Looking hurt, Tadpole and I did so: nothing but grubby handkerchiefs and a tube of Polos.

'Well, don't loaf around under these trees—there may be snakes!'

We followed her out into the playground. Tadpole turned around and waved, blew a kiss and said, 'Bye, see you soon!'

Ms Hawakhanewalli whirled around. 'Who were you talking to?' she demanded.

'The tree, ma'am,' Tadpole said. 'Just saying bye to the tree.'

'You kids!'

I winked at Tadpole and we went off to our classrooms.

Back home that afternoon we finished our homework and whistled to the dogs.

'Mom, we're going out to play!' Tadpole announced gaily. Mom looked at her fondly.

'I'm so glad we moved here,' she said, 'it's so good that both of you spend so much time outdoors!'

If only she knew we were talking to trees, we'd be back in a sterile flat on the twentieth floor in two ticks!

We were both anxious to see what damage last evening's storm had done to our new friends.

'I hope they're all right,' Tadpole said as we slipped through the gate. We headed straight towards Ustadji and the Peepal Princesses. Twigs and leaves lay strewn all around, though thankfully, none of the trees had fallen.

'Hello, good afternoon Ustadji, I hope the storm didn't hurt you.'

'Good afternoon, beta! Oh, actually it was very exhilarating—it got us rid of all those itchy dead branches and leaves that were just hanging on and we swayed and danced.'

'He and his girlfriends are fine, so he thinks everything's hunky dory!' the DDT Didis said petulantly. 'One of the Mangoes lost a pretty big branch, but does he care?'

'Apparently it was infested with borers, so just as well, otherwise they would have attacked the whole tree,' Ustadji replied calmly.

'Ustadji, how many babies do you have?' Tadpole asked suddenly.

'Tadpole! What a question!' I was hugely embarrassed.

'Oh sweetie, I've lost count. Thousands probably! I'm having babies all the time—the birds and bats know that. The hornbills and barbets and parakeets and mynas and green pigeons and bulbuls and bats eat their fill of figs and scatter my babies all over the country. I've got relatives everywhere.'

Just then, the dogs all stood in a row facing the gate and began growling softly.

'Intruders,' Ustadji whispered urgently.

'They always come after a storm.'

We could hear the voices of men and women, chattering as they approached. A small group appeared; they were carrying sickles and long staves armed with curved blades at their ends. They saw the dogs and stopped. Then they saw us.

'Hold the dogs!' one of the men said.

I whistled to the dogs. They came up to us and sat down, watching the intruders.

They took no further notice of us but stood in front of the Peepal Princesses and bowed their heads. Two women bent down and left some marigolds and stuck some agarbattis in the ground before them. Then they went off towards the palace.

'What was that about?' I asked. 'Will they tell the Baba that they saw us here?'

'Don't worry, dear,' Princess Bo said. 'They're the local villagers. They were just paying homage to us. Now they'll go to the patch of forest behind the palace and pick up fallen branches and cut bunches of leaves.'

'Does it hurt when they do that?' Tadpole asked.

'I've heard it sort of tingles sometimes,' Princess Bo said.

'It's okay, except sometimes they chop off really big, fresh branches and that does hurt!' Princess Ficki said. 'You can sometimes hear those poor trees scream when they do that. And it takes ages to re-grow them.'

'Are they allowed to do this?' I asked.

'Strictly speaking no! They can't touch us. But you know—they need fodder for their buffaloes—which then produce the excellent dung you sweetly gift us—and wood for their fires so they can cook. If they had gas cylinders why would they waste their time lopping branches off us?'

Our own gas cylinders still hadn't been delivered and I knew Mom had been going round the bend because even the electricity was so erratic. She had actually got the farmhands to collect firewood and had bought charcoal for the backup clay oven.

I wanted to see the Oleanders closely today, so I took Tadpole with me to the lake, where they grew. I was a bit curious about these trees. They were so glossy and green, their flowers so brilliantly yellow and they leaned over invitingly. But I have to say, there was something strange about them.

They bled pure white.

I know a lot of plants bleed white, but it's weird. I mean we bleed red, which is fine. Some plants and trees have amber or gold coloured or even green sap and resin—even that's healthy. But pure white? That's completely evil!

We sat down rather gingerly next to a few trees that promptly dropped a couple of golden flowers into Tadpole's lap. She picked one up and squinted down the hollow stalk.

'Can I suck it for the nectar?'

'Please…please do…' the trees whispered.

'Tadpole, don't touch them!' I snatched the flower away from her. 'They're poisonous!'

One of the women who had been collecting branches and leaves from the palace forest had come down to the lake to wash her face. She looked across at Tadpole and called out, 'Don't touch them, the milk is poisonous.'

Tadpole dropped the flower and wiped her fingers on her jeans. 'Okay, okay, I get the message!'

The sun was beginning to go down, and flocks of mynas and parakeets were returning after the day's work, flying in at high speed and chattering at the tops of their voices about the day they'd had.

Suddenly Mithoorani and Gingianus swirled out of the mob and landed neatly on Tadpole's shoulders. She beamed.

'Hi Baby,' Mithoorani said in her usual affectionate way, nibbling her ear.

'Yo Chicklet! How goes it?' Gingianus chuckled throatily.

'Such a day I had!' Mithoorani went on. 'Just got an invite from the big VIP Seemal at Teen Murti House to attend his open house in March! And then the Mahuas on Rajesh Pilot Marg will start flowering and of course the Coral Trees and Dhak on the Ridge and...it's crazy I tell you!'

Gingianus rolled his eyes. 'It happens every year...the social calendar is jammed between February and July, and she behaves as though she's the only one being invited to all these dos!'

'Who appeared on Page 3 five times last year, and who didn't make a single appearance eh?'

'Only because you were seen cuddling up with that macaw that had escaped from the zoo and was on the run! I don't harbour escaped cons!'

'He was not a convict, he was seeking political asylum! And now he's been rescued and is being rehabilitated. So there!'

'My dears, the number of marriages we have to fix in the season...you have no idea! Trees everywhere flowering away to glory, pollen dust in the air causing hay-fever on an industrial scale, we take it from one tree to another after matching horoscopes.'

There came an alarming humming and buzzing sound and instinctively I ducked. A couple of huge furry bees were hovering around us.

'Hah, they believe they're the only ones fixing weddings. My dears that's our calling in life! We may visit as many as 2,000 blooms in a day! We get paid in nectar and take pollen from one bloom to another—after ensuring compatibility. And when the marriage is a success a fruit grows and all that these greedy bozos—and lots of animals—usually do is to eat it and then scatter the seeds as faraway from the parents as possible... Via their bottoms! Eww!'

'I'll have you know, most trees and plants and shrubs won't have it any other way. They don't want their babies to grow anywhere near them...though later some do ask after them.'

'And boast about them too,' Tadpole added wisely. 'That

Ustadji goes on and on about all his famous relatives in Corbett and Rajbagh and places like that.'

'Well our ancestors took the seeds and dropped them there,' both Mithoorani and Gingianus said together. 'So the credit's ours!'

Mithoorani perched on Tadpole's head and leaned over clownishly. 'Besides, that stupid bee has nothing to do with Ustadji's kids, or those of the Peepal Princesses. They have special emissaries for carrying pollen around.'

'What's emissary?' Tadpole asked at once.

'Like a messenger or courier boy,' I said. 'But what do you mean, Mithoorani?'

'Ask them,' Mithoorani retorted succinctly. 'It's so complicated I get mixed up every time I tell the story, but they should know it.'

Tadpole grabbed my hand. 'Come on, Bhaiyya,' she said urgently, 'let's find out!'

She stood under Princess Bo and asked straight out: 'Princess Bo, Mithoorani told us you have special emissary to carry your pollen, not just bees and birds like everyone else.'

Princess Bo rustled her emerald leaves. 'Come up here, both of you, on to this branch which has these drupes and I'll tell you.'

The branch was not very high up and easy to climb on to. We sat side by side our legs dangling down.

'Okay, let's hear it Princess Bo!' Tadpole said chirpily.

'Look!' Princess Bo said urgently, 'Look at that bright red fig on the twig nearest you. Look closely at the top. Do you see anything?'

We peered as closely as we could, our heads touching.

'There's a tiny black insect trying to get inside,' Tadpole said. 'Now it's gone in!'

'It's called a fig wasp. And she'll never come out!

'What? Have you trapped her? Can she bite or sting?'

'No. But ah, now let me ask you a trick question: have you ever seen our flowers?'

'Flowers?' Tadpole and I looked at each other blankly. She shook her head.

'No, I don't think so. Where are they? Do you have any at all?'

'Hundreds!' Princess Bo chuckled. 'Some are gentlemen flowers, some are lady flowers and some are neither, which we call gall flowers...'

'But where are they?'

'They're all crowded together *inside* each fig. It's rather like a bazaar inside there. Most of the gentlemen flowers are near the top, the others crammed below.'

'Oh, wow!'

'Yes, and that little fig wasp has just gone inside to lay her eggs in the gall flowers. She'll lay all her eggs, one in each flower, and then die inside.'

'Oh!' Tadpole's eyes were big and she clutched my hand. 'That's sad! Poor thing!'

'Well, the eggs hatch and the tiny gentlemen fig wasps, which are blind and without wings emerge first and bite and eat their way out of their gall flowers.'

'What about the lady wasps?' Tadpole asked.

'They're still inside their gall flowers—and there are usually many more ladies than gentlemen. Anyway, the gentlemen fig wasps are desperate to meet the ladies. So they bite and eat their way through their gall flowers and mate with them.'

'Eww! Do they even knock or just barge in?' Tadpole frowned.

'They break in, mate—and then they die!'

'It *** them right for being so rude! You can't enter a lady's bedroom without knocking. If Bhaiyya did that I'd whack him one!'

'I guess! Anyway, the lady wasps now start leaving the fig

through the opening at the top. They brush against the gentlemen flowers waiting at the top, all laden with pollen. Some ladies have little carry bags which they fill with the pollen before flying off. They fly off long distances trying to find another tree with ripe figs. And when they do, they—as you just saw—wriggle inside the hole at the top of the fig. They push their way inside and lay their eggs one by one in the gall flowers, but in doing so brush against the lady flowers of the fig and deposit their pollen on them. The lady flowers thus get the pollen they need in order to make seeds. And then, when a bird or bat or animal eats the fig, it deposits the seed faraway...and a new tree grows!'

The shrill voices of the DDT Didis came wafting over again: 'Yes they deposit those awful sticky seeds on the heads of some poor defenceless other tree and then...'

'Oh shut up with your whingeing!' Princess Bo snapped. Her voice softened. 'And do you know, for every one of us fig species, there is a special type of fig wasp. What works for us Peepal Princesses, won't work for Ustadji—he has his own brand of fig wasp.'

'Wow! Why can't any wasp do that?'

'Oh, you know the entrance hole at the top? It's like a keyhole. And only the wasp with the correctly shaped head can squeeze its way in—any other won't fit. So it's like each of us have our own lock and only one type of wasp has the key and can enter.'

'Wow!'

'It's almost a sort of prestige thing. Like the wasps are custom made for each of us.'

'Oh yes we're very prestigious trees,' Ustadji called out. Obviously he'd been listening in. 'I for one, am a keystone species!'

'What?'

'So many depend on us banyans—animals, insects, birds,

reptiles, humans. If we were to go, they would all go; the whole forest would go. We provide food and sustenance and shade and wisdom and medicines throughout the year—whether it's our figs or leaves or bark or...'

'Ustadji *bas*—enough!' the DDT Dozen groaned.' And yet you depend on this tiny little wasp that's one millimeter long to keep your species going. Think of that and be humbled, oh, great all-knowing tree of knowledge! If there were no tiny fig wasp there would be no giant banyans! Good riddance I'd say!'

Ustadji bristled, his leaves trembled. 'Billy?' he called, 'will you make a deliverable on those silly Neems, please?'

'Deliverable? What's that?' Tadpole asked.

There came a loud flapping sound and a branch near Tadpole bent. One of those dinosaur-like hornbills was perched on it, swinging his tail and grinning.

'He means eat some figs and deposit the er...seeds on the Neems!'

'Hey, are you touchy or what? We were only joking!' the DDT Dozen protested together. 'Where's you sense of humour Ustadji? And you're all knowing!'

That evening, we had barely got back home when Tadopole suddenly slapped her forehead.

'Bhaiyya we've been such idiots!' she exclaimed.

'What do you mean?'

'I mean we've met the trees in Medley Gardens next door and some in school—but we haven't said hello to the trees in our own farm! How do you think they must be feeling?'

Actually there weren't many trees on the farm and none were fully grown. A few scraggly green trees, which Mom said were Ashokas, lined the driveway, and there were a couple of other ragged trees near the southern boundary wall, which looked suspiciously like more Julies. There were a few others which introduced themselves as Crepe Myrtles and one which said it was an Easter Tree. Tadpole was right. When we first went up to them to say 'hello' (we had to be careful no one was watching us), they sniffed and shivered their leaves.

'So you've finally noticed us!' the Ashokas said frostily. 'So nice! We live here too, you know.'

'Of course they prefer all those oldies next door. Ancient trees with ancient beliefs and stories…'

I realized that these guys were pretty young and had very little 'tree experience'—in fact they had been planted by the landscape fellow who Dad had employed when he had bought the farm.

One thing Tadpole and I got to know pretty soon was that— as the schoolyard Neem had told us—word got around pretty quickly. While we did sneak a quiet word or two with the trees in the schoolyard, and met a few new ones—a gulmohur (who said his ancestors had come from Madagascar) and something called a Devil's Tree—we did not remotely anticipate what would happen when we went on a school picnic to Lodi Gardens.

5

On the morning of the picnic the buses dropped us off in the car park on Lodi Road and we were all herded by harassed teachers led by Ms Hawakhanewalli towards the tomb of Muhammad Shah Sayyid. It is perched on a green hillock, surrounded by straight and tall ash grey palm-like trees. Tadpole's class—the junior-most in the group—went off first and my class—the senior-most followed last.

Ms Hawakhanewalli blew her whistle shrilly and we all stopped in our tracks.

'You will stay inside the perimeter of these palm trees. Spread your mats and settle down. You may play badminton or with a Frisbee or catching ball. No cricket or football—is that clear? Now march!'

Bringing up the rear I watched as Tadpole's class moved ahead, the kids lined up two by two. Then I saw Tadpole suddenly stiffen and turn her head towards one of the stately grey palms. She gave a delighted grin and suddenly saluted the tree. Then she moved on, her face turning pink as her friends began teasing her. I followed and suddenly started.

'1st Royal Bottle Palm Regiment *Ten Hun!* Ready for guard of honour inspection! Present arms!'

My head jerked sideways towards the tree that had obviously barked the order. It stood stiff and ramrod to attention as did all the others. I nodded briefly, imperceptibly I hoped, and slowly made my way down the line of trees. Once I leant towards a tree to examine its trunk. Some moron had carved a heart on it and scrawled, 'Sushi loves Khushi'.

'Did he?' I asked raising an eyebrow, 'or did he...just you know...'

'He did too *sir*! Very much, *sir*! They met here, *sir*! Eloped and got married, *sir*! Have five kids and a Dalmatian, which pees on us, *sir*! Thank you for talking to us, *sir*!'

Automatically I stood to attention and snapped a smart salute.

'What the hell are you doing yaar, saluting a tree?' Ashwin my best friend hooted digging me in the ribs. He peered at the tree. 'He also wants to draw a heart and write his name, but he's shy. Anyone has a penknife? Let's write "Vish loves Zafia!"'

I went red. Zafia was the tall brown-eyed girl who I rather fancied (and helped in Chemistry and she helped me in History) but she was absent today. In fact, she had been absent from school for a week now, down with viral fever.

I grinned sheepishly. 'Cut it out and shut up. But they're like a guard of honour aren't they, and I'm just practicing for when I become Prime Minister.' I could see Tadpole was watching me with bug eyes, a hand over her mouth.

'You! Prime Minister!' My friends all fell about laughing and clapping each other on the back and shoving and jostling and forgot about what I had been doing. It had been a close save. Tadpole and I would have to be very careful.

It wasn't easy. After lunch, Ms Hawakhanewalli decided that we should walk around the gardens. Herding us like sheepdogs the teachers escorted us along the paths, pointing out the tombs. Somehow (and she's good at this sort of thing), Tadpole sneaked up and joined me and took my hand. Normally we would rather be dead than seen together like this in school, but I knew there was a problem.

'Bhaiyya,' she whispered.

I nodded. 'I know!' We had barely left the Royal Battle Palms and were passing by a cluster of rustling bamboos and a small mango grove when they all started greeting us with friendly 'hi's' and 'hellos' and 'how're you doing kids?' and 'regards to Ustadji,' and stuff. We couldn't say anything except grin fatuously back at them and wave weakly. Fortunately everyone was too busy doing their own thing to notice us. But man, did our ears flap as we overheard every word of what the trees were saying as we walked along the pathway.

'Such sweet kids! Look at them, hand in hand!'

'So shy! They don't talk to us!'

'But Mynawati told me that Adrakbai had told her that Teekhiboli had told her that Seetimaro had told her that Gingiyaar had told her that they talk a lot—and to Ustadji at that! And even to Kapok Maharajji! The little girl keeps asking cheeky questions!'

'Well they're with all their dumb friends here, so naturally they'd want to speak to them rather than us...'

'Yeah, I mean who talks to us, except ourselves!'

'But hey, just listen to this—the Battle Palm Regiment reported that the kids saluted them and the boy asked one of them questions about his tattoo.'

We could have sworn a cheer broke out, certainly a cool breeze rustled through the trees making the branches wave and the leaves dance and swirl—and some drop lazily.

'Mithoorani said they're sweet and respectful. They don't swipe at branches or slash leaves like most kids do,' a big Peepal said, its leaves flickering as we walked past.

'Huh!' a big fellow just west of the Bara Gumbad snorted,

making both of us jump. 'They're sweet now because they don't know... Let them find out and...' I didn't know what he was, but his leaves were arranged fanwise in hands of seven leaves. (Later Ustadji told me he was the Devil Tree or Satparni or Blackboard Tree and hailed from the Himalayan foothills and got popular in Delhi because his kind grew very fast.)

'Shaitan, button your lip!' came a chorus from a group of trees I couldn't identify. 'Just shut up will you!'

'Huh! They're all the same! They'll be out with...'

'*Shut up Shaitan!*' It was quite a chorus and I looked startled as Tadpole gripped my hand.

'Bhaiyya, what are they saying? Why are they telling him to shut up?'

'Beats me. Now let go of my hand Tadpole, someone might see us!'

'Sorry!' She gave me a sheepish grin and looked around. 'But Zafia hasn't come today. You don't mind when she holds your hand!'

'Oh, I didn't notice she hadn't come.'

There was a rustling sound from the trees; it seemed that they were chuckling huskily. Tadpole grinned.

'You were looking all over for her when we got off the buses. I saw you!' She pointed at the trees. 'And they know too—they're giggling!'

'Are not!'

'Are too!'

'Why don't you join your class? They're way up front.'

'Oh, okay!' She grinned and ran off.

As we walked around the gardens I kept hearing snatches of half-whispered intriguing conversations on the breeze. Obviously Shri Shaitan or whatever hadn't kept his mouth shut.

'Imagine, they *live* there and they don't know!'

'Thank God for that! But then no one's known for 300 years!'

'Yes otherwise....'

The little girl is cute but Mynawati told me that Adrakbai had told her that Teekhiboli had told her that Seetimaro had told her that Gingiyaar had told her that Ustadji said she asks too many questions.'

'Best that they never know.'

'Shh, the fellow's ears are flapping!'

'Eavesdropper!'

'Can't mind his own business!'

'None of them can!'

I put my hands in my pockets and looked at the sky and whistled innocently. The whispers continued:

'Their whole species is like that!'

'Interfering busybodies!'

'And so destructive!'

'Did you hear? They even attacked that sacred Mangarban forest outside Delhi?'

'What?'

'Yes! It's scandalous!'

'And this, just after the Great Metro Massacres.'

'So many revered members of my family brought down on Barakhamba Road.'

'And mine! I lost so many family and friends on Alipur Road.'

'So many sacrifices!'

'And they say they plant ten new saplings for every one they kill. Plant them where? Out in the boondocks amongst the Juliflora thugs?'

'About which, they do nothing.'

'Invading everywhere! Imperialist colonial running dogs!'

'Shh…his ears are flapping again.'

'Let them! Let him know what damage his kind has done!'

'But he and his sister must never know.'

'Never!'

'Otherwise poor old Ustadji and…'

'Shaitan! Shut up will you?'

'Sorry, wasn't thinking!'

'Do you ever?'

'Hey!' Ashwin slapped me on the back, starling me. 'Why are you standing under that tree with your mouth open like a goldfish and that stupid look on your face? Catching flies?'

'Oh…nothing…' I went red.

'Guys, he's dreaming about Zafia! She's absent today. Poor fellow, he's missing her!'

'Just cut it out, will you?'

'Who's Zafia?' the big peepal tree next to the Bara Gumbad we had gathered under a little while later (while Hawakhanewalli droned on and on about the tomb) rustled. 'I'd love to meet her. You can tattoo a heart with her name and yours on my trunk—I'd be flattered. We believe in free love—that's why we have heart-shaped leaves after all! We dedicate one leaf to every lovey-dovey couple in the world!'

'Just cut it out, will you,' I whispered fiercely. Fortunately all the kids were now making such a racket (the lecture had just gotten over) that no one overheard me.

'Yes, we'd love to meet her! You can walk hand in hand with her under us,' came the chorus borne on the breeze.

'Shut up, will you?'

But I couldn't help wondering what would happen if I did introduce Zafia to say, Ustadji and the others. She'd probably think I was nuts and dump me. But it would be so nice to share this with someone, apart from Tadpole of course: someone like Zafia for example.

I rang her up that evening. She said she was feeling much better now, so I invited her over on the coming Saturday. She could catch up with some of the classes she had missed, especially Chemistry.

'Please come and spend the day, you have to see the farm. I'll ask Mom or Dad to drop and pick you up from our school bus stop. And there's something special I want to show you.'

'I'd love to,' she said, 'And I really have to catch up on my Chemistry.'

6

*T*hat night, Tadpole came into my bedroom again. 'Bhaiyya! Did you hear those trees in Lodi Gardens?'

I nodded. 'Yeah, it was so embarrassing.'

'They're keeping some big secret from us!'

'What?' I was actually wondering whether to ask one of the Peepal Princesses—or all of them—if they would mind terribly if I carved a heart with my name and Zafia's on their trunks.

'You're not listening! Those trees are keeping a big secret from us. We have to find out what it is! Should we ask Ustadji?'

I shrugged. 'Sure we could. He's the tree of knowledge after all: The all-knowing, all-seeing one, blah blah blah!'

'I will!' Tadpole's eyes were big and solemn. 'They shouldn't keep secrets from us!' she said sounding offended. 'We are their friends!' I figured I would have to tell her what I had planned— she would come to know anyhow.

'Tads, Zafia's coming over for Chemistry lessons on Saturday.'

'Chemistry lessons? Ooooh, woo-woo-woo!'

'There's nothing woo-woo about it. I'll teach her what she missed and then I thought we could go over to Medley Gardens.'

Her eyes widened. 'You want to tell her that we talk to trees and they talk to us?'

'Um…maybe…'

Tadpole put her hand on her hips and cocked her head. 'Don't be stupid. You want her to dump you? That's what she'll do if you tell her. She'll go home screaming!'

'She's not like that. I just thought she could meet the trees, that's all. No one said anything about talking to them.'

'What about Mithoorani and Gingianus? They'll see me and fly down on my shoulders!'

'So what? That'll be cool. Zafia would love that. And maybe you can tell them to perch on her shoulders too!'

I was very excited on Saturday morning. We were to pick Zafia up from our school bus-stop at eleven, which meant we had to leave the house by ten-fifteen. Straight after breakfast, however, Tadpole came up to me and grabbed my hand.

'Bhaiyya, come on, let's go to Medley Gardens!'

'We have to pick up Zafia!'

'Ooof, there's so much time still. We can go, say hello to the trees and come back. We can tell them that we will be bringing your girlfriend who you would like them to meet. And that they should be nice to her.'

'She's not my girlfriend! And stop talking like a grandmother!'

'Come on!'

We scooted off next door with the dogs. Then I realized why Tadpole had wanted to meet the trees so badly first thing in the morning. She went and stood right in front of Ustadji.

'Hello Ustadji, I hope you slept well, namaste! You know, yesterday we went to Lodi Gardens and all the trees there said that there's some big secret you are hiding from us. What is it? We're your friends after all. There should be no secrets between us!'

A shimmering ripple ran through all of Ustadji's leaves as well as those of the Peepal Princesses.

'Baby, you musn't listen to those Lodi Garden gossips. Just because they live in Lutyens' Delhi they think they know everything. It's all rubbish! They pick up all kinds of nonsense and rumours from the fools who walk there everyday.'

'Lutchins' Delhi? What's that?' Tadpole looked blank.

'Mr Lutyens was the dude who designed New Delhi and his horticulturist, or gardener if you like, a Mr Mustoe, planted all the trees there. They now think they're VIP trees and talk all sorts of nonsense!'

'Oh…but…there was this Mr Shaitan who said…'

'Shaitan?' Ustadji's voice was filled with contempt. 'Don't you listen to Shaitan! He and his family are the biggest gossips and rumour mongers of them all! That's why his kind is used for making blackboards at school! What does Shaitan know of our great and ancient traditions? Pah! Barely sprouted yesterday and thinks he knows everything! These fast-growing types—so shallow and greedy! He should have remained in the Himalayan foothills where he belongs!'

'Oh.' Tadpole half closed her eyes and then nodded. 'Okay,' she said at last and shrugged. 'Sorry I asked.'

I looked at my kid sister shrewdly. Oh no, Ustadji, that wasn't the last of it. And I think I knew what Tadpole's next move would be. She would not rest until she got to the bottom of the mystery.

As for me, I was feeling a bit distracted because I was thinking about Zafia. I glanced at my watch. Shoot, still only nine-thirty. I cleared my throat.

'Ah, Ustadji—we'll be bringing a friend to meet you all later today. I hope you don't mind.'

'Your *girlfriend?*' the Peepli Princesses all tinkled together and giggled. And I could swear even the dour and usually bitter DDT Dozen also giggled.

'Well, Zafia is a girl and a friend… Actually I have to teach her Chemistry.'

'And so, a girlfriend!' Ustadji said in his rich baritone. 'Well done, beta! Yes, you bring her here, I'll teach both of you Chemistry! The Chemistry of All Life! How from thin air and with some sunlight and water and a few minerals we enable all life to thrive.' Tadpole clapped and nodded.

'He *loves* her Ustadji! He wants to *marry* her!'

'You know,' said Princess Bo mischievously, 'you both can climb up on me and you know, start to kay eye ess ess eye en jee!'

'As if!' I blushed.

'And we don't mind if you tattoo your names on us with two hearts intertwined. We'd love that! No one does that sort of thing to us here! Ooh, it'll be so romantic!' said Princess Ficki.

'Hey, just because they have heart-shaped leaves they think they have a monopoly on romance. You bring your girlfriend to us, we'll make sure no mosquitos or flies bother her and that her breath smells sweet when she kisses you!' the DDT Dozen chorused.

We arrived at the bus stop to pick up Zafia at eleven o'clock. We parked under the big tree with feathery leaves and waited for her. While Mom waited inside the car, Tadpole and I got out so that Zafia saw us when she arrived.

'Hi kids, you wait here everyday for your bus and never say hello to me! What are you doing here on Saturday?'

Both of us jumped about two feet high.

'Wha...?'

'Who...?'

'Him!' Tadpole said fiercely pointing to the huge tree. Its leaves trembled and a lot of them showered down.

'Hi, kids, glad to catch your attention at last. I'm Tamar-i-Hind!'

'Who?' I asked blankly.

'Tamarind, idiot!' Tadpole hissed.

'Oh hello!' I muttered.

'My regards to Ustadji! By the way, there's a relative of mine growing in Medley Gardens too; behind the palace—I don't think you've gone there yet—he hasn't mentioned meeting you both. His name is Shri Imliji. In fact there are a whole lot of us there with some other riff raff.'

'We haven't been to the forest behind the palace yet. It's too near the building. The Baba will kick us out...'

'Oh, but he might not. Take him a small gift and he'll let you wander about everywhere. And his wife, Mataji is one lonely soul—she keeps talking to herself—she would love to talk to Baby.'

'She talks to herself?'

'Look, Zafia's here!' Tadpole said as a blue Honda drew up and stopped behind our car.

The parents exchanged greetings as we got into our car.

'So we'll wait for you here at six,' Mom told Zafia's dad, getting back behind the wheel. We drove off, and I was thrilled, because Mom was firm about her rule about no kids sitting up front. So it was I, Zafia and Tadpole (who bagged a window) squeezed at the back. I glanced sideways at Zafia: she had such a gentle face and big golden brown eyes, and long curving eyelashes... Her nose was small and her ears too, pink as shells when the sun shone through them. Her hair, long and brown was in a loose ponytail, and brushed against my arm. She smelt heavenly. I gulped. What would this...this angel...say if I told her I talked to trees and they talked back to me? Would I lose her forever? Could I take the risk? And yet, how could I not tell her such a wonderful thing?

I guess I had got it badly.

Well we balanced a few equations and checked out the Periodic Table (which I thought was so cool) and Tadpole kept popping her head around the door asking, 'Are you done yet? Hurry up!'

'Hurry up? What for?' Zafia asked smiling. She had lovely, even white teeth too.

'Oh well, um…we discovered this um secret forest next door which we want to show you. You know it's in the grounds of a palace actually…'

'Wow! That's cool.'

'And Bhaiyya thinks that you'll be the Princess of Medley Gardens,' Tadpole said gleefully. 'Though there are already three princesses there.'

Zafia raised her eyebrows.

'Kids!' I shrugged and grinned, 'You know what Tadpole's like!'

We had an early lunch and set off soon after, whistling to the dogs. They knew the drill and raced ahead.

'Come on,' I said as I ushered Zafia through the barbed wire gate. She looked thrilled.

'Wow, this is so cool,' she said looking around. 'Are you going to show me the palace?'

I shook my head. 'No, there's an ogre and ogress living there and they'll chase us out. We go to the forest at the other end. There are some huge old trees…'

'Oh!'

I glanced around. Tadpole had gone running ahead with the dogs.

'I'll let you into a secret,' I said, 'You know, Tadpole talks to the trees here and says they talk back to her. Don't tell her that I told you though…'

Zafia's eyes widened and she eyed me strangely.

'What?' I asked.

'Nothing!' she shrugged.

'You're looking at me all funnily.'

'Am not! Well what's so great about that? I talk to my plants too. I have a little garden on the terrace and talk to my plants every day. They get very sulky if I don't. I even play them music.' She made a face. 'They don't like rap though. They prefer old-fashioned stuff.'

'Oh…you do?' I grinned. 'Do they talk back to you? Tadpole says the trees are talking to her all the time.'

Zafia looked at me funnily again and then away. 'Um, maybe they do…maybe they don't…' she murmured.

We reached Ustadji and there was Tadpole standing in front of him, hectoring and pleading with him again.

'Ustadji please, *please* tell me the secret! I won't tell anyone, I swear!'

The dogs barked and Tadpole looked around. 'Hi, come on Zafia, meet our new friends!'

'She's sweet!'

'Lovely!'

'Hello sweetheart! Welcome to Medley Gardens!'

The Peepli Princesses approved.

'Namaste betiji, I'm Ustadji as mahasheyji here might have told you. The Tree of Knowledge. The All-Knowing, All-Seeing One.'

'Who keeps secrets from us!' Tadpole added petulantly. I wasn't bothered about Tadpole right now. I was looking at Zafia, and knew I was going scarlet.

'May your visit here be a happy and prosperous one!' Ustadji went on genially.

'Thank you ji,' Zafia said calmly as my mouth fell open. 'With your blessing, I'm sure it will.'

What sounded like wolf whistles rent the air—a brisk breeze whistling through leaves probably—leaves of the Oleander siblings.

'Wow!'

'Dishy darling!'

'Come and visit us!'

'You witches, shut up!' I blurted turning around and facing them. Then I went red. Zafia didn't seem at all perturbed. Then (tubelight!) it suddenly struck me…

'You….you just said "thank you" to that tree,' I stuttered.

'Yes,' she said calmly. 'He wished me a happy and prosperous stay so I thanked him. Wouldn't you?'

'You *heard* him?'

She smiled and for the first time ever, took my hand and squeezed it. 'Bozo, how else would I know what he said?' she asked gently. I wanted to kiss her right away. 'And so did you!'

'Me? Nah…well…'

'Dufus! You just told those witches to shut up when they whistled, didn't you?' She giggled.

'But…but…when…how…'

'Zafia didi even you can talk to them?' Tadpole's eyes were the size of grapefruit. 'How cool is that! Come on, let's meet everyone!'

'But…but…when….how?'

'Does it matter?' she asked me her hand still squeezing mine.

'Now come along and sit down and I'll give you a Chemistry lesson: The Chemistry Lesson of All Life!' Ustadji rustled. The Peepli Princesses groaned.

'It's Saturday, for chlorophyll's sake!'

'Give the kids a break, will you!'

'Baby,' said Ustadji, 'Do you know why we reach up towards the light?'

'All the better to see with,' Tadpole chimed and Zafia giggled.

'Yes, because we use the sunlight. We take the energy of the sun and turn it into food and fuel so we can grow!'

'But Ustadji *please* tell me the secret now!' She smiled as sweetly as she could.

'Go on Baby, take that root and swing, enjoy yourself!'

Well, I was certainly enjoying myself. Imagine, I had a (girl)friend who also spoke to and was spoken to by, trees.

'When did you start talking to your plants and when did they start talking back?' I asked as we slipped in and out of Ustadji's multifarious prop-roots, still holding hands.

'Dunno, while gardening I think. A rosebush pricked me and said, "sorry," when I said "ouch".'

'You know, at that school picnic you missed at Lodi Gardens— they were all talking so much!'

'Yeah, they can be very chatty at times.'

'And they did mention some big secret that was being kept from us. Tadpole's determined to find out what it is.'

'Come on,' Zafia said, 'let's go behind that fat Peepal tree...'

'Excuse me Miss, I'm not fat! My figure's perfect for my age!' Princess Peepli was quite outraged.

'Sorry!' Zafia apologized. 'You've got a great figure, ma'am! Very healthy!'

So healthy that both of us could sneak behind her trunk and be hidden. Zafia looked at me her eyes shining then put her arms around me.

'Darling, did he brush his teeth after lunch?' one of the DDT

Didis shrilled. 'Don't kiss him if he didn't. There'll be millions of bacteria in his mouth!'

'Eww!'

'Here, give him this little twig from me and make him chew on it. Then he can kiss you all he wants!'

Stupid spoilsports. Zafia drew back, grinning.

'They have a point, you know!' she said as Tadpole came running up.

'Come on, let's meet the others,' I said, taking Zafia's hand.

'Hello there ...walk amongst us...'

'Girlie, girlie, so cute no, this way please!'

The dreadful Julies were at it, stretching out and trying to snag Zafia's dupatta with their spikes.

'Come this way, avoid those saplings they've got huge thorns and only want to impale you!' I said, taking Zafia's arm and leading her away from the thorny patches. Tadpole skipped ahead.

'Meet the Mangoes,' she said, as we entered the grove. 'They're great to climb!'

'Good morning dear, sorry we have nothing to offer you, but do come back in May and we'll have a basket of our most luscious ready.'

I glared at them: 'I like that, you forbade me from climbing and said I would use catapults and now you're offering her...'

'You're a fifteen-year-old boy!'

'Almost sixteen!' I reminded indignantly.

'Which is even worse. And she's a sweet young girl...'

Zafia smiled. 'Don't mind them silly,' she said, 'they love teasing.'

'Hey, you guys, what's this big secret everyone's talking about?' Tadpole asked. She was indefatigable. 'You all are keeping something from us.'

A rustle coursed through the grove.

'There's no secret. Who told you there was one?'

'Oh all the trees in Lodi Gardens were saying...'

'Pah! Them! Prima-donnas the lot of them. Forever demanding makeovers from their malis! They've been spoilt sick! Nothing to do all day but gossip! Never believe what they tell you!'

We spent a bit of time with the Mangoes and then went off to meet the Semuls.

'That big guy, he's the Raja. His full title is His Royal Highness and Ultimate Exalted Majesty Raja Bomabxji Kapok Maharaj, Shahenshah Semul Shambolji Cebia VIIIth! You'd better curtsey before him then he might allow you to call him RSC,' I told Zafia.

'That's because he wears red silk cotton underpants!' Tadpole added in a loud whisper.

'Wow, he is grand!' Zafia said looking up at the huge tree.

'Hello my dear...so nice of you to visit. I would like to cordially invite you to my Open House to be held between the middle of March and beginning of April. Do RSVP one of my secretaries here.'

'Thank you so much,' Zafia said politely. 'I'd love to come.'

'Er... Your Majesty, what's this big secret everyone's talking about?' Tadpole asked casually. I swear the six stalwarts around the Raja stiffened and bristled.

'Secret?' The Raja laughed but I knew he was faking it. 'There's no secret here!'

Tadpole stamped her foot. 'There is too! Every tree in Lodi Gardens was saying so...'

'Baby, they're just jealous of us. We're growing here, more or less wild and free, whichever way we want to. Have you seen what they do to trees there? Those poor Ashoka fellows for example: they make them look like upside down exclamation marks! We call them popsicle trees. How undignified is that! And other trees are hacked so they look like animals and birds. Just before winter people lop off huge branches so they can sit in the sun and then complain in summer that there's no shade. I mean we're trees sweetie, we have our dignity! We're in charge of the whole world. We have great responsibilities!'

'Okay, okay.' Tadpole wagged a finger. 'But I'll find out, I really will! Just you wait!'

'Tads, that's no way to talk to Maharajji,' I said, horrified.

Tadpole grabbed our hands. 'Come on,' she said fiercely, 'let's go behind the palace and check out those trees we haven't met there. Maybe they'll tell us!'

But just then Mithoorani and Gingianus flew down and perched on her shoulders.

'Hi Baby, missed you!'

'Yo Chicklet, your bro's got a chick.'

'You two know anything about a big secret that's being kept from us?' Tadpole asked. She really was like a bulldog with a bone.

'Secret?' Mithoorani rolled her eyes. 'Baby I know so many secrets...'

'Me too!'

'Well tell me then!' Tadpole said impatiently.

'Did you know that Shri Julahaha the baya weaver married three wives this season? Three wives! And none of them knew he was already married—twice already!'

'And did you know that just because someone wrote a book on them, all the birds living in Rashtrapati Bhavan are demanding that all other birds need visas and passports to visit!'

'Such arrogance!'

'Secrets about trees!' Tadpole said exasperated. 'Oh, okay, never mind!'

We passed by the (Jealous) Jacs and then the Laburnums.

'I believe the girl grows firangi flowers on her terrace,' one of the laburnums said in a slightly sneery tone.

'My dear Lovely, you know humans, no taste at all.'

'How they love the inferior botanical species! Flowering bushes and plants! My word, whatever next? Weeds and grasses and creepers and lichen?'

'And rosebushes!'

'Dahlias!'

'Chrysanthemums!'

'Petunias…I tell you Petunias!'

'Vegetables darling, she'll be growing vegetables next!'

'Gobi!'

'Kaddu!'

'Mooli!'

'Bhindi!'

'Tori!'

'Shut up!' I said angrily. 'You're being very rude!' I turned to Zafia who was looking a bit surprised. 'Sorry, they just think too much of themselves.'

'Us trees, especially us native flowering trees, no one can touch us for beauty! We have 5,000 years of history and culture behind us. And they were grown yesterday and think they're the cats' whiskers! Out with them I say!'

'Well the laburnums are very pretty when they flower,' Zafia grinned and then winked, 'but the rest of the year…well a bit pathetic I guess. No one notices them. That's probably why they're so cranky most of the time. And I do grow vegetables too and they're very tasty!'

'Did you hear that? She called us pathetic!'

'And cranky!'

'Miss, we'll have you know that your stupid fat dahlias and cauliflowers...'

'You know,' Gingianus interrupted sotto voce, 'the scientific name of laburnum is *Cassia fistula*! You'd think anyone who is called fistula would keep a low profile!' He rolled his eyes. Even I didn't know what it meant so later I quietly Googled it. My God, Gingianus was right! Look it up for yourself, if you want to!

I led Zafia away and was happy to see all the four dogs raise their legs against the 'Lovely' Labs. So much for 5,000 years of history and culture.

7

'*B*haiyya, not this way, we should go from the back. There are lots of hedges there we can hide behind and no one will see us,' Tadpole said excitedly. Zafia had extended her hand and to her delight Mithoorani perched on her fingers.

'Got any sunflower seeds darling?' she drawled. 'These two always forget to bring them.'

But Tads was right; there was no way we could approach the trees growing behind the palace building from the main driveway. We'd be spotted straightaway. There were convenient hedges growing that led towards the thick copse of trees behind the palace.

'Come on,' I said, 'let's go!' I whistled to the dogs which milled around us excitedly. 'Quiet, you guys!' I hissed, taking Zafia's hand and ducking down. A narrow path between the tall hedges gave us cover.

'Are you children hiding from someone?' the hedges whispered, making us jump. They were on both sides and sounded like stereo speakers!

'We're mehandi hedges, so if you like...' they whispered, 'you can ask Mataji who lives in the palace and she'll make your hands look so lovely...'

'No thanks and no we're not hiding,' Zafia answered calmly, going a bit pink, 'we're just playing.'

Good grief, now the hedges were talking to us too, whatever

next? I was astonished at the size of the 'forest' that stretched back from the rear of the palace building. The main driveway ran right around the palace, and there must have been garages or stables here because there was a row of dilapidated buildings, several of which had peepal trees (probably cousins of the Princesses) growing out of them. But beyond them, it was all jungle that sloped downwards in rocky steps. We approached carefully. Tadpole looked absolutely thrilled.

'I bet these guys will tell us the secret,' she said, running up to an enormous tamarind tree. Behind him were various other trees—and lots of twisted Julies too.

'Are you Shri Imliji?' Tadpole asked politely. 'If you are, your cousin Mr Tamar-i-Hind sends his regards. We wait under him for our school bus every day.'

'So at last you've come to see us!' Shri Imli sounded disgruntled. 'Everyone here has been talking about you children and yet you never even looked this way and ignored us.'

'Sorry Imliji, you see we're scared of the old couple. They'll kick us out if they see us!'

'Oh they're harmless and toothless and they'd love to talk to you!'

'Imliji, everyone says there's some big secret here...' Tadpole would just not give up. Prickly voices from beyond Imliji wafted over; those awful Julies again.

'And so there is...and wouldn't you like to know it dearie! But we're not going to tell you, are we?'

'Keep quiet, you fools!' Imliji snapped. He shivered his feathery leaves, sending clouds of them cascading down. 'There is no secret—it's all rumour and gossip,' he said in a more gentle tone. 'You shouldn't believe what those thorny, prickly types tell you.'

'But we heard it from the trees in Lodi Gardens and they're not prickly...'

'Them? Bah!'

'Baby, you should ask the avenue trees in New Delhi. They'll tell you some very interesting things,' the Julies said maliciously.

'Avenue trees? Who are they?'

'Oh, you know the tamarinds on Ashoka Road and the jamuns at India Gate and the neems on Shahjehan Road and those arjun fellows at Motilal Nehru Marg.'

'Will you stupid Julies keep quiet?'

'Come on, Tads, forget about the so-called secret, let's explore this forest,' I said. We moved in amongst the trees, looking around in astonishment.

We could recognize some of them, but not all. They all murmured greetings to us as we walked past them. There were quite a few of those awful Julies too, what with their twisted trunks and terrible spikes. The 'forest' extended for quite a distance behind the palace building, sloping downwards in rocky steps and apart from the trees there were creepers and bushes. Some areas were open and rocky and others had a fresh green cover.

'You're so lucky to live next to a forest like this,' Zafia said, her eyes shining.

Tadpole grabbed my hand and the dogs lined up in their usual way, looking alertly down the path we had come. HighQ barked tentatively.

The caretaker's witch-like wife was tottering towards us, carrying a huge bundle of peepal leaves on her head. She was in a ragged orange and green sari, and was bow-legged and as crookedly bent as one of the Julies. Her face was wrinkled and her eyes were cloudy grey. She saw us suddenly and stopped.

And then she smiled.

One yellow tooth stuck out of her lower jaw and her eyes crinkled up.

Tadpole quickly got between Zafia and me and clutched our hands.

'Namaste Mataji,' Zafia said politely, smiling back. 'Kaise ho? How are you?'

I just grinned like an idiot.

'Children!' The old crone sounded delighted. 'Children haven't played here for many years...' She wiped her eyes with her pallu and smiled at us again. Her hair was bright orange too.

'Bhaiyya, why is she crying?' Tadpole asked.

'Come,' the old woman went on. 'See the palace and have some lassi!'

The dogs went up to sniff her and I was about to call them back when...

'And how are you all?' she asked them, patting Dufus on the head as the others pranced around her whining delightedly and wagging their tails.

We followed the old lady back to the palace. Her husband was asleep on a charpoy in the backyard under the shade of a neem tree.

'Wake up, children have come!' the old lady yelled. 'Feed them!' She dumped her bundle of leaves in front of a tethered buffalo in the backyard and went back to the charpoy and shook it.

'I'm getting up!' the old man grumbled, sitting up and yawning. He saw us and nodded a greeting.

'You know, Zafia, I've never been inside a palace before,' Tadpole whispered as we followed the old couple into the building. We entered what seemed to have been a kitchen. There was a long bank of clay ovens built into one wall. The old man scuttled inside another room and emerged dragging a couple of chairs. There was a long rickety table in the kitchen which we stood around.

'Please sit,' he said and disappeared inside to get more chairs.

'Whose palace is this?' Zafia asked as the old lady poured out thick lassi from an earthenware pot into small tumblers.

'It was the Sultan's palace first, and then the white sahibs snatched it!' she said proudly. 'Then they went away and sold it to an adha-angrez (half-English) fauji who had married a desi and had two daughters who played here! Now they are old women like me!' She looked sad. 'The palace is falling down! No one looks after it!'

We could see that. There were cracks zigzagging down the walls, the paint was peeling everywhere and there were huge dark damp patches on the ceiling.

'Could we look inside?' Zafia asked.

They nodded.

It was amazing, like a museum that had not been opened for a hundred years. There was a huge entrance lobby with creaky wooden floor and a wide marble staircase winding up from either side. At one end was a wooden stage, like a bandstand, and what looked like a grand piano concealed under a dust cover. Two huge cobwebby chandeliers hung from the ceiling. The drawing and dining rooms, which were enormous, were full of creaky ancient furniture, also covered. There were some ornamental vases and marble statues of naked ladies on tables and sideboards and paintings of snooty British army officers and ladies on the walls. Two rather tatty tiger-skins adorned the walls as did swords and shields and coat of arms.

'It must have been quite something,' Zafia said as we looked up the grand sweeping staircase that led to the first floor. We followed the old lady up the steps. She jangled a large bunch of heavy brass keys in her hand. Tadpole remained quiet—she was still wary of the old lady. The dogs bustled about in their usual happy way. All the bedrooms or bedchambers opened out into a wide, airy gallery that ran around the whole floor. The bedchambers were enormous, with huge old four-poster beds and dressers as tall as giraffes though the mirrors were badly stained and warped. The bathrooms too were huge.

'We're inspecting this place as if we're going to buy it,' Zafia suddenly giggled. 'But I really would love to live in a palace like this!'

'Me too,' Tadpole said suddenly. She grinned. 'Then we could sit under the trees and have a mad tree party every evening!' She looked at me. 'Bhaiyya, do you think they'd know about the secret?' she asked.

'Don't know, why don't you ask them?'

'Nah, not now. Maybe later.'

'She won't eat you Tads, she's a sweet old lady.'

'Look she's caught a mouse!' Tadpole gave a small scream and pointed. Sure enough, the old lady was holding up a small mousetrap, which had a mouse in it.

'There are so many,' she said, smiling and holding it up for us to see. Then she looked at the mouse. 'How many times have I told you not to come inside the house? But do you listen? Now, see, you've been caught! I'm going to take you out and free you—but don't you come back here! The old man doesn't like it, you hear?'

Tadpole was beaming at her. Then she went up to her and took her hand.

'You silly thing, no sense you have, coming here and getting caught all the time!' Tadpole scolded the mouse. She smiled at the old woman. 'Let it go! I hope she has learned a lesson!'

I grinned at Zafia. 'That's Tadpole softening her up for the kill! Wait and watch!'

What I loved about the palace was the wide breezy galleries that ran right around the rooms on the first floor and the terrace which was crowned by what the old lady called, 'chattris' (umbrellas). Cool places to roller skate in, or use a skateboard. From the gallery on the southern wing you could see our farm (and Circuit House), looking all new and shiny. The eastern flank overlooked the 'wild' forest, while from the northern side you saw the great trees of the 'sacred grove' that we had met and befriended. The western side overlooked the big unkempt lawn that was divided in four parts by pathways and what the old lady (who was quite chatty) called a 'charbagh'.

'Mataji,' Tadpole said, blinking innocently, 'some people told us that the trees around the lake are a part of a sacred grove and no one can pick or cut anything there. Why is that so?'

'Ah, she's using the flanking maneuver!' I murmured.

The old lady smiled. 'Child, the trees there are very old and sacred. So no one must cut or pick anything from them,' she said.

'Oh, but aren't the trees in the forest behind the palace sacred too?'

'No, that's not a sacred grove. It's just jungle! '

'Oh, so who planted all those trees in the sacred grove?'

'Ask the old man all these questions, he'll tell you.'

We went back down. 'Can we come here and play?' Tadpole asked in her sweetest voice, eyeing the huge 'ballroom'.

'You can come any time you want,' the old woman said, 'I know you are good children because you spoke to that mouse!'

'Thank you!' Tadpole beamed.

That's as far as Tadpole got that afternoon, because the old man was snoring loudly on his charpoy and it would not be nice to wake him up.

'Can we walk a bit in the jungle?' I asked the old lady as she settled down to clean some rice. We hadn't really explored it because we had run into her and I was curious about it. It seemed to be a wild, exciting place to explore.

'Certainly, but go carefully. There are lots of thorny plants there and stinging insects and scorpions.'

'We will be careful. Come on guys, let's check it out,' I said.

Tadpole cast a wistful glance at the old man, willing him to wake up, but to no avail. The path that led into the jungle went all the way down the rocky slope to the eastern boundary wall and then turned left parallel to it. It went up to the northern boundary before heading westwards again, towards the mango orchard and then back south, forming a full circuit around the 'jungle.' The jungle was crowded with trees. They rustled at us in a friendly manner, and murmured amongst themselves.

'Why are they whispering like that?' Tadpole asked, eyeing them suspiciously. 'There is some secret and they're keeping it from us.'

'Or they're talking about us,' Zafia said, smiling. 'I hope they're saying nice things!'

We sat on boulders in the shade of one of the Julies, taking a break when suddenly it whispered.

'Hey kids, do you know the great secret of Medley Gardens?'

'What?' I asked, surprised.

'No! Tell us, tell us, tell us!' Tadpole said, unfazed.

'Oh that sucks! We thought *you* knew. We know there *is* a secret but we don't know *what* it is. It's been driving us crazy for years!'

'Who knows?' Tadpole demanded.

'Those prima donnas in their so-called "sacred" grove know!

Your precious Ustadji and his girlfriends. Those neems and the mangoes—all of them I think—even our Julie cousins who grow there. But will they tell us? No! Never! Even the birds, won't tell us, no matter what we offer them! Bah! It's so frustrating it makes us grow wildly!'

'Sunflower seeds!' Tadpole said thoughtfully. 'Next time I'm going to offer Mithoorani sunflower seeds, maybe she'll tell us then!'

'Come on, time we got back,' I said. 'But this is a great place to explore!'

It was getting on to five o'clock and a cobweb grey mist had begun to descend, turning the 'wild' Julies into ghostly, twisted figures. We would soon have to drop Zafia off at the pick-up point.

'See you guys,' I said, waving to the trees.

'Come back soon,' some of the wild Julies whispered. 'And tell us what the great secret is!'

'We'll try!' Tadpole assured them. 'Promise!'

Zafia's mom, Zaheeda Aunty was waiting in her Honda under Tamar-i-Hind when we drove up to drop Zafia off. She was a very erudite (that's learned) and famous historian and taught at Jawaharlal Nehru University. It was said she had a huge collection of rare old historical books and manuscripts in her library.

'Hello children, had a good day?' she asked, getting out of the car.

'I had a great time, Mamma,' Zafia said. 'They live in a fantastic place!'

And then I had my brainwave. 'Aunty, we live next to this old palace called Medley Gardens. Someone told us that it was built by some sultan and then taken over by the British who sold it to an army officer. His daughters are now fighting over the place.

Would you be able to find out more about the palace?' I told her the location and our address.

'Well, well, I'm very impressed Vishwajit,' Zaheeda Aunty said, 'to think that you're so seriously interested in your neighbours!' Her brown eyes twinkled. 'Would you know approximately when it was built?'

I shook my head. 'No, Aunty but over 250 years ago definitely. There's only an old Baba and his wife living there now and they're quite vague and wooly headed. But I'll try and find out from them again.'

She smiled. 'Great, you do that and I'll look up what I can about the place—you search for it online too. If I find any literature or written material in my library, I'll let you know. Then you can come over and research it for yourself! How does that sound?'

'Great!' I was exultant. One, I had impressed Zafia's mom. Two, I could hopefully find out more about Medley Gardens. Three (and most important): in doing so, I could spend more quality time with Zafia! Learning history of course! 'Thank you so much, Aunty!'

'I want to find out too!' Tadpole said. 'I'm interested in it too!'

I almost retorted, 'you're too young for this,' when I clammed up. After all it was chiefly because of Tadpole that all this had happened.

'Okay, okay...but don't be a nuisance,' I said and she glared at me.

I did Google Medley Gardens later that evening, but got nowhere. It turned out to be the name of a street in a small town called Tipton in England.

'How can a street be called "Medley Gardens"? Tadpole asked. 'It should be called "Medley Street"!'

I grinned. 'Next time you meet someone from England, you can ask them!'

A few days later, on a Friday evening, Zafia called me.

'Hi, can you and Tadpole come over tomorrow?' she asked. She sounded upset.

'Why? Has your mom found something about Medley Gardens?' My hopes soared.

'No, not yet...it's a bit difficult to explain. You know I was walking past the shopping complex in our locality when I heard this gurgling, strangling sort of sound...'

'Oh...and...?'

'I looked around, but none of the people around seemed to be making that noise. It sounded like someone was choking.'

'And?'

'It was the tree I was standing under. A gulmohur, I think. Its leaves were sort of trembling and shivering and every now and then it would emit this horrible choking gurgle.'

'Did you ask it why?'

'Idiot! There were so many people around. But I saw why it was making that sound. Its trunk right from the ground up has been tightly cemented. They've built this new low wall right around it, choking it. It's a young tree and must still be growing.'

'Oh shoot!'

'Can you and Tads come over and check it out? Then I'll tell Mamma and she'll get them to break the wall, I don't think they're allowed to build right around the trunk and roots of a tree like that.'

'Okay, sure.'

We went to Zafia's place the next day. She was right. The poor tree was being slowly garroted to death. We took her mom along to see it and she got in touch with a botany expert at the university who contacted the authorities who had done this stupid thing. The wall was broken down in a week's time. We went back to see the tree afterwards.

'Thank you so much,' she said. 'I'm Gully, by the way. It's such a relief.' She sighed heavily.

'What's the problem?' Zafia asked very softly. 'You can breathe and grow properly, can't you?'

'Yes,' Gully replied in a martyred tone. 'It's not me I'm thinking of. It's those poor Bonsai trees in the Bonsai Park at Lodi Gardens. Can you imagine what it must be like to be a Bonsai?'

'Gully, what's Bonsai?' Tadpole asked in her usual blunt way and unmindful that someone might overhear her talking to a tree.

Gully shuddered. 'You know,' she said, 'your species does a lot of horrible things to us. You lop off our branches—how would you like it if we cut off your arms or legs? You strip our leaves to feed your goats and buffaloes—how would you like it if we stripped off sections of your skin and ate them? You chop us down with axes or power saws to make chairs and tables and newspapers. It may take us 100 years to grow and you bring us down in thirty seconds flat. And you do that to forests, which are the size of entire countries! You deliberately grow forests so you can cut them down again, how sadistic is that! You set fire to us and burn us down. But with Bonsai what you do is the worst. You deliberately stunt our growth by snipping away at our roots and branches. And it's for no real reason at all though you say it's spiritual! You want mighty redwood and banyan trees to be one foot tall! And you think we look beautiful like that! How perverted and gross is that! How would you like it if we could do something so you became dwarves and midgets and hobbits and never grew beyond six inches high?'

We looked at each other nonplussed. We had never thought about it that way.

'I think you should go and visit those poor Bonsais at Lodi Gardens. At least you freed me…but there's nothing you can do for those pour souls except maybe give them some comfort.'

'Sure we will!' we all chimed together, feeling terrible. 'We promise!'

'Thank you,' Gully said, with a sniff. 'You really are good kids.'

Frankly we didn't feel all that good. I knew Zafia was particularly upset because she said that one of her aunts had a couple of Bonsai trees.

'I'm never going to speak to her again,' she said stormily, wiping a tear. 'Always snipping, snipping, snipping at them with her secateurs.'

'Maybe if you tell her, she'd realize what she'd done and stop.'

Zafia sniffed. 'Yes, maybe, but it's too late for the ones she already has. I don't think they'll be able to grow into towering trees now.'

'I guess.'

An old woman selling dark red roses noticed us and waddled up.

'Buy your girlfriend some flowers, make her happy!' she said, thrusting a bouquet of deep maroon roses at me. I blushed as Tadpole giggled.

'Yes, yes, Bhaiyya, to show you love her!'

Now poor Zafia blushed!

'Tadpole!'

'Don't be stingy! Buy her those roses! See she's upset.'

'Will you just pipe down?' I hissed.

'We would be honoured if you bought some of us and presented us to the lovely lass!'

'Eh? Who said that?' I stared suspiciously at Tadpole, whose mouth was open in surprise and then widened into a grin of pure delight.

'They did, they did, they did!' she said pointing to the flowers, as Zafia looked on, her face still pink. 'Now you just *have* to buy them!'

The old crone thrust a bouquet at me. 'Buy them, she'll be happy, she'll love you very much!'

'Er...' I said hoarsely to the bouquet, hardly knowing what I was doing. 'You don't mind?'

'Not at all! We've been raised for this! They grow us in a flower farm and cut us and then sell us so we can make people happy.'

'Except when they pull our petals apart, or use us to string garlands with, which are put around the greasy necks of politicians. Yuck, what a fate! Those people smell terrible, and are full of sweat and grunge and lies!'

'We've got maybe two or three more days to live, so we might as well make people happy during that time! Especially young people in love like you!'

All the roses in the bouquet were speaking—turn by turn it seemed.

'Okay,' I said hastily, going scarlet. 'How much?' I asked the crone.

'Only a hundred rupees,' she replied.

That would clean me out for the week but I had no choice. I dug into my pockets.

Zafia went deep pink with delight when I presented her the bouquet.

'Hope this makes you happy!' I mumbled, going even deeper scarlet myself. Tadpole clapped and whistled and quickly took a photograph with her phone.

'Tadpole, will you cut it out!' I hissed as she grinned and winked.

'Thank you,' Zafia said softly, 'No boy has ever bought me flowers before, let alone talking roses!' She sniffed them appreciatively. 'They're beautiful and smell wonderful. Let's go home and I'll put them in a vase!'

'You know,' I said slowly, 'this is beginning to get out of control.'

'What is?' Zafia asked, as Tadpole went off to the kitchen for a nimbu paani.

'First the trees at Medley Gardens started talking to us, then other trees and bushes in town, and now even cut flowers are talking to us. We'll be having conversations with cauliflowers next.'

'That should be interesting and intellectual,' Zafia said. Then she leaned towards me and pecked both my cheeks, her eyes shining. 'That's for the roses,' she said. 'It was so sweet of you. Wait till I tell my girlfriends—they'll be so jealous!'

I would normally have reacted to that, but another monumental thought had just struck me.

'Zafia, you know we're going to Rajbagh over the Christmas break. What happens if the entire forest starts talking to us? We'll be deafened!'

'They'll have so many interesting things to tell you,' Zafia said. 'You'd better take a recorder along!'

'Very funny.' I looked at her. Her brown eyes were sparkling and she cocked her head to one side and raised her eyebrows.

'What?' I asked.

'Oh, so your mom hasn't told you?'

'Told me what?'

'That Mamma and I are coming along too. Your mom invited us... Papa can't make it, but we can...'

'You're coming to Rajbagh with us! Awesome!'

'Isn't it!' Her eyes shone happily.

Her room door opened and Tadpole and Zaheeda Aunty entered.

'Bhaiyya, Zafia and Aunty are coming with us to Rajbagh!' Tadpole said excitedly. 'Aunty just told me!'

'I know.'

'Hello beta,' Zaheeda Aunty said, spotting the roses immediately. I went red.

'Aunty, did you find out anything about Medley Gardens?' I asked, hoping to distract her.

'I'm sorry I haven't had the time, but will certainly look it up. How about you? Any luck on the internet?'

That's what I liked so much about Zafia's mom. She spoke to you as an equal. I was not even sixteen and she was a famous scholar and she was talking to me as if we were equal partners in an important research project. I nodded.

'All I discovered was that Medley Gardens is a street in a small town called Tipton in England,' I said ruefully.

'Medley Gardens is quite a big palace, so there must be something written about it, somewhere,' she told me. 'Don't worry, we'll ferret it out sooner or later!'

8

$\mathcal{A}$s the weather got colder we noticed that the trees in Medley Gardens seemed to become quieter and moodier. Ustadji became all grumpy and even the Peepal Princesses didn't giggle or tease us like before. As for Kapok Maharajji, he seemed to go into a shell, dropping leaves left right and centre so that the branches started looking bare.

'They always get like this at this time of the year,' Mithoorani assured us. 'Nothing to worry about! They're under a lot of stress because they're all making preparations for the big Open House Festival which begins in March. They have to transport food and drink to the places they'll start budding from—it takes a lot of work and coordination, so they end up being quite moody.'

'Oh,' I said, 'I suppose it's all right then.'

We had also noticed that several new birds had suddenly arrived in Medley Gardens at about this time and asked Ustadji about them.

'Oh, they're our winter guests,' he said. 'Those fellows there on the grass, running around and wagging their tails are wagtails. They and several others have flown down all the way from Central Asia and Siberia—just imagine.' There was another black and russet fellow, with an ashy cap, who kept shivering his tail and bowing, which Ustadji said was a black redstart. But he got really excited one morning and was waving his roots at us madly as we approached.

'Children, I'd like you to meet Chhotu,' he said and a tiny ash grey and yellow bird with a small truncated crest whirred on to a branch near us. 'He's a grey-headed canary flycatcher and lives in the Rajbagh National Park, where my Nani is. He'll spend the winter here with us at Medley Gardens. His family has been doing that for generations.'

'Hello there,' Tadpole said, 'you know we're going to Rajbagh too, for three days soon.'

The little bird emitted a cheerful little whistling song and zoomed off.

'He's a bit shy,' Ustadji said fondly, 'he says that Nani is getting on a bit but doing very well. She's around 700 years old after all and is the grandest matriarch in all of Rajbagh. My father of course as you know, is the famous Jogi Mahal banyan in Ranthambore, and my mother is related to… well you must have heard of the great banyan in the Botanical Gardens in Kolkata…'

'There he goes again, dropping names and boring everyone with his famous relatives,' the DDT dozen chimed, exasperatedly. Tadpole and I hid our grins.

We had also made friends—sort of—with the villagers who came regularly to the forest behind the palace to pick up leaves and dry branches. Tadpole would wave madly and smile at them and they'd smile back. The women loved her and would pat her head or pinch her cheeks and offer her little tidbits. When they got to the forest they would often hunker down, kindle a small fire and make tea—which we had to drink too. They seemed to sense that all three of us—and Tadpole especially—had this affinity with the sacred grove and the forest. Every time they came they would first 'pay homage' to the Peepli Princesses and

Ustadji, leaving small offerings of flowers and agarbattis before setting off for the forest. Often they brought their children along, and would scold them soundly if they tried to pick leaves from branches in the sacred grove. Tadpole would sometimes join them in their little ceremonies, and later cheekily ask the Princesses or Ustadji: 'See now, I've prayed to you, so please tell me what the secret is!'

And the Princesses and Ustadji would rustle their leaves and fan her cheeks with a cool breeze, but that was all.

There was a freak thunderstorm in the beginning of December and while some of the trees in the jungle section of the palace grounds did lose fairly large limbs—and one or two keeled over, our friends in the sacred grove remained standing. When we went to check on them all, there was bad news. Imliji was very upset.

'I've just heard that Tamar is not doing too well,' he told us. 'Some of the birds are saying that he's listing to one side after this storm. He is very old, but he's grand too. Could you check on him and let me know exactly how he is? These birds are never very good at reporting facts.'

When Mom dropped us off at the school bus stop the following day, we realized that the rumours had been true. The huge tamarind tree was leaning over towards the road, though it still seemed to be holding firm. Tadpole rushed over and hugged him.

'How are you feeling?' she asked. 'We were told you were not well.'

'Tadpole, back off!' I said, looking around. Luckily none of the other kids who were picked up from this stop had arrived. A few passers-by glanced curiously at her.

'Hello Baby, no I'm not doing too well,' the grand old tree admitted and creaked. 'That last storm was terrible. The soil under my roots is coming loose and my roots can't get a grip.'

'Can we do something?'

'No Baby, but thank you for being so concerned.'

A couple of cars and motorcycles drew up dropping off the other kids. Tadpole stood near Tamar-i-Hind, giving him sympathetic looks while trying to talk to her friends. This was Zafia's stop too, and soon her mom dropped her off and waved to us. I drifted up beside Zafia.

'Hi,' she said, her eyes twinkling. 'I had a very interesting discussion about the state of our country with a pumpkin, a kaddu growing on my terrace—it was like those TV talk shows.'

'I told you this would happen!'

'She said that if all the political leaders in the country really did have kaddus for brains, the country would prosper and race past China and the US in one year flat!'

'Oh!'

'Hi Zafia. You know, poor old Tamar is not feeling well,' Tadpole said, joining us, her eyes worried. 'Can your mom ask her botany professor friend to do something for him?'

'Hey, what are you phuss-phussing about?' Mohit Kanoria, who was big and hefty, and a known bully, thrust his pasty face at us, leering. 'Hey Zaf, why do you hang around with wusses?' He laughed.

'I'll hang around with who I feel like,' Zafia said sharply. 'You stay with your own rodent kind.'

'The chick has spirit, I love that!' He leered at me. 'And the boyfriend hasn't jumped to her defence!'

'Will you…' I started hotly, beginning to bunch my fists. Then Tadpole suddenly grabbed me.

'Bhaiyya,' she said tearfully. 'Tamar is saying that he can't stay upright any longer!'

'What?' Both Zafia and I turned towards the huge tree. Low creaking sounds were emerging from it.

'Kids, she's right. I can't stand anymore. Move away from me now! Quickly!'

'What?' I looked around. There must have been about fifteen kids milling around the bus stop, chatting and fooling around. The bus should be arriving at any minute.

'Yes and you were saying?' Mohit thrust his face into mine, grinning.

'Oh get lost, Mohit,' I turned back to the tree. 'Are you sure?'

'Yes, my time has come...'

'What time has come Bhaiyya?' Tadpole asked with tears in her eyes.

'Hey, who are you talking to?' Mohit inquired belligerently. 'I'm right here.'

Zafia had taken Tadpole by the hand and had begun moving away.

'Everyone!' I suddenly shouted. 'Move away from the tree. It's about to come down! Move, move, move!'

'What?'

'Yeah, move away, Iron Man here is going to push this tree down with his pinky finger!' Mohit hooted, and leant against Tamar.

Some of the other kids began moving away, and now Zafia too was ushering them aside. Tamar creaked a little louder.

'Will you get out of there?' I shouted, 'you'll be smashed to pulp when it comes down!'

'Sure, sure...'

'Not long now,' the great tree groaned. 'I'm so glad I met you all… Good luck…!'

'Can't you hang on just a little while? We could get help .'

'The soil won't hold me any more, beta.'

I glanced up at the tree.

'Abandon tree, abandon tree, mayday, mayday, mayday!' Mynas and parakeets screeched as they zoomed out of the tree, and a pair of kites that had built a huge nest right at the top, just circled around, mewling helplessly. There was nothing they could do.

Zafia now did a very brave thing. She stepped out into the middle of the road and put her hands out stopping the traffic. Tadpole grabbed hold of a couple of her friends and went and joined her and soon all the kids had joined hands and were standing across the road. The traffic screeched to an indignant halt.

'Mohit, get the hell out of there!' I yelled, backing away, because by now, Tamar-i-Hind had begun keeling over. It was imperceptible at first, but becoming obvious. If Mohit didn't move he'd be squelched all over the pavement and who wanted to see his brains? I grabbed his hand and yanked hard, pulling him out of the great tree's shadow.

'Thank you,' Tamar groaned, 'I would have hated to kill someone in my last moments… Even a bully!'

And then, as everyone watched stupefied, the great tree fell. We felt the ground shudder as he came down, raising a cloud of dust, his great roots ripping out of the mud. He brought down the roof of the bus shelter as well as wires and cables that sparked and fizzed, and smashed the divider in the middle of the road. But, thanks to Zafia and the other kids standing firm across the road, not a single vehicle or person was crushed under his great weight and all the kids were safe too. Mohit's face was chalk-white as he stared at the fallen tree.

'How did you know the tree was about to fall?' he stammered.

'You saved my life, man!'

'It told me,' I said unthinkingly, 'it warned me. Didn't you hear it?' Mohit gave me a strange look.

'Whatever, but thanks...I would have been chutney.' He wiped his face. By now our school bus had joined the long queue of vehicles hooting and tooting in frustration behind the fallen tree and we walked up to it and got on board. Zafia was still consoling Tadpole who was crying.

'One minute,' Tadpole sobbed suddenly freeing her hand. She jumped off the bus and scampered back to Tamar, now lying flat on the road. Zafia and I followed even as Ms Hawakhanewalli, also on the bus bellowed:

'You! Get back here at once, where do you think you're going? There may be live wires on the ground!'

But Tadpole was standing in front of the tree, tears running down her cheeks.

'I'm sorry,' she said, 'I'm so sorry this happened.'

'Come on Tads,' I said putting my arm around her.

'Look!' Zafia said, pointing. Thousands of ants were vacating the tree, some carrying tiny white capsules, which I later realized were their eggs. 'They've lost their homes too!'

It wouldn't be long before men with axes would arrive and hack off Tamar's huge branches, to clear the road. Already we could hear the sirens of emergency vehicles.

'We'd better go,' I whispered to Zafia. 'Before they start hacking. It'll upset Tadpole like anything.' Tadpole reached forward and broke off a couple of fruit pods.

'Will these grow if I plant them at home?'

'I don't know Tads, we could try.' We took her by the hand and led her back to the bus where Ms Hawakhanewalli had smoke coming out of her ears.

'You kids, you have detention for a week!' she thundered.

Amazingly, Mohit and some of the other kids put up their hands.

'Ma'am, but they saved our lives!' Mohit said. 'They warned us that the tree was about to fall and made us move away. How they knew, I don't know—Vish said the tree told him! We didn't have any idea!'

'Oh, very well,' Ms Hawakhanewalli seemed unwillingly mollified. 'But it was still stupid to go back after it had fallen.'

'Better than before, Ma'am,' Mohit said cheekily and everyone laughed. She glared at him, as the bus began extricating itself from the huge traffic jam. But she was looking strangely at the three of us and suddenly I realized why. She was remembering the incident with the trees in the school playground—especially when Tadpole had turned around to say 'bye' to the neem we had just befriended. I was now sure we had not heard the last of this, because once she got her teeth into something she would not let go until she had all the answers.

Sure enough all three of us were called to the principal, Ms Mahajan's office during the lunch break. 'What have you kids done now?' Ms Shalini, her PA asked, ruffling Tadpole's hair.

'We've done nothing, Ma'am!' Tadpole said.

We were called in and stood before the huge, gleaming desk, behind which our principal sat. She had short no-nonsense silver grey hair, but liked wearing necklaces and bracelets with enormous multicolored stones. Hawakhanewalli eyed us like we were Martians and indicated we sit.

'Vishwajit, Zafia and little Sameeha...what's all this about this tree fixation you seem to have? I hope you are not under too much stress.' She riffled through some papers on her desk. 'It doesn't appear so, your academic performance is good. So what is it? Would you like to talk to Ms Diwani, the counselor? Is there something troubling you?'

'Ma'am, it was so sad when the tree fell,' Tadpole gulped, wiping back a tear. 'It was such a big, friendly fellow...'

'She means tree!' Zafia and I chimed together. Ms Mahajan looked at us askance and Hawakhanewalli had an 'I told you so', expression on her face.

'All of you have friends in school, don't you?' Ms Mahajan asked. 'I remember seeing you all running around in the grounds, so it's not that you're lonely.'

'Yes Ma'am, we have friends!'

'So why do you have to talk to trees? Ms Hawakhanewalli said she distinctly heard Sameeha talk to a neem tree in the playground. What do you have to say about that?'

'But Ma'am they must be so lonely!' Tadpole said. 'They stand in one place their entire lives with no one to talk to. They can't go to the malls or video parlours, it's just so sad for them.'

Ms Mahajan smiled. 'So you think if you talk to them they'll be happy?'

'Yes, Ma'am,' Zafia said, 'I mean it's a known fact that plants like music and grow better when they hear it.'

'Not the kind of music you kids listen to, these days!' Hawakhanewalli retorted.

Ms Mahajan had fixed her grey eyes on me. 'How did you know that tree was about to fall?'

'Um, it was creaking and groaning away, besides leaning over the road. And then suddenly all the birds flew out of it...'

'None of the other children seemed to have heard or noticed anything.'

'Ma'am, they were all listening to music or talking. If they had paid attention they would have heard it too.'

'Very well. You certainly have saved some of their lives, we're very proud of you. You reacted quickly and sensibly. Well done!'

'Thank you, Ma'am!'

'But kindly don't indulge in this sort of thing in school,' Hawakhanewalli said sternly. 'It is disruptive.'

'Yes, Ma'am.'

'But if the trees wish us good morning, it would be rude not to reply,' Tadpole said indefatigably. She got a glare from Hawa but a smile from Ms Mahajan.

'Okay, you can go,' she said. 'Zafia dear, do stay back a moment...'

I waited outside for Zafia.

'What did she want?' I asked her all agog when she came out. Zafia grinned.

'She asked me what sort of music I play to my plants. She said all her house plants look pretty miserable and need to be cheered up. So I told her that my plants like classical stuff, not jazz or anything with too much percussion. She's asked me to record some of it for her!'

Imliji—and some of the others in the sacred grove—were very sad when we told them about what had happened to Tamar.

'You know, Tamar always looked so big and strong, but he really wasn't. He was growing too close to that terrible road and imbibed poisonous traffic fumes all his life. They probably weakened him. They say he had breathing problems. Well, at least he's out of his misery now, poor fellow.'

'He said the soil had come loose under him.'

'That's probably because you people must have been digging under him and not covered up properly afterwards.'

'Imliji, I picked these pods from him after he had fallen. I'm going to plant them in our farm,' Tadpole said. 'So in a way he'll be with us forever.'

'That's so sweet of you.'

'Don't do that, Baby! Don't you know it's bad luck to plant tamarind trees? Plant us instead...' Those evil Julifloras just couldn't mind their own business.

'Go to hell!' Tadpole yelled at them. 'I'm going to plant them, so there!'

Tamar unfortunately was not the only casualty caused by that storm. An old, long dead fish-tail palm in Zafia's garden keeled over and was found leaning tiredly against the side of their house the next morning. Zafia only noticed it after she got back from school that day. When she rang to tell me she was in tears.

'Old Fish-tail's fallen,' she sobbed. 'I think he had died some years ago, because he had no leaves, just this cheese plant creeper growing up his trunk and he wouldn't talk. But even so, he had hollows for magpie robins to nest in and love seats for parakeets to court and kiss and cuddle each other without being hassled by crows. Mama says we'll have to bring him down because he's dangerous and could fall any time. I hate these storms! Could you come over please?'

'Sure!'

Tadpole and I were dropped over at her place that weekend and she took us out to the garden. The sad old tree—only the trunk was left—leaned against the building.

'When are you going to pull it down?' I asked. 'We'll be here with you.'

'Thanks,' Zafia said in a small voice. 'Mama says she's written for permission to the Tree Officer in the Forest Department, who has to come and inspect him and give us permission. Mama sent them photographs and then she had to get an affidavit from the court. It was quite a rigmarole.' She gave a small smile. 'She said they wanted to know who the tree's father/husband was and all kinds of intricate and very silly details like who planted it and the name of their father/husband.'

'Your mom must have had fun filling in the form.'

'Yeah, now let's see what happens.

Actually nothing did, for weeks. Then, one foggy morning in December, just before our trip to Rajbagh and when Tadpole and I had gone over to Zafia's place again, two men turned up from the Forest Department and wanted to see the tree.

'Hmm,' frowned the Tree Officer, looking up the trunk. 'But it's alive, it's green!' He was a short portly, balding man in a grey pullover and muffler and trousers.

'That is a creeper growing on it,' Zaheeda Aunty pointed out. 'You can see the tree is dead.'

The second man, who must have been the TO's sidekick, gave the tree one look, and snorted, 'It's dried up, it's dead!' and shrugged. The Tree Officer took several pictures from different angles.

'So when will you let us know?' Zaheeda Aunty asked.

The Tree Officer nodded importantly. 'A report will have to be written. It will take time.'

'I hope it will be the Final Report and not the First Interim Report!' Zaheeda Aunty said, a smile twitching on her face. We giggled.

'We'll write a report!' the Tree Officer repeated woodenly.

'Really,' Zafia's mom said shaking her head after they'd left. 'I can't believe how ridiculous it is—technically that tree has fallen—if it had fallen the other way it would have been lying flat in the garden.'

Back in Medley Gardens that evening, Tadpole excitedly recounted to Ustadji what had happened.

'So these fellows have to write a big report,' she said. 'Can you imagine?'

'I wonder how many thousand pages it will be,' Ustadji mused. 'It's wonderful that you people take so much care and trouble over bringing down even a dead tree.'

'Yes,' I said, 'I didn't think of it that way. The government does care about trees and nature after all...'

'And yet, for a housing project or shopping mall or coal mine, they'll hack down 500 fully mature trees without batting an eyelash. I mean how many grand old trees have been martyred for the Metro project?'

Then, on the evening before we were to set off for Rajbagh, Zafia rang up.

'Hi,' she said, 'I have good news and bad news depending on how you look at it.'

'Eh? What do you mean?'

'Mom can't make it to Rajbagh. Some urgent work has come up and she has to finish it.'

'Oh, shoot!' My heart sank. I had really been looking forward to the trip with Zafia.

'That's the bad news,' Zafia said. 'Do you want to hear the good news?'

'What can be good after that?' I said heavily.

'She said I could go if I wanted. She's spoken to your mom about it. So I'm still coming.'

'Oh wow! Great! Your mom's something else!'

Zafia giggled. 'I think you made a big impression on Mama when you asked about researching Medley Gardens. And by the way—she has unearthed this massive tome, which lists the famous buildings and tombs and palaces that were built in and around Delhi during that period. She said that Medley Gardens should be mentioned in it. It has pictures and black and white sketches and architectural drawings plus information on the structures.'

'Wow! Can you bring it along with you tomorrow?'

'I'll ask her, but I think it should be okay.'

That evening Tadpole and I went over to Medley Gardens again to say goodbye to the trees.

'We'll be meeting your relatives in Rajbagh,' Tadpole said solemnly. 'Do you have any message for them?'

'Give Naniji my regards,' Ustadji said. 'She's the famous Rajmahal banyan in Rajbagh, everyone knows and loves her. As I told you, she's very old now and may not hear or remember as well as before, so she might have a bit of a problem remembering who I am.'

'I'm sure she'll remember you,' Tadpole said, hugging one of Ustadji's prop-roots.

'Enjoy yourselves dears—don't get eaten by tigers and be careful of the elephants,' the Peepal Princesses said. 'Sometimes they like shoving you over just for the heck of it.'

'And don't forget to apply Neem mosquito repellent,' the DDT Didis chimed. 'Or you'll be bitten black and blue!'

We picked up Zafia from her house, early next morning. Tadpole of course had grabbed one window seat and Zafia happily agreed to sit in the middle, next to me. She unzipped her backpack and took out a huge, brown-paper covered volume.

'Here's the book,' she said, her eyes shining. 'We can look through it as we drive.'

'All aboard?' Dad asked, looking back. 'Kids, belt up please, thank you! Off we go!'

He started the big Prado as Zafia and Mom waved to her mom and we set off. We opened out the book on our laps and already underneath it, Zafia's hand had snuck into mine and I squeezed it gently.

'Let's browse through,' she said. 'Sometimes, anticipating is better than actually finding what you're looking for.'

'Show me too,' Tadpole said, 'I want to see it too!'

9

We entered the Rajbagh National Park at around two in the afternoon. By this time, we had long packed up and put away the heavy tome and Zafia was asleep with her head resting on my shoulder, her silky hair cascading down my arm and chest. Of course I pretended to be asleep myself as I breathed in her lovely perfumed shampoo. Tadpole was asleep too, her head lolling against Zafia's shoulder. We drew up outside the Wildlife Department Office and Dad went to meet the Field Director, Dr Arnab Mahatre, who was an old school buddy of his. Dr Mahatre was a big, ruddy faced man with closely cropped snow white hair and a trim moustache, and wore stylish Ray Ban shades. He came out to the car to meet us.

'Welcome to Rajbagh,' he boomed, poking his head through the window and waking the girls up with a start. 'The best run national park in India!'

'Hello,' Mom said politely, getting out of the car.

'I've booked the Rajmahal Forest Resthouse for you, for three days,' Dr Mahatre said cheerfully. 'You should find it quite comfortable.' He smiled at Tadpole.

'So what would you like to see? Tigers? Elephants? Leopards? Wild buffalo? We have them all.'

'Some trees,' Tadpole blurted looking around, and rubbing the sleep out of her eyes.

'Trees, eh?' Dr Mahatre looked surprised. 'Now that's very

interesting! You are interested in botany?'

'We all are,' Tadpole averred looking at Zafia and me for support. Zafia nodded and I mumbled 'uh-huh'.

'Well we have some magnificent trees in the park. Stands of sal and sisoo, banyan and peepul like you've never seen before, khair, bael, wild mango, also climbers and lianas and shrubs and grasslands.'

'It would be nice to see a tiger too,' Dad grinned.

'Sure. A couple of riding elephants have been stationed at the resthouse, and you can use them twice a day, morning and evening. You can drive around too, but must take the forest guard with you. No getting out of the car for any reason or wandering around on foot outside the resthouse premises alone. Okay?'

'Okay, Uncle,' we chorused.

The Rajmahal Forest Resthouse was about 25 kilometres away from the office and we would have to be shown the way to it.

'Arre Ajay Singh, chalo!' Dr Mahatre yelled and a small wiry man scuttled out of the office. He had an ancient shotgun over his shoulder. 'Right, he'll go with you and stay at the resthouse—he's the guard and caretaker—and he knows the jungle inside out. He'll cook for you as well.'

As we drove into the jungle, we looked out of the windows in awe. These forest trees were something else.

'Look at them,' I whispered in awe, 'they're at least three times the size of the trees in Delhi.'

'They're scary,' Tadpole said, 'do you think they'll be friendly?'

'I hope so,' Zafia said, looking at the trees crowding the narrow jungle track we were bumping along.

'They're wild trees, not domesticated like the ones in Delhi,' I said.

'Tall, dark and handsome,' Zafia said with a grin.

'Like me!'

'Haha!' But she did squeeze my hand tightly again!

'Well at any rate the langurs don't seem to be scared of them,' I commented, watching a troupe of monkeys leap exuberantly in the canopy, whooping and yelling, tearing leaves and snapping twigs.

'Bhaiyya, do you think they'll be friendly?' Tadpole asked again; she was quite worried.

'We'll know sooner or later,' I said.

'You know,' Zafia suddenly said, 'they might talk a different language. I mean if people living in different places talk different languages then why not trees?'

It was a sobering thought. If they did, would we be able to understand what they said?

We bumped along the narrow jungle track, panicking flocks of partridges and flame-coloured jungle fowl. The peacocks were really stupid and kept running in front of the car instead of getting out of the way.

Soon we emerged into a huge golden meadow, where the grass was singing like a lovely choir and dancing and swaying in the cool breeze. Ahead, blue hills loomed and there was the silvery glint of a river, studded with polished white rocks.

'Look—chital and sambhar,' Ajay Singh suddenly said pointing to a herd grazing some distance away. Dad stopped the car so we could watch them.

Not too faraway, the grass suddenly agitated violently and a pair of wild boar emerged with twelve striped piglets in tow.

'Piglets! They're so sweet!' Tadpole said, thrilled. The family trotted away briskly, their tails stuck up like antennae.

The meadow gave way to dense jungle again going up a thickly forested hillside. We were about 250 meters from the forest edge when all three of us stiffened.

'Go forage somewhere else, you bullies!'

'Leave us alone. You got your hafta so what do you want now?'

'Goddamn bulldozers!'

'What do you think we are? An eat-all-you-can buffet?'

'Okay guys, poison up leaves—on the double! Spread the word! Thorns and spikes at the ready: nicotine, tannins and cyanides to the frontline!'

The shrill, agitated voices were borne clearly on the breeze.

'Look!' Tadpole cried pointing through the windshield. Ahead, the trees at the edge of the jungle were being pushed. Leaves twirled down and dust rose.

'Elephant!' Ajay Singh said in a low voice. 'Sahib stop.'

A herd of elephants was attacking the trees. We could hear the trees yell as the elephants ripped great swatches of bark off them, or tore down branches and stripped their leaves. Occasionally one would trumpet shrilly, when it probably got pricked by a thorn.

'Freaking maniacs—get away from us!'

'Will you take your filthy trunk off me?'

'Aaargh! Help! I'm going down!'

'Hoodlums!'

'Vegetarian barbarians!'

'Why can't you be self-respecting carnivores?'

'Stop shoving like that!'

'Oh my God,' Zafia said, clutching my hand. 'Look...that poor tree!'

Even as we watched in horror, we saw a large, handsome tree, just at the edge of the forest, sway violently back and forth, its branches and leaves trembling and shivering in fear. Then we saw the elephant—an enormous tusker—was shoving it with his trunk and tusks, back and forth, back and forth. He gave it a final mighty heave, and slowly the tree keeled over and crashed to earth in a cloud of dust. Birds called in alarm and peacocks screamed. The tusker was now ripping off tender leaves from the fallen tree's canopy and stuffing his face.

'Wow!' Dad said, lowering his camera. 'Did you kids see that?' There came a sob from the back row.

Mom looked back at us. 'What's the matter?' Tadpole was in tears and even Zafia's eyes glimmered suspiciously.

'Mama, that elephant just killed that tree,' Tadpole sobbed. 'He just pushed it over. Like you run over someone with a car on purpose.'

'Baby, he has to eat. He's so big and must need so much. He probably needs about 250 kg of vegetables a day!'

'But look at all the other trees they've hurt, pulling branches off them and stripping their bark. Ustadji told me that if their bark gets stripped they die slowly and painfully.'

'Who told you?'

'Ummm, our Botany teacher at school,' I said hastily. 'Ms Varghese.'

'Look at him,' Tadpole went on 'he's just eaten a few leaves from the top and now is moving off. He killed the whole tree just for that!'

'It's all right,' Ajay Singh said gently and we turned to him in surprise. 'Now that tree has fallen, other small saplings that were growing around it and being shaded by it will get a chance to grow big and strong. Otherwise they would have stood no chance to grow at all. That tree had lived a good life. Its time had come.'

'Oh,' Tadpole said in a small voice, wiping her eyes.

But there was one very positive outcome of the encounter. All three of us had heard and understood what the trees had cried out. We were still on the same page. We could still communicate with them. Of course whether they were friendly or not was a different matter, but at least we would know what they said.

We watched the destructive herd eventually emerge into the meadow and head towards the river where they began playing and bathing, trumpeting happily and oblivious of the carnage they had wrought.

'Chalo sahib,' Ajay Singh said as Dad started up and we drove into the section the elephants had just ravaged.

It looked like a battlefield. Many trees had great strips of bark torn off their trunks, and were moaning. Others had huge branches sheered right off. Smaller branches and torn leaves lay scattered on the forest floor. Bushes and grasses had been flattened and trampled. At least three trees had been uprooted.

'So much for being harmless vegetarians,' Zafia muttered darkly. 'This is like a butcher's shop as far as the trees are concerned!' Already chital, sambhar and langur had started feeding on the fallen trees. 'Just look at the destruction!'

We reached the Rajmahal Forest Resthouse at around four-thirty, a little chastened by our encounter with the elephants. Here we got the biggest surprise of the day. The resthouse was located on the lip of a thickly forested ridge, like a cliff top, and overlooked a valley, which was studded with blue lakes and golden-green meadows. We could see animals grazing in the meadows, and the blue waters of the lakes sparkled invitingly. But what took our breath away was the resthouse itself and the approach to it.

At first we didn't notice it at all. As Ajay Singh directed Dad and we climbed up the ridge, both Tadpole and Zafia suddenly grabbed my hand and pointed.

'Bhaiyya look!'

'Vish...oh my God...'

We seemed to be driving straight into the most enormous

banyan tree in the universe. We had thought that Ustadji was huge, but this one dwarfed him. We drove straight into the tree—and through it! Its massive prop-roots formed a tunnel-like arch under which we drove turning and twisting for quite a distance. Above us, the great tree rustled and creaked and squeaked, and hornbills squealed in the massive canopy.

'My word, this is like driving through a tunnel,' Dad said. We finally emerged at the far end, and there was the Rajmahal Forest Resthouse. A few of the banyan's aerial roots were gently brushing against the turreted terrace of the resthouse.

'What a tree!' Mom said in awe as we got out of the car and looked back at it.

'It's like a forest itself,' Dad agreed.

'How old is that tree?' Zafia asked Ajay Singh.

'Around 700 years old,' he replied proudly. 'It's one of the oldest and biggest banyan trees in the world.'

The resthouse was a granite two-storey structure that looked like a miniature replica of an English castle. It had two turrets at either end of the terrace and crenellated walls. There was a big living and dining room downstairs, along with the kitchen. An external staircase led to the bedrooms on the first floor; these were the round turreted rooms at either end, which opened out into the stone-flagged terrace. Wild rose creepers and ivy crawled up the walls, shimmering with bees. The two round bedrooms had huge dressing rooms and echoing bathrooms (with resident spiders) attached. Tadpole, Zafia and I would have to share a bedroom and a spare cot was dragged out for me and put in the adjoining dressing room. Our room faced the great rustling banyan and we stared at it in awe. Unlike a genuine castle (I guess), our rooms had huge floor to ceiling windows and not narrow gun slits, so we got a beautiful green view of the great tree rus.

'Bhaiyya, do you think this tree is Ustadji's grandmother?' Tadpole asked me in a whisper.

'It must be,' I said. 'I don't think there could be another such tree nearby. And he did say she was the famous Rajmahal banyan.'

'Ask her,' Zafia said, tying her hair into a ponytail and smiling.

Tadpole took her hand. 'Come with me Zafia, I'm feeling shy.'

That was a new one—but if you saw the tree you would understand. They went downstairs and stood in front of the great tree, just ahead of the arch we had driven through. I leaned over the crenellated terrace and watched them.

'Er...hi, sir, ma'am,' Tadpole said clutching Zafia's hand. 'I'm Sameeha and live next door to Medley Gardens in Delhi. Are you Ustadji's nani?'

'Hello little girl! Are you referring to that puny little rascal grandson of mine that's settled near Delhi and thinks he's God's gift to banyans?' The voice was raspy but not unfriendly. Tadpole and Zafia looked thrilled, and I went down to join them.

'I think so ma'am, everyone calls him Ustadji on account he's the all-knowing tree—the Tree of Knowledge!' Tadpole said shyly.

The great old banyan emitted what can only be described as a snort of laughter. Her roots trembled and shook with mirth.

'Him? Tree of Knowledge? The All-Knowing One? Now I've heard everything. Pipsqueak was only born yesterday and calls himself Ustadji. Wah! But how's he doing?'

'He's doing well, ma'am.'

'Still cuddling up to those gossipy Peepal girlfriends of his?'

'Yes ma'am.'

'And the others?' There was a shrewd, inquiring note in the banyan's tone.

'They're all good, ma'am and send you their regards. The

Julies of course are trying to advance everywhere.'

'Them! They can't touch us. We'll squeeze the life out of them! Colonials! The old Baba is looking after the place well?'

'Yes, ma'am, we made friends with him and his wife.'

'Have the owners come to visit the place?'

'No ma'am, not that we know…'

'I see.'

Suddenly it struck me that the big old grandmother banyan was asking all the questions, not us. But Tadpole would change all that pretty soon, once she got her confidence back.

'Er ma'am what should we call you?' she asked innocently. 'I mean we call Ustadji that…so…'

'Ustadji—I love it—that duffer! You can call me Naniji, okay?'

'Okay, Naniji.'

There was a sudden agitation up on Naniji's branches. A troupe of langurs had turned up and were glaring down at us. Some plucked leaves and figs and chewed them, others whooped around the branches.

'Got something to eat? Banana chips, chiwda, chaklis, gulab jamuns…better bring them next time or else…' A big fellow bared his teeth at us and grimaced.

'Behave yourself!' Naniji snapped at the langur, 'or should I tell Asha that you're sleeping in my canopy these days?'

'Behenji nahin, I was only teasing them,' the langur pleaded apologetically. 'After all it's not everyday that you meet kids who can speak the language. One's got to have a bit of fun with them.'

'Who's Asha?' Tadpole asked.

'She's the resident leopardess,' Naniji replied. 'She's probably out hunting or on patrol at the moment. I could introduce you to her if you like.'

'No, that's fine,' I said hastily.

Then Mom called us in for tea.

'We'll rest today,' she said. 'Daddy's driven all day and must be tired. We'll go for our elephant ride tomorrow morning, okay?'

'Mom, can we go and play on that tree?' Tadpole asked.

'I guess so, but maybe you should ask Ajay Singh first.'

Ajay Singh said it was okay, but not to go in very deep. The animals didn't really come up to the resthouse when it was occupied—most of the time. But we would have to come indoors once the sun went down.

Tadpole grabbed my hand as we made our way to the tree. 'Bhaiyya, when should I ask her about the big secret?'

I shrugged. 'Anytime I guess. But I don't think she'll know.'

'Bhiayya, she's 700 years old, of course she'll know. If she doesn't, who will?'

'Okay, ask her then!'

'I will, but maybe later.' I could understand why. It was already getting dark and the swaying aerial roots of Naniji seemed a little menacing, as if they would like to wind around your neck and draw tight. I'm sure she wouldn't do anything of the sort, but well, she was a big wild tree in a big wild jungle so you never knew—even if she was Ustadji's grandmother.

We were messing around Naniji, swinging from some of her aerial roots and finding comfortable perches to sit when a mighty commotion erupted from above us again. The langurs, still up on the higher reaches of the tree were screaming blue murder.

'Get out! Evacuate! Evacuate! Mayday! Mayday!' The whole troupe just leapt out of the tree and skedaddled as fast as they could in every direction.

'What? What?'

I grabbed Tadpole and Zafia by the hand. 'Maybe the leopard's come back,' I cried. 'Let's go in!'

We rushed back inside and went up to the terrace and peered hopefully at the tree.

'Naniji, why did they all run away like that?' Tadpole asked.

The big old tree chuckled hoarsely. 'Ajgar just woke up and stretched.'

'Ajgar?'

'Oh, the old python that lives here. He's been asleep for days. Now he's awake and hungry...and the monkeys panicked.'

'Where is he?'

'VIP Hollow 501, Branch 458 A, 4th story, West Wing. He's coming down now.'

We flashed our torches at the tree. Suddenly we saw the snake. He was thick as a fat person's thighs, but beautifully patterned and polished, and moved with liquid grace, his beady eyes unblinking, tongue flickering.

'He's awesome!' Zafia said.

'Wouldn't like to get into an embrace with him.' I remarked.

'We won't be able to play on Naniji if he's there,' Tadpole said.

'Baby, don't worry,' Naniji said gently. 'I'll warn you when he's hunting or feeling peckish. Most probably he'll catch something fat tonight and then sleep for the next month or so as he digests it. Nice lifestyle he has!'

'Thank you, Naniji.'

After dinner, Zafia and I took out the big tome again and started looking through it properly. Tadpole was sleepy and went off to bed. We dragged a trestle table out onto the terrace, and put a hissing petromax lamp nearby and sat side by side, flipping through the pages.

'I never knew there were so many ruins in and around Delhi,' Zafia said softly.

'Let's look at the index, maybe Medley Gardens has been listed there.'

It wasn't, but the index was not very comprehensive or properly done. The sketches of the ruins were beautiful though and of course we got side-tracked as we pored over them, our heads occasionally touching.

'Maybe the palace had a different name before it was called Medley Gardens. Do you know who was the sultan who built it?'

I shook my head. 'Ustadji never told us his name. He just said that the fellow was enormously wealthy and once filled more than 25,000 giant lotus leaves with jewels and set them afloat on the lake to impress his bride. Apparently they covered the entire surface of the lake. Ustadji said he "wanted to make her heart happy".'

'Would you do that for me?' Zafia asked softly, and I glanced at her sharply. Her eyes were sparkling and there was a smile twitching at the edge of her lips. I turned scarlet.

'Um...if you give me the jewels,' I grinned.

'If I give you the jewels! You cheapskate!'

'Actually, I'd sell them and buy myself a Rolls-Royce maybe,' I said. 'Then my heart will be happy!'

'You wouldn't dare sell my jewels!'

'You don't have any jewels!'

'That's what you think! Come on now, let's look for this rich sultan. Maybe I can marry his descendants. Then I will have all the jewels!'

'You know,' I said thoughtfully. 'I really wonder what happened to all those jewels...'

'If there were any in the first place.'

'Ustadji was pretty certain there were.'

'They must have got looted—what else happens to jewels? Ustadji said that the sultans probably took the treasure with them when they fled. Or else I guess the goras must have taken them when they sacked the palace. They're probably in the Tower of London along with all the other looted stuff.'

'I guess.'

We were scrolling down the index once more, hoping that some name might ring a bell.

'What are the other names of banyan?' Zafia suddenly asked. 'The palace could have been named after Ustadji.'

'Bargadh, baddh,' I shrugged. 'We'll have to check it out.'

But there was nothing with those names.

'Look at this,' Zafia said suddenly. 'There's a Dilkhush Kanwal Mahal listed here. And you said the sultan had filled the lake with lotus leaves crammed with jewels. Well, kanwal is lotus in Urdu—and he wanted to make his bride's heart happy—that's dilkhush.'

'Crammed with jewels.'

'Whatever! But kanwal is lotus, and dilkhush fits too, so let's look it up.'

Then suddenly I remembered. 'We've got it!' I cried, 'Ustadji said that the palace's original name was Dilkhush Mahal before the Brits changed it to Medley Gardens. I'd forgotten. We've hit the bullseye!' We looked at the faint black and white sketch. Dilkhush Kanwal Mahal had been built well over 300 years ago by an extremely wealthy descendant of the emperor Aurangzeb, though the exact date when it was built was not known. Right from the beginning, it was used more as a pleasure pavilion and hideaway, where the sultans kept their harems and organized all-night dance parties around the bejeweled lotus-filled lake. It was here that he and his descendants came for rest and recreation after conducting looting expeditions, sometimes allegedly even without the emperor's knowledge or permission, so they could keep all the loot for themselves. There were several gazebos and chattris around the lake—all of which had been destroyed or pulled down. But we knew we'd found what we were looking for, because the palace and garden in the sketch fitted Medley Gardens perfectly. The lake and island were there too.

'Is there anything about the trees?' I asked, my eyes running down the text.

'Look!' Zafia suddenly grunted. 'This footnote! It says that well before the British took over the sultan had consulted a fakir-baba who told him to plant a sacred grove of trees around the lake, which people of all faiths would revere. He put a spell on the place, saying that anyone who cut or harmed the trees there would meet a terrible fate.'

'That's like what happened with the Tughlaqabad Fort in Delhi, isn't it? Actually Ustadji told us that it was a burial place for soldiers, and to protect it from desecration the fakir-baba called it a "sacred forest" and planted all the trees. But cool, we've almost solved the mystery!'

'But there's no mention of any jewels,' Zafia said sadly.

'Look,' I said, 'there's a long list of chapter references, which may have more information. We could ask your mom if she could show them to us, when we go back.'

'And let's Google Kanwal Mahal…'

We did, but no luck. All Google told us was that 'kanwal' meant lotus in Urdu. Big deal.

'Maybe we could ask Naniji about the secret tomorrow,' I said. 'Grandmothers usually know about such matters. It's their job.'

Zafia gave me a strange look. Then she leaned forward and

pecked my cheek.

'Sometimes you say the darnedest things.' she said, staring at me. I was just summoning up the courage to kiss her back, when a deep moaning hoot emerged from somewhere within Naniji, followed by a series of blood-curdling screeches and screams.

White-faced, we stood up and stared at each other, our hearts pounding. Then the thing shrieked and screeched again and this time, a peacock gave a desperate squawk, followed by a horrible gurgling sound and the heavy flapping and thudding of wings. Then it seemed as if all the peafowl in the forest had begun screaming and somewhere close, a sambhar gave his hollow sounding 'dhok!' alarm call. Zafia and I clutched each other for dear life, trembling like leaves, too petrified even to flee indoors.

'What was that? Ghosts!'

'You should be ashamed of yourself, scaring those poor children like that—kindly do your hunting elsewhere while they're visiting, it's not polite!' Still trembling, we looked over towards Naniji. Some of her aerial roots were swinging indignantly and she sounded cross.

'Sorry children, HuHu just took down a peafowl. She's a forest eagle owl,' she explained gently. 'She doesn't mean any harm to you.'

'Oh.' Slowly we approached the edge of the terrace and looked down. It was a beautiful full moon night, the forest bathed in an eerie silvery glow.

'Look...' Zafia pointed. Just near the entrance to Naniji's arch, an absolutely huge owl—looking like a sack of potatoes—was viciously plucking the peahen it had just taken down. For a moment it fixed its enormous blazing golden eyes on us, glaring menacingly. Then it dug its claws into the bird and flapped off heavily into Naniji's branches.

'She's a big girl,' Naniji said fondly. 'Sometimes she forgets how scary she can be.'

'You bet!' Zafia squeaked faintly. 'My heart's still doing 200!'

'Sweetie was that because you were holding your friend in your arms?'

We looked at each other and blushed furiously.

'Naniji...' Zafia protested.

'Only teasing! Don't mind me!'

'Okay, goodnight Naniji,' Zafia said.

'Goodnight, sleep well. See you tomorrow morning!'

We went off to bed, but I couldn't sleep. That bloodcurdling scream still rang in my ears. But gradually I began tuning in to other sounds of the forest outside. Naniji creaked and groaned, her leaves rustled as the breeze blew through them. Somewhere a jackal howled, and then I heard the faraway, but distinct, 'aaooom-aaooom-aaoom' of a tiger. And then, excited hushed whispers from the wild roses peeping through the window:

'Those kids are something else! They've been talking to Naniji ever since they got here!'

'She'll be gossiping with them all day now.'

'Who could imagine city kids could talk to us!'

'They're sweet. Especially that little girl.'

'And those two lovebirds...'

'Hey Rosie, your petals are about to drop, aren't they? Ask Hawaji to blow them onto the girl's bed. She'll think he's scattered them over her.'

'Sheesh! He can do it himself.'

That's when I guess I must have dropped off. Tadpole shook me awake, early next morning, highly excited.

'Bhaiyya wake up. We have to go for our elephant ride. Hurry up and get ready!'

Zafia was already up and ready. She gave me a funny look.

'Hi,' she said sidling up to me. 'You know, when I awoke this morning my bed was full of rose petals. They were on my pillow and in my hair. They smelt divine.' She cocked her head. 'You know anything about that?'

'Who me? No. Maybe you should ask the roses.'

'I will,' she said and gave me yet another quick peck. 'Thank you.'

10

Ajay Singh was waiting for us outside, with our elephant, punctually at six o'clock the next morning. The elephant's name was Sheetal and she had the usual smiling face of her kind and small twinkling eyes. She seemed friendly, but we knew what she could do to trees and bushes. Still I guess she had to eat too...

That first elephant ride was magical. The forest was ringing with bird song, the air was cool and fresh as a salad. Cobwebs lay strung about like strings of pearls, and leaves dripped dew from their tips. We passed under Naniji's arch.

'Good morning, children!' she said in a kindly voice. Because Mom and Dad and Ajay Singh were on board with us, we couldn't of course wish her back, but just waved and smiled inanely. But we overheard Naniji talking—well sort of to herself! Her various prop-roots were telling each other how HuHu the owl had scared us last night. Some of the outer, younger and cheekier prop-roots were giggling. Zafia and I went red and exchanged glances while Tadpole asked us straight out.

'What scared you? And you hugged each other? Woo-woo! Did you kiss too? Why didn't you wake me?'

'Dekho! Pugmark!' Ajay Singh suddenly grunted, stopping Sheetal and pointing to the ground.

'Leopard,' he said.

'Asha?' Tadpole asked and then bit her tongue. Ajay Singh

looked at her strangely, and nodded.

'Yes, it could be, but how did you know her name, Baby?'

'Um…just guessed,' Tadpole shrugged nonchalantly, but went a bit pink.

We emerged at last from under Naniji's huge canopy and entered a stand of very tall, straight trees, with ramrod trunks, deeply scoured.

'These are sal,' Ajay Singh explained. 'This park is famous for its sal trees.'

'They're so tall!'

'Handsome too!' Zafia said.

'Thank you dear,' one of the trees said, sounding a little diffident. 'But you know, you really should not mix too much with those epiphytes…'

'Epiphytes? What's that?' Tadpole asked, forgetting that Mom and Dad were with us. Luckily they were too engrossed in enjoying the ride and didn't hear her.

'Those banyans and peepuls and their kind! That horrible fig family! The Ficus clan!'

'Is epiphyte a bad word?' Tadpole asked hopefully.

'Could be, sweetie.'

'Bhaiyya, remember even the DDT Dozen told us the same thing, but then Ustadji told them to shut up. Please tell us what you mean!' Tadpole pleaded. Mom looked at us questioningly.

'Vish, don't tease your little sister,' she said. 'Tell her what she wants to know.'

'Okay, Mom.'

Tadpole grinned. 'Mama, he's keeping secrets from me. He's telling Zafia but not me. Bhaiyya tell me what epi whatever means.'

'Epiphyte!'

'Whatever! What does it mean? Tell me!' Her eyes were

shining—and I knew exactly what she was doing. She was really talking to the Sals—through me. She was asking them.

'Little girl an epiphyte is a plant that lives on another plant—not exactly like a parasite but something like one. More than that we are not at liberty to divulge. You'd better ask the mother of all epiphytes—Naniji.'

'I will!'

She leaned over towards me, 'These trees have so many secrets!'

Sheetal had now started going downhill and soon we were at the base of the ridge, and entered a big meadow, rather like the one we had driven through yesterday, with wavy fronds of silver-green grass, about waist high. Ahead a blue lake sparkled, sequins of gold and silver sunlight bouncing off its surface.

Chital, sambhar, and nilgai grazed peacefully in the grassland, and a herd of wild buffalo raised their heads to look at us warily. Parts of the lake were fringed by tall feathered fronds of grass and in other parts the grass had been cropped short by the animals.

'Hey you waddling pachyderm—stay on the straight and narrow, will you!'

'Mind where you plant those oversize feet of yours!'

'Gross eco-footprint you have! You should be ashamed!'

'And keep your stupid trunk to yourself!'

'Yeah, why don't you roll it up and swallow it?'

We looked at each other in surprise. The grasses around us were very clearly telling Sheetal where she got off! Not that it made a jot of difference to her, because every now and then she would yank out a sheave of grass, dust it against her legs and stuff it into her mouth.

'Welcome to the famous Rajbagh grasslands! Remember you are in the presence of the most successful plant families in the entire world, so do mind your manners and be respectful!'

We looked at each other, eyebrows raised.

'They're just grasses and they think they're so great!' Tadpole said, rolling her eyes. 'Cows and goats and buffaloes eat them!'

'Yes, we are the greatest!'

'Three cheers to us!'

'High fives all round!'

They hummed and swayed and danced in the cool breeze and began singing:

'Without us grasses, you won't have bread!
Without us grasses you'll all be dead!
Without us grasses you won't have cake
Without us grasses you'll have nothing to bake

No rotis, no nans, no hamburger buns
No idli, no dosa and not even a samosa!
No bamboos for pandas
No grasses for goats
And how can you be healthy
If you don't eat your oats?

No roti with your dal
No rice with your sambar,
No puris with your aloos,
Or pastries in the mall!

So bow and scrape before us
And treat us like gold
For this is the best lesson
You will ever be told!

Without us grasses you won't have bread!
Without us grasses you'll all be dead!
Be dead, be dead, be dead, dead, dead!

We stared at each other in astonishment as the song faded away. These guys were real ego-maniacs. Then suddenly an urgent whisper ran through the grasses like a flame.

'Grasses fix bayonets! Big herd of chital emerging from forest at two o'clock with intent to graze!'

I looked at the grasses through my binoculars. The edges of their blades glittered like shards of glass like serrated hacksaw blades: they were sheathed with silica, which is glass. They would try to slash to ribbons the lips and tongues or any animal that tried to eat them.

'Inform all biting fly squadrons in the locality to scramble at once and intercept the herd!'

Then, a few minutes later, we heard something that made us sit up very straight indeed.

'Grasses at ease! Tiger spotted at edge of forest, emerging into grassland, just left of the lake. Has spotted chital herd and is waiting in ambush. Guys, this is going to be fun!'

'There's a tiger nearby,' I whispered. 'They said to the left of the lake, at the edge of the forest...'

'Bhaiyya, we know, we heard too!' Tadpole said. She turned to Ajay Singh. 'Bhaisahib, *sher abhi aane walla hain*. He's going to emerge just now.' She pointed. The forest guard looked at her, a frown crinkling his brow.

'How do you know?' he asked, but he stopped Sheetal and raised his binoculars, looking in the direction she had pointed. 'I don't see anything there!' After a few moments he suddenly stiffened.

'Sahib, memsahib, *dekho sher*! Baby ne *pehele dekh liya*,' he said in an awestruck voice. 'Your eyesight is very good,' he told Tadpole who bridled. I raised my eyebrows heavenwards and winked at Zafia. We were all looking in the direction of the tiger and the stupid herd of chital had no clue. They drifted up closer to it. Tadpole took a deep breath.

'Should we warn them? They're walking straight into the tiger's mouth...'

'We shouldn't interfere,' I said. 'Just think how many people have seen a tiger, let alone watched one hunt, that too on their very first visit to a national park?'

Tadpole swallowed.

'Tads, if the tiger doesn't hunt them, the chital will eat up all the grasses,' I said.

'Those stupid grasses were boasting so much, it serves them right if they get eaten!'

The tiger burst out of the grasses like a streaked, fiery missile, heading for the chital. They panicked and fled every which way, their hooves drumming as they ran. The grasses bent over double and swished with laughter. We sat stupefied, watching the hunt. The chital were trying to flee back into the forest, and as one darted towards it, the tiger swerved and sprang. We didn't see it actually bring down the animal because they had both just entered the forest, but we heard the snarl and the despairing bleat... The rest of the chital herd vanished into the trees.

'Goaaaal!' yelled some of the grasses.

'Got it! Good man!' yelled another lot.

Mom and Dad were absolutely stunned and thrilled.

'That poor deer,' Mom said, quickly wiping her eyes. Poor Tadpole and Zafia were in tears too.

'She was such a pretty doe,' Zafia said, as Tadpole swallowed a sob.

'And those stupid grasses were laughing! I hate them!'

'Ah, Baby don't cry,' a section of the grassland just to the right of us, said kindly. 'We win some, we lose some! We need tigers and leopards otherwise there'll be so many deer that they'll eat up all of us and then where would we be? Extinct! Plus, if we go extinct then the deer too will starve and go extinct. And then the tigers will starve and they'll go extinct too! So it's very important for tigers and leopards to eat deer and nilgai and keep their numbers under control. That's why we cheer every time there's a successful hunt.'

'Oh, but it's so mean!' Tadpole wiped her eyes. 'Everyone's eating everyone else!'

'What to do, Baby? That's the way Mother Nature works. You could ask her to change her way but I don't think she will. She's pretty upset with your species anyway. You've screwed up her climate control mechanism pretty good.'

We headed back shortly thereafter and were soon passing by the patches of grass that had been singing and boasting. They were still at it.

'Hah, we showed those stupid deer, didn't we?' they exulted as if they had themselves hunted the poor thing.

'Oh big deal,' I snorted, 'that tiger was a master hunter and would have caught them regardless.'

'Sonny boy, don't take that tone with us! We're the most successful plants in the world! You harvest our seeds. Wheat, rice, corn, millet, bajra, oats...what'll you live on without them? You fatten your animals on that too and then eat them. And you clear more and more land; you cut down enormous forests so you can grow more of us. We've taken over most of the land in the world! We're the rulers of the world! You came, you planted, we conquered!'

'We only grow you to cut you down with those monster harvester machines,' I said cruelly. 'So where's the dignity in that?'

'You can't ever kill us off completely, like you're doing to other species! You have to keep growing us after you harvest us. You can't stop or you'll starve! We're the champions of the world! You have to keep our seeds and even develop new varieties of them to grow so you can eat. Without us, your kind will be kaput. Extinct! We're number one! We will always live! Long live grasses! Jai ho!'

I made a face. Just then Sheetal twirled her trunk around a sheaf of grass—the very one I think that had been shouting all this, and yanked it out by the roots.

'Take your filthy trunk off me you mastodon! Oww that hurt!' It screeched as Sheetal deposited it into her mouth.

'You talked too soon, didn't you?' I said with quiet satisfaction. 'Now tell us what it's like inside Sheetal's stomach!'

Suddenly Mom put her hand on my forehead. 'Vish, are you feeling okay? You've been muttering away to yourself. I hope that tiger hunt didn't upset you.'

'Mom, I'm good,' I said, going scarlet, as Zafia hid a giggle behind her hand and Tadpole rolled her eyes dramatically.

We messed about around Naniji after breakfast, swinging from her aerial roots and finding comfortable branches to sit on. She was very sweet and rebuked a platoon of ferocious forest ants that objected to having their path blocked by us.

'Go around them, will you! They're very important visitors from Delhi! Where are your manners?'

Tadpole was readying herself for another round of questioning.

'Naniji,' Tapole said frowning, 'how do you know that Ustadji is your rascal grandson? I mean you've never been to see him, have you? You've been stuck here for 600 years.'

'Seven hundred, Baby, and some parts of me are very

arthritic indeed! Well his mother put down roots about a hundred kilometres from here—after her seed was deposited there by our khandani hornbill airline. The birds ate my delicious figs and deposited the seeds in a forest next to a village called Bargadpur, when I must have been about 200 years old already. She grew up there. Bargadpur is over 200 kilometres from Medley Gardens so it was difficult for the hornbills and mynas that were in service with her, to carry her seeds in situ all that distance. But what happened was that a homing pigeon who had been raised in Medley Gardens by the Sultan was brought to Bargadpur for a race and released and he ate some of my daughter's figs before taking off for home. He got back there very quickly indeed and deposited little seedling Ustadji on a...um...in Medley Gardens and hey presto, he took root...' Suddenly she clammed up.

'Deposited little seedling Ustadji on what?' Zafia asked.

'Nothing my dear, nothing. He just made the deposit...leave it at that.'

'Naniji, some of those grasses were calling you epiphuts,' Tadpole said, making bug eyes.

'Epiphytes,' I corrected.

'Whatever. What does that mean? Is it a bad word?'

'They said it means parasite.'

'We're not parasites!' Naniji snapped. Then she took a deep shuddering breath, 'Well at least not full-time ones,' she went on. 'I guess you children are old enough to know. We belong to a family called strangler figs.'

'That's what those DDT Neems told us,' Tadpole said excitedly. 'And then Ustadji shut them up.'

'So you're like a creeper then?' I asked.

'No, what happens is that as seeds we are sticky and we get

deposited by birds on the high branches of other trees where we stick...'

'And?' Tadpole asked.

'And then we start growing from there. We send some roots earthwards and others twine tightly around the host tree's trunk. Once the roots hit the ground they behave like stems carrying nutrients up to our leaves and then we really get a grip on the host plant and put the squeeze on them...'

'Oh, how awful.'

'Well to cut a long story short—though it takes a long time, we...er...strang...er hug our host tree to death, crushing it with our great weight, depriving it of light and air and nourishment and squeezing it so it cannot grow. It dies and over a period of years, its trunk begins to rot away until there's just this hollow tunnel left where it had been.'

'Naniji, did you do this?' Tadpole asked in a horrified whisper, with tears in her voice. 'How cruel!'

'Yes dear, I'm afraid I did. That tree—I have forgotten its name, died hundreds of years ago.'

'And Ustadji too must have done the same thing?'

'Yes. I think he was probably deposited on a neem. That's why they hate him.'

'But...you're *murderers*!' Tadpole cried. 'I'll never talk to you again!'

'Well darling, what do you think all the creatures that eat other creatures are then? We only do it because it's the only way we can survive when our seeds are deposited up in the forest canopy.

'Don't forget darling, we still provide all of you with lifegiving oxygen, We do a lot of good...' She tailed off. 'Sorry if it upset you darling, but it's just the way things are.'

'Just imagine! Ustadji is the Secret Strangler of Medley

Gardens! How cool is that!' I said to Zafia who promptly pinched my arm.

'Sometimes,' Naniji went on gently, 'there are things in life which are not at all nice, but we just have to accept them because we can do nothing about them.'

'I guess,' Tadpole said in a small voice, sniffing.

'We're just made that way. We strangle our foster parent and then we try and make up by growing big and wide and giving everyone food and shelter and wood to…sorry I'm getting carried away again. But there are a lot of you kids who do things like that too!'

Tadpole gulped. 'Is this…is this, the big secret you all were keeping from us?' she asked Naniji.

'Darling it was hardly a secret…you would have learned about it sooner or later.'

'So there is *another* secret then?' Tadpole perked up and so did Zafia and I.

'I've said too much already!' Naniji muttered, 'I'm just a garrulous old woman of a tree who can't keep her mouth shut!'

'Naniji please tell us!'

But Naniji lapsed into silence. We looked at each other and shrugged. Tadpole looked sulky.

Zafia gently stroked one of Naniji's swinging roots. 'At least tell us what it was like when you were a very young tree. What was this place like, who lived here, what did they do? And tell us what you know about Ustadji when he was a young and handsome fellow!' Zafia went on, grinning, 'Who else he might have strangled!'

'Ah my dear, it'll take me some time to dredge up those memories. Only my innermost prop-roots might remember— they're the oldest ones. These outer ones know nothing and couldn't care less about anything that happened before their time. Call themselves Generation Next! Generation Halfwit, I say!'

'My God, Naniji, it's like you are living in different time periods. Your different roots remember different things depending on when they emerged.'

'Yes, dear. So I'll try and coax my oldest roots and see what I can get out of them. Can't promise you anything though.'

'Thank you, Naniji. Ustadji did the same thing when he told us about Medley Gardens.'

Somewhat mollified we went back to the resthouse for lunch. Later I Googled 'Dilkhush Kanwal Mahal' again. All I got was a list of people who were named Kanwal and who were on Facebook and Twitter and stuff like that. Really! I drew a blank with Kanwal Palace too.

At about three o'clock Dad announced that Mahatre uncle had recommended that we spend some time in a forest machan, overlooking a waterhole, so we could see the animals come down to drink. We would drive there, accompanied by Ajay Singh. We set off and soon were driving through the grasslands we had crossed on elephant back that morning. Those grasses were really awful.

On seeing the Land Cruiser approach they started to shiver violently and cry. 'Please, please sahibji, don't run us over—oh, no we're all going to die!' The car of course drove over them and flattened them. The first time this happened, Tadpole put her hand to her mouth in shock and Zafia looked pale and hid her face in my shoulder (not that I minded).

We had no choice, because the path was so narrow and the Land Cruiser so broad that some grass would have to get run over. We passed over them and then suddenly we heard mocking laughter from behind the car.

I turned around. 'Look Tads, Zafia, they've just been fooling with us!'

Behind us, the 'run over' grasses had sprung up again and were laughing gleefully at our discomfiture. The grasses that the tires had gone over were staggering back to their feet and I guessed that was because the soil or sand was so soft that they got completely cushioned when the massive tires went over them.

'You cruel people, you killed us!' the grasses pretended to wail. 'You cruel, cruel people, you just drove over us!'

Tadpole made a rude face at them.

The machan was located in a section of the forest beyond the grasslands. It had been constructed on yet another large banyan tree overlooking the waterhole and was about 30 feet up.

Ajay Singh dropped us here and parked the Prado some distance away, so the animals wouldn't get spooked by it and returned to the machan on foot. We climbed up the rickety ladder and settled down. It was amazingly quiet. A soft breeze whispered through the foliage and insects (cicadas I think) sang shrilly. Mom and Dad settled themselves on the cushions and promptly dozed off. We stared at the waterhole, willing some animal to come down to it from the surrounding jungle.

'Hey, you the children from Medley Gardens in Delhi that everyone's talking about?' The voice was hoarse and creaky. We looked around surprised. At first I thought the machan tree had spoken, but then Tadpole grabbed my arm and pointed adjacent to a huge clump of green bamboo. It was creaking, and squeaking— and speaking.

'The old woman has been sending messages that you're to be treated like VIPs,' the bamboo said hoarsely. 'So welcome!'

'Hello, what's your name, Uncle?' Tadpole asked.

'Laathi Maaro!' the bamboo replied. 'That's laathi and maaro with double "a's"!'

'Hello, and when do the animals come here?' Zafia asked.

'They'll start arriving soon,' Laathi Maaro replied. 'I think your arrival might have disturbed them.'

'Oh, tell them we just want to see them.'

'I'll send a message!'

We heard a lot of rustling and creaking and then the hushing of the trees on the other side. Some branches and fronds nodded as if greeting us and Tadpole waved back at them.

'So what's it like being a jungle tree?' Tadpole suddenly asked.

'I'm not a tree darling, I'm a grass,' Laathi Maaro answered. 'But it's great living in a forest.'

'You're a grass? We met some awful grasses on the meadow near the lake,' Tadpole said, even as I held her arm warningly.

'Oh, yes those shorties! Don't mind them. Their egos are in inverse proportion to their size! We bamboos are the ones you need to respect!'

'Why?' Tadpole asked curiously.

But Laathi Maaro suddenly seemed to be embarrassed. 'Never mind,' he said gruffly. 'The monkeys should be coming down any minute.'

'But why?' Tadpole persisted in her usual bulldog way. Zafia put her mouth to her ear.

'Because policemen use lathis to beat people up with,' she whispered. 'And those lathis are made out of bamboos! So they're ashamed of being taken advantage of like that.'

'Oh,' Tadpole said, nodding. 'I get it!'

'Children, we're hurt and upset. We're growing wildly all over the forest and you haven't even noticed us!' The voice was petulant, with a complaining note in it. We looked around.

'Please, who said that?' Tadpole asked.

'You're looking at us but don't see us! We're everywhere yet invisible! How do you think that makes us feel?'

We gazed around the waterhole. The trees, some sal and others we didn't recognize, waved their fronds at us in a friendly fashion.

Zafia grabbed my arm. 'It's them!' she hissed, pointing to bushes growing all around the waterhole. 'The lantana!'

'We're the Lovely Lantana, kids!' the bushes chorused. 'Do you know that legend has it that many, many years ago a sweet lady brought one of us over in a pot from South America because she thought we were pretty? We got free here and now look at us! We're sprawling all over the hillsides and forests, we've conquered vast areas—and you don't even notice us! For shame! We're a huge success! We deserve fame and honour and recognition!'

'You sound like those awful Julies,' Zafia pointed out.

'Dear, we think that India is a kind and hospitable country with a lot of kind and hospitable flora which we can easily push over and dominate and trample. What more could we ask?'

'You're weeds!' I said.

'Every successful person is one then,' the Lantana replied cheekily. 'He too rides roughshod over others and takes advantage of the weak and bullies the disadvantaged and flourishes where he's not wanted.'

'Okay, okay, point taken.' I wanted them to shut up, but they went on murmuring under their breath about how wonderful and colourful they were, and how many types there were and how butterflies and bees loved them. Luckily, a small herd of chital emerged out of the forest and tiptoed to the edge of the water, looking around warily. A few bent their heads and began to drink, while others looked around nervously and grazed intermittently. A family of bristly sambhar deer too emerged and promptly waded into the water. Birds started flying out of the trees and landed next to the water, dipping their bills for a drink. Some monkeys emerged and started fooling around in their usual way.

Suddenly we heard a deep rumbling followed by a shrill trumpet. The branches and bushes on the other side of the waterhole were violently thrashed and flattened. A huge tusker emerged—possibly the same one we had seen earlier, shaking his head angrily, snatching up swathes of grass and branches and stuffing his face with them.

'Oh...oh it's Pagal Raja! It's the Mad King!' the bamboo whispered hoarsely. 'Brace yourselves!'

Pagal Raja trumpeted shrilly and the other animals fled helter-skelter.

Something had obviously made Pagal Raja pretty mad indeed, for he ripped up a small bush and trashed it angrily on the ground, even as it screamed for mercy.

'It really is a jungle out there,' I whispered to Zafia.

We both held Tadpole's hands comfortingly. Mom and Dad had awoken and were looking at the elephant apprehensively. Ajay Singh was watching the animal too.

Pagal Raja's cold red eyes looked in our direction and he raised his trunk up high as if trying to catch a scent.

'He can smash this machan like matchwood if he wanted to,' I whispered, scared. The elephant was now skirting the waterhole, ripping up the bushes growing next to it and striding towards us.

'Pagal, that's enough! Get into the water and cool off! You've been consuming mahua again!'

Our banyan had spoken!

'Yes, get the heck out of here or we'll beat you over the head!' Laathi Maaro added, creaking loudly.

'You old hag, I can knock you down anytime I want!' the elephant trumpeted.

'You can knock part of me down Pagal, not all of me!' our banyan replied. 'And then, when you're resting or sleeping a little bird will drop one of my seeds on your head and you know what will happen afterwards? I don't think you want to hear this.'

'Eh?' the tusker cocked his head, his trunk still feeling the air. 'What rubbish are you talking? Besides, I smell humans! Are you nursing them to your bosom?'

'My seed will send down a root, between those big flapping ears of yours into your brain and suck up the gooey matter in it. Other roots will pin those banana leaf ears to the side of your head and writhe around that stupid trunk of yours.'

The elephant took another step closer, his eyes still red with rage, but a little unfocused.

'Desist! You've seen what we've done to the turrets and walls of mighty forts and palaces? Inserted our roots into them and split them asunder. And those are made out of solid granite! You think your big soft head will be any challenge? Now step back before I scramble my seed dispersing squadron!'

The elephant paused and swung his trunk around uncertainly. With a grumbling rumble he turned and splashed into the waterhole and started spraying himself.

'Thanks,' I said to our banyan, 'you saved us.'

'What's your name?' Tadpole asked.

'Oh, that Pagal is a drunken fool. He'll get into real trouble one of these days. Baby, you can call me Bargad Aunty.'

Pagal Raja splashed around in the waterhole for a while, sending tidal waves racing to the shore, before climbing out. He cast another look at our tree and then disappeared into the forest as soundlessly as a shadow. Ten minutes later, Ajay Singh climbed down and set off to fetch the car.

'That was quite an experience,' Mom said, 'that elephant really looked angry.'

'Bargad Aunty told him off!' Tadpole said matter-of-factly. 'We should thank her.' Then she bit her tongue.

'What dear?'

'Nothing, Mama!'

But she hugged a prop-root hard and whispered, 'Thank you.'

'You're welcome darling,' the tree replied.

'Bargad Aunty, do you know any secret about the trees in Medley Gardens?' Tadpole asked hopefully.

A few of Bargad Aunty's leaves brushed Tadpole's face. 'Sweetie, all I know is that there is some great secret, but what it is…'

'Oh,' Tadpole said disappointed. 'Never mind.'

11

*I*t rained during the night and the next morning a dense fog shrouded Naniji and the rest of the forest. The valley below was completely obscured. We could barely see the tips of our noses!

'We'll have to stay indoors,' I said, 'what a waste!'

Mom and Dad seemed quite content to put their feet up and relax in front of the fire Ajit Singh had lit in the living room downstairs. Luckily the rain had stopped, and we could sit outside on the gleaming flag-stoned terrace, though it was shivery cold when the wind blew. We snuggled into our windcheaters, our noses red, our fingers wrapped around mugs of hot chocolate.

'I wonder if trees feel cold,' Tadpole said, looking at Naniji. 'Do you feel cold, Naniji?' she asked softly.

'Brr... sometimes we do—when the temperature falls to near freezing. Our leaves don't like the frost forming on them. They can't do their work properly then and it sometimes even kills them. Even now, in this fog it's a bit difficult. But it'll pass, not to worry and thank you for asking.'

'Did you ask your old prop-roots if they remember what it was like when they were young?' Tadpole was not one to give up—ever. I grinned at Zafia, who was looking so cute with her hair cascading out of her yellow woolen cap, her cheeks pink, her tiny nose red. She smiled back and for some reason blushed.

'Yes dear, we sat up at night and tried remembering,' Naniji said. 'But it's rather like remembering a dream. They said they

142

remember that there was always a lot of fighting between your species—men galloping about on horses brandishing swords and firing guns. They cut a lot of us down to build fires and shelters and hunted animals all the time—we all suffered a lot.'

'I'm sorry.'

'It's all right. Apparently all the sultans and princes at that time would ride out and raid and burn towns and hamlets and villages and return laden with treasures. Many got very, very rich that way.'

'What did they do with their treasure?' Tadpole asked, her eyes round.

'They built fine palaces and lived well. They drank wine and bought dancing girls and had a good time.'

'Medley Gardens was also such a palace,' Tadpole said thoughtfully.

'And it was built by one of the richest sultans who filled the lake with huge lily pads and loaded them with jewels and gold coins,' I added.

Zafia's eyes were bright. 'We must find out more when we get back to Delhi.'

Naniji creaked. 'Whatever you do, remember dears, what lies buried beneath us trees is often much too valuable to be dug up and taken out and frittered away.'

'What do you mean, Naniji?' Tadpole asked, looking puzzled.

'Baby, we actually hold the world together. With our roots we keep the earth together and make sure it doesn't break up. We suck up water from deep down, and when it rains the water just doesn't drain away wastefully like from a tap that's left running. If we weren't around, you'd only have rocks and desert with sand and grit blowing about everywhere. Uproot us at your peril! Yet you cut down forests, ravage and poison the earth and leave it in ruins, rendering it useless for all life. All so that you can get your greedy hands on gold or silver or diamonds or coal or oil or those dangerous elements you make bombs with so you can kill each other.'

'But why are you telling us all this?' Zafia asked. 'What does it have to do with what happened here hundreds of years ago?'

'You'll have to figure that out on your own or with the help of your friend here who hasn't been able to take his eyes off you all morning! He's thinking he's never seen anyone so beautiful before.'

It was my turn to go red.

'How did you gue...' I started and shut up, blushing furiously.

'The look on your face my dear: I've seen it so many times before. I think you call it besotted.'

Tadpole frowned. 'Naniji, don't you trees feel scared? If something bad is about to happen you can't run away. If men with axes came towards me, I'd run away and hide. But you can't do that.'

'No we can't, sweetie. We have ways of protecting ourselves from many enemies but not your kind. We defend ourselves with thorns and spines, many of which are poison tipped, our leaves produce poisons like cyanide and nicotine and tannin and alkaloids which can give animals and insects horrible stomach aches and heart attacks if they try to eat them. Some of us—like our acacia cousins—hire armies of ants, who they supply with sweet energy drinks. In return the ants savagely attack any animal or insect that dares to eat the trees. But against men with power saws and axes—and terrible chemicals which defoliate us—we can do nothing. We just have to stand and take it. Stand and fall rather.'

'But that's so terrible!' Tadpole gulped.

'Well, we try to look at it like this: When you fall ill, you can't run away from your illness, can you? You have to stand and fight it—with medicines or by having operations or whatever. Sometimes nothing works and you just have to take it on the chin. So we think that your species is kind of a sickness or disease which makes war on us from time to time, against which we can do little. But at least we have one consolation: we know that if you destroy all of us, you'll be destroying yourselves too. You can't survive without us. I think it's what your species calls MAD.'

'MAD?'

'Mutually Assured Destruction!'

'It's not very nice to be thought of as a disease,' Tadpole said in a small voice.

'Of course not—and you're not one by a long shot. You're sweet and considerate and kind. But enough of this dark dire discussion: let's talk about happier things now!'

A mischievous note entered her voice.

'Young man, I hope you've been running around the trees in Medley Gardens serenading your love like they do in all those Bollywood films.'

Zafia blushed and giggled and Tadpole clapped.

'Naniji, he's such a dork—he never dances or sings!' She rolled her eyes. 'Poor Zafia!'

'It's never too late to start! Ah, did I ever tell you? A Bollywood blockbuster was shot here—and the hero and heroine spent three whole days running around my prop-roots singing and dancing, wiggling and jiggling, getting dizzy and falling down. They would have gone on forever except they irritated HuHu who emitted one screech and the whole film crew fled thinking they were being attacked by chudails and rakshasas! The hero fell off his white horse and fainted and the heroine had to carry him away in her arms. Such fools!'

'I wouldn't like to irritate HuHu,' I said.

'Oh, she won't mind if you sang and danced a bit! Let the weather clear a bit and you can start practising!'

Fortunately the weather did clear by the afternoon and we set off for our first jungle trek with Ajay Singh. Mom and Dad didn't accompany us this time—they said they wanted to relax at the resthouse. It was great because it was easier to talk to the trees and grasses this way. We climbed down the ridge slope, being careful not to slip on the muddy, squelchy ground and set off in a different direction to our elephant ride.

'There's a stream nearby, we'll walk along that,' Ajay Singh said. 'You can see some beautiful birds there.'

After the rain, the forest looked beautiful, what with raindrops sparkling on every branch and every leaf shooting rainbows like lasers. Our socks and jeans were soon soaked through, though we didn't mind. This was real jungle trekking, so much better than being carried on the back of an elephant. We brushed through the soaking grasses and ferns.

'Look at us!' they crowed. 'We're covered from root to tip with diamonds!'

'The drops will soon dry and disappear!' Tadpole remarked tartly.

'What does it matter? We don't have to bother looking after it when we're not wearing it. We just enjoy it when we do have it.'

'Dears, don't let those silly grasses upset you with all that talk.' A large peepal tree spoke. 'Look at us—and there are many like us. We don't do rain jewellery! Our leaves have drip tips and channels so the water runs off them. Otherwise the water blocks our pores and we can't make food properly. Besides, we're beautiful anyway! We don't need any silly jewellery!'

We were walking through a narrow gully, shouldered by

high fern covered banks, following Ajay Singh closely. Suddenly Tadpole stopped.

'Look at these plants,' she exclaimed, 'they look like cobras!'

She was right. The plants stood on tall stalks and their leaves looked like the hood of a cobra.'

'It looks a bit like a jug too,' said Zafia, examining one of them.

Ajay Singh grinned. 'It eats insects!' he said.

'They're pitcher plants!' I exclaimed. 'They probably have nectar somewhere near the entrance and when an insect goes for it, it slips and falls inside into the plant's stomach where it is digested.'

Tadpole's eyes went round.

'Actually,' Zafia said thoughtfully, but her brown eyes twinkled. 'I think all plants are non-vegetarian! I mean they grow on the decomposed flesh and bones of all kinds of creatures that have died and rotted—ants, termites, rats, snakes, monkeys, deer, elephants, people.'

'Eww! Zafia!'

'Yeah, I guess in some senses we are all man-eaters!'

'Bhaiyya, stop it!'

We came to the stream at last and started picking our way through the smooth grey, white and maroon river rocks. The sky had completely cleared by now and the sun was sharp and brilliant, lighting up the leaves and etching out the rocks of the cliffs that rose on either side of the stream. Ajay Singh kept his eyes glued on the sandy bed—he was looking for pugmarks. We didn't see any, but we did see some lovely birds—one of which, very smart in black and white with a long forked tails, kept diving into the water and emerging, looking very pleased with itself. Then far ahead we saw a herd of chital emerge from the forest to drink. We heard a sudden, raspy, husky sound and looked up.

Seven or eight huge black and white birds with enormous yellow bills were flying in a convoy across the sky.

'Great pied hornbill,' Ajit Singh said.

'Hornbills? They're the birds Ustadji and Naniji use as couriers for their seeds! Just look at them. How do they manage to pick up figs with those enormous beaks?'

'I wonder if they know Naniji,' Tadpole said.

'I guess every hornbill in this place knows her. She's been around for so long!'

We started heading back by a different route. Occasionally, Ajit Singh would make us stop and tell us to listen to the sounds of the forest: we heard the drumming of a woodpecker, the cry of a startled bird; the hushed murmur of cool wind through the forest canopy; the pistol-shot crack of a twig as one of us stepped on it; 'dhok' the faraway alarm call of a sambhar.

And much more than Ajit Singh could ever guess. We stopped for a break in a small clearing, sitting on the trunk of what must have been a forest giant that had recently fallen.

'Look at it,' I exclaimed, 'it's been uprooted.' Indeed the massive roots that had anchored this giant to the forest floor for scores of years lay exposed, with vivid orange fungi festooned all over them.

'It fell two months ago, during a storm,' Ajit Singh informed us. We hardly heard him. We had tuned into young, shrill excited voices all around us.

'Can you believe it? It's been two months since Dadaji fell!'

'Poor Dadaji! But it was about time he fell! He was more than a hundred!'

'So old and gross and doddering! No sense of style!'

'Look at me! I've grown 30 centimetres in the last month thanks to all the sunlight I'm now getting. I'll be a six-footer before you know it.'

'What kind of tape measure are you using? Bet I'll reach the top before you!'

'Race you. First one to the top wins! See you there in sixty years!'

We looked around in amazement. There were a lot of saplings growing around the fallen tree trunk. They were slim and sprightly, waving their leaves around and bending in the breeze, looking happy.

'Ah, the sunlight! What bliss!'

'Thank God for the storm!'

Tadpole pursed her lips. 'Hey you kids, that's no way to talk about your elders!' she scolded sternly, hands on her hips, glaring at them.

'What?'

'It's that brat! That kid talks!'

'Oh yes, one of the woodpeckers was drumming away about them: The kids who talk to trees and plants, and who have come to visit. They've completely won over that old hag, Naniji!'

'Such a sentimental old fool she is!'

'Shh…these guys might carry tales.'

'They really are rude, aren't they?' Tadpole said to Zafia and me, shaking her head. 'They're like the Julies. Their Dadaji never taught them any manners.'

'Don't mind them, dear,' a kindly voice said from the edge of a clearing. A stately deodar waved its branches at us.

'Their old Dadaji was quite a tyrant. First of all, he allowed them to fall far too close to him and then he was a neurotic, over-protective parent. Didn't allow them any freedom! His canopy ensured that they got no light and they were given very little sustenance from the soil. He grew bigger and fatter all the time. Poor things remained in the soil for decades wondering if they'd ever germinate. Then that storm came around and knocked Dadaji flat, opening up the canopy. Now the sky's the limit for these little guys and they're shooting up like rockets!'

'Just remember, that if it hadn't been for Dadaji you wouldn't be here in the first place,' Tadpole told the saplings, happy to have someone she could lecture to and who couldn't run away.

'Hey, never thought of it that way...'

'Good old Dadaji!'

'Such a sweet old fellow, he was! Tsk, tsk!'

'If you don't stop that, I'll yank you all out!' Tadpole said angrily, stamping her feet.

'Yeah, do that and see what happens!' one of the cheeky saplings jeered. 'We're in a national park and protected by the Wildlife (Protection) Act. Yank us out and you could be in jail for seven years!'

'You know,' Tadpole went on sweetly, 'I really don't have to do that. All I have to do is tell the nearest herd of chital or sambhar or nilgai or elephants or even caterpillars that there are these tasty, young, very fresh saplings growing here which they might want to sample. If I can talk to you, I can talk to them!'

'Please, we were only teasing you!'

'Not elephants. We know what they can do!'

'And not caterpillars—they're worse!'

'Maybe that's what Dadaji was protecting you from,' Tadpole went on righteously, and beginning to sound like a nun.

'Yes, he was so brave! So upright! So strong!'

'Remember that time when the earth shook? That must have been elephants stomping around.'

'And we remained hidden under the soil, safe and sound in the dark.'

'Thanks to Dadaji. He must have taken quite a bashing!'

'But even they couldn't knock him over.'

'If they had...'

'We would have been halfway up the canopy by now!'

'You guys!' Tadpole was exasperated.

'Please don't tell the elephants about us; at least not for another fifty years till we can look after ourselves properly!'

'After all, we've only just come out of the dark!'

'Oh okay, okay.' Suddenly Tadpole smiled and cast a quick look at Ajit Singh. He was busy whittling a piece of driftwood with his pocket knife. Swiftly she went around and lightly kissed the saplings one by one.

'Be good now babies, okay? Promise me!'

'We promise, Didi!' the saplings said solemnly.

Zafia and I had been watching the encounter with amazement and amusement. Tadpole came up to us.

'It's so nice to feel like a big sister,' she told us.

That evening Dr Mahatre called up Dad and spoke to him for a while. Dad and Mom were both on the terrace and Dad kept glancing towards us while speaking. After the call Dad had a brief chat with Mom and then they both headed towards us.

'Kids, that was Dr Mahatre,' he said and tousled Tadpole's hair. 'Apparently Ajit Singh has been hugely impressed by you kids, especially Tadpole. He told Dr Mahatre that he's never seen children who are so...empathetic and sensitive and receptive to Nature, and so observant.'

'Empathetic? What's that?' Tadpole asked at once.

'Understanding and kind. Anyway, he's given us permission to go into the core area of the park where normally tourists are not permitted. He says that you all should experience the real Rajbagh jungles He's instructed Ajit Singh to take us there. We'll be leaving by five tomorrow morning so that we reach there by around seven. Be ready!'

You could only enter the core area of Rajbagh National Park through a narrow gorge bounded by steep craggy cliff faces. A rocky road, barely wide enough for the Land Cruiser bumped alongside a green river that rushed excitedly out of the gorge. Once you drove through the gorge whose entrance was blocked by a thick steel chain linked across two cement pillars and a padlock the size of a cabbage, you entered a forested valley. This was the real jungle. We sensed a wildness even in the trees—they were huge and rugged, towering more than a hundred feet into the sky. We recognized sal and deodar of course, which were everywhere and peepal and banyan. The peepal trees here would make the Peepli Princess back in Medley Gardens seem like tree-hobbits!

'Look,' Ajit Singh said, indicating that Dad should stop. He hopped out of the car and pointed to a gigantic forest tree. 'Strangler fig—you can see what it's doing to its host!' It was horrifying. The huge tree had a mesh of great roots clamped tightly around the trunk of its host tree, like a straitjacket from hell.

'That poor tree,' Tadpole said, almost in tears.

'*Mar jayega*. It will die and rot away, and the other one will grow.'

Some of the great trees in the core area were really the rough and ready kind: they'd obviously heard about us humans but rarely encountered any of us—and some were not very polite about it. Others however, seemed pretty savvy.

'What, you're telling me that those skinny, puny things rule the world? How?' one great giant said, shaking a few of its branches in disbelief. 'They look sillier than langurs.'

'Don't underestimate them. You know they make weapons that can knock us over in minutes. Just be grateful that you're standing here and not in the middle of an area earmarked for a highway or coal mine,' its neighbour said.

'Yes,' Tadpole said, looking up at the giant. 'Because then you'd have no chance at all!'

'Tell me little girl, the birds tell us that the trees that grow in places like Delhi are puny little saplings which need to be fed and watered and trimmed all the time and don't know how to look after themselves? You people have to put tree guards around them to protect them. Is that true?' And we could have sworn the tree giggled and sniggered.

'Well, some are fed and watered—otherwise they'd die.'

'Pipsqueaks!'

'Wimps!'

'Apparently they're always whining and complaining about monkeys and parakeets and peafowl and people cutting off their limbs!'

'They wouldn't last a day here!'

Tadpole looked up indignantly. 'Listen, many of them live on their own, okay? And many live in places where very important people live too: the kind of people who can decide whether you should remain standing or be cleared and turned into dining tables or newspaper, right? By just growing there in that ferocious weather—which you couldn't take—and by looking beautiful and green they cool and soothe these powerful people. They offer them jamuns and tamarinds and sweet mangoes and beautiful flowers so they just might like all trees and make sensible decisions about them.'

Zafia and I looked at Tadpole impressed.

'Yes,' Zafia added, 'those city trees do your public relations for you, so show a little gratitude!'

'Look!' Ajit Singh said suddenly, taking Tadpole's arm. 'Vine snake!' He pointed to what looked like a stem with a leaf. It was completely still.

'It looks just like a plant!' Tadpole said, staring at it. 'It's not moving at all.'

'Tadpole, a great many creatures mimic plants,' Zafia said. 'Apart from spiders and praying mantises and snakes and chameleons, even tigers camouflage themselves as dried grass.'

'Baby, just touch us! Just once! Please, please...pretty please! Look how beautiful our leaves are! Take one! Caress us! Love us!'

Tadpole crouched down staring at the earthen bank on one side of the path. We had stopped again, to scan the craggy cliff faces on the other side of the river, where some goral were perched precariously on the rocks and bouncing around in a hair-raising manner.

'Bhaiyya, Zafia come here...look!' Tadpole said hunkering down on her haunches. She pointed towards a plant growing on the bank; its leaves were emerald green, dramatically etched and laced with fine glassy spines around the rim.

'It wants me to touch it,' she said and grinned. 'Silly thing thinks I don't know it's the bhicchu-booti!'

It was the notorious stinging nettle—and Ajit Singh had shown it to us and warned us about it.

I took out my pocket magnifier. 'Let's have a good look. Wow—it's got these glassy hypodermic needles all over its leaves. Each one loaded with venom.'

Tadpole peered through the magnifying glass. 'You really are beautiful,' she breathed.

'And like many beautiful creatures, deadly,' I said. 'Touch it and you'll get a horrible itchy painful rash.'

'But I would like it for my leaf collection,' Tadpole went on. 'Bhaiyya, give me your penknife—I'll use Papa's driving gloves so I don't touch it.'

'Please missy I'm sorry, just let us be!' The plant pleaded as Tadpole opened the penknife and put on the gloves.

'Don't try to mess with me, okay?' she said, gently stropping the blade against her palm.

'Okay, so sorry ma'am!'

We grinned as Tadpole put the penknife away and took off the gloves.

'Just pat us goodbye, miss,' the cheeky plant said and Tadpole glared at it and then turned her back.

Ajit Singh came up to us. 'Look there, under that overhang,' he said pointing up the cliff face. 'A huge beehive! These are the ferocious rock bees.'

The hive was huge and dark and mysterious as a cave. Through the binoculars we could see it teeming and simmering with bees.

'It's a good thing we are so faraway from it,' Mom said, unwrapping a pack of sandwiches and paranthas. 'Come on kids, let's have some breakfast.'

She laid out all the breakfast things on the bonnet of the Land Cruiser and we began to help ourselves.

I was just about to plunge my knife into the jar of honey, to spread some on my roti, when I noticed the two furry bees on the rim of the jar, peering inside.

'Look, they want to get it the easy way!' I said grinning. 'Readymade!'

Tadpole came over and looked at them. We were able to tune into them.

'Look at this!' one of them said in a disgusted tone. 'Looted property! God knows which hive this was stolen from!'

'But it's not too pure...it's been adulterated!'

'We slave our butts off and they come with smoking sticks

and dope us and rob us and then adulterate our honey and give us a bad name.'

'And then the stupid Queen goes and ups our load from 2,000 to 2,500 blooms per day!'

'Stupid Queen? Hush, don't say such things! Someone might hear and you'll be in trouble!'

'Fat lot I care! She's just upped our flower load grossly and no one says anything, just "yes, Your Majesty, certainly Your Majesty, thy will be done Your Majesty!" Do you know how many extra hundreds of kilometres of flying that means? And no sign of any bonus! This is exploitation of labour, plain and simple! We need to form a union.'

'She is the Queen!'

'Well only until there is a palace coup! Then we eat her alive! Hah!'

'Shh, even so, then there'll be another Queen who'll do the same thing or be worse!'

'Listen! What's that?'

'The Code Red Hum!'

'The hive's under attack!'

'Banzai!'

'Tora, tora, tora!'

'Kamikaze here we come!'

'Stingers away!'

'Go, go, go!'

And even as they whirred off, Ajit Singh came over excitedly. '*Dekho, bhalu!*'

A sloth bear had shambled up the rocky cliff, into the cave and now was standing on its hind legs, raking the hive with its claws, trying to break a piece off, while the bees went mad. We could hear their angry hum over the sound of the river.

'Get inside the car!' Ajit Singh barked, rapidly clearing our breakfast things and herding us into the car. 'Put up the windows!' We stared transfixed through the windows.

'Cool dude, that bear!' I remarked, as the bees seemed to hardly irritate the bear at all. Occasionally he would swipe at them as they buzzed around his face, which seemed to make them madder still. He broke off a large chunk of the beehive, and slobbered all over it. Finally the massed attack seemed to have an effect and he started shambling clumsily down the rocky cliff face. The swarm chased him all the way down and then he just disappeared into the foliage, still clutching the chunk of hive under one arm!

'God, I wouldn't have liked to have been that bear for all the honey in the world,' Dad said. Several bee patrols flew over the car, some actually hovered around the windows, peering inside which gave us delicious shivers.

'Let's go, sahib,' Ajit Singh said and Dad started the engine.

Back at the resthouse that evening, we messed around under and on Naniji as usual.

Tadpole told her all about our 'bear 'n' beehive' experience that morning.

'Really Naniji, I think bees are more dangerous than elephants!' Tadpole said. She quickly added, 'is there a beehive anywhere on you?'

'There may be a couple but not anywhere near where you are—on some outer suburban limbs. Yes, some of the birds were telling me about the bear's raid—they said the bees lost over 500 soldiers in the raid and yet the bear got away safely. They really do need to be better trained; some of them just lose their heads and sting blindly! But we think bees are much better than elephants. You've seen what elephants can do to most trees, while bees—without them most of us would be extinct. We give them nectar and pollen and they arrange our marriages so we can have kids! Where would we be without them? So we don't mind them at all. If they build hives on us, it gives us further protection from other creatures and all they ever want in return is a little bit of pollen or nectar.'

'I guess, but they're pretty scary when they're angry.'

'And I'm sure so would you be,' Naniji said, 'if someone tried to steal something you've worked very hard to get. It can take ten years to build a good hive and five minutes for a bear—or you people—to destroy it. Think of that! Now I hear you're leaving tomorrow morning?'

'Yes, we'll miss hanging around with you!'

'So will I miss you, my dear. Give my regards to that rascal and so-called Ustadji, will you?'

'Sure!'

On our way out of Rajbagh the next morning, we stopped to thank Dr Mahatre and say goodbye. He sat behind his office table (at 6.30 in the morning) and offered us tea and biscuits.

'I hope you enjoyed your visit,' he said and then leaned towards Tadpole, Zafia and me. 'Ajit said you were the most remarkable children he's ever taken around. You didn't keep hankering after tigers and elephants but were equally interested in the trees and plants and even insects. That's very, very unusual.'

'Uncle, but we did see a tiger hunt on our first morning. It was awesome.'

'Hmm, and Ajit told me that you, little girl, knew the tiger was around before it could be seen.'

'Uncle, Tadpole's very good at spotting,' I said hastily. 'Sometimes we think she has X-Ray vision!'

Tadpole went red. Dr Mahatre nodded. 'Well whatever, it's

been a pleasure having you as visitors and I do hope you'll come again soon.'

And as we drove out, I could swear the trees too were waving farewell to us.

It was dark by the time we reached home. Zafia would spend the night with us as her parents were out of town and would return only tomorrow. The dogs gave us their usual noisy, licky, waggy welcome. All of us were dying to go to Medley Gardens to meet our friends—and suddenly realized how much we had missed them. The great forest trees at the Rajbagh National Park had been wonderful and impressive, tall and statuesque, wise and canny. But they were wild trees, used to dealing with elephants, tigers and wild boars—they were tough customers that kept their distance and dignity. The trees of Medley Gardens, quite simply, were our friends.

And as much as we wanted to tell them about Rajbagh and Naniji and those rude grasses, they were equally keen to tell us their news. Big news: news that could change things forever in Medley Gardens.

12

$\mathcal{W}$e charged off to Medley Gardens first thing the next morning. It was a Sunday, foggy and cold. Tadpole raced away ahead of Zafia and me with the dogs running alongside her barking joyfully. She ran up to the Peepli Princesses and hugged them hard one by one squealing, 'We're back, we're back, did you miss us, we missed you!' Then she stood before Ustadji with a big grin on her face. 'You have so many prop-roots and trunks I don't know which one to hug, Ustadji!' she said.

'That's okay,' he said gruffly. 'And how is Naniji?'

'She's good! She sends you her love.' Tadpole's eyes sparkled. 'She was a bit puzzled when we referred to you as Ustadji, she didn't know who we were talking about. I wonder why?'

'She must be getting on and becoming forgetful, that's all,' Ustadji said, as Tadpole nodded. The Peepli Princesses giggled.

'Hello children, we hope you had a good time and weren't bothered too much by mosquitoes,' the Neems said. 'Is it true that they're as big as sparrows there?'

'So what's been happening here?' Tadpole asked, swinging from one of Ustadji's roots.

'Well, we've had visitors! Very important visitors,' Ustadji said gravely. 'The two old ladies, the owners of Medley Gardens are here! They visited last evening and walked around the sacred grove.'

'What?'

'Ustadji, are they staying here?' I asked, thinking that if they were staying at the palace our forays here would be curtailed.

'I don't think so; they drove away later in the evening. I don't think the palace is quite habitable as yet.'

'Maybe we can ask the old Baba and his wife,' Zafia suggested.

'Zafia, let's first say hello to the rest of the trees,' Tadpole said. 'We've been away three whole days!'

So we did. At this time of the year, the trees were all quiet and contemplative, some even looked as if they were depressed, and had their leaves drooping sadly.

'Are you feeling all right?' Tadpole asked one of the mangoes in the orchard.

'Yes dear, it's just that time of the year. We shut down most of our operations and take it easy for a while and put all our food into storage and start preparing for the spring. In a few weeks we'll be very busy again, but now it's like we're hibernating.'

'Oh sorry if we disturbed you!'

'Not at all, dear.'

The Julies didn't seem very troubled by the climate. 'Hello girlies…come, come step this way please! Did you step on any of us in the forest?'

'No we didn't and you stay away from the place, understood?' Tadpole said sternly.

Even Kapok Maharajji and his six bodyguard princelings were looking a bit gaunt. They'd lost leaves and some of their branches were looking quite bare.

'Good morning, Your Highness RSCji!' Tadpole said, curtseying before the great tree. 'How're you doing?'

'Good morning, my dear. I'm doing very well, thank you and making preparations for the Open House in a couple of months. All other operations have been shut down. How was your trip to Rajbagh?'

'Good. The trees there are just huge.'

'Yes—and a bit feral if I may say so.'

'Well, they do have tigers and bears and elephants to deal with.'

'I suppose so, but it can't be worse than what we city trees have to deal with.'

'They send you their regards.'

The great tree lapsed into silence and we moved on. The others, the Jacos and the Laburnums were all looking a little sorry for themselves. Only the Oleander Siblings were still glossy and green and dropping their bright yellow blooms on the ground.

'Come on, let's say hello to Babaji and Mataji,' I said. We found them both busy sweeping the great ballroom. Clouds of dust rose from the wooden floor. They stopped when they saw us and smiled.

We greeted them and promptly picked up the extra brooms that were lying around and started helping them.

'Did someone come here yesterday?' I asked. They nodded beaming.

'Both the memsahibs came!' Mataji said. 'They didn't inform us, just turned up!' She confirmed that the two sisters owned Medley Gardens jointly and they would be visiting again this afternoon.

'Well, we'd better not be around then,' I said.

'Come on, let's check out the forest area,' Tadpole said.

It was dry and biscuit crisp in the forest; more paper bag brown than green.

'It's like walking on bags of chips,' Tadpole said as we crunched our way around. A bluish haze had begun to descend and the Julies here were looking a little ghostly and malevolent. Their branches stuck out crookedly, as if beckoning us into their embrace from which there would be no escape. 'Did you learn the secret of Medley Gardens? Tell us, tell us....' they whispered gleefully.

We returned home shortly before lunch to find Mom and Dad and Amma busy in the kitchen, from where delectable aromas were emerging. The dining table had been laid for seven people.

'Have you called someone over for lunch?' Tadpole asked as Dad peered into the oven and basted a huge roasting chicken.

'Yes dears. Our neighbours will be coming over.'

'Neighbours?'

'The two ladies who own Medley Gardens next door. They're sisters and they're in town.'

'What's their name?' Tadpole asked as Mom strained bright green peas and vivid orange carrots out of boiling water. She looked at us warningly.

'Now don't giggle or laugh. Their name is Periwinkle!'

'What? Periwinkle? Mom, you can't be serious!'

'Petunia and Poppy Periwinkle,' Mom said and we knew she was stifling her own giggles.

'Petunia and Poppy? Are you serious?'

'Yes. They rang us up and said they'd like to see us so we invited them over for lunch.'

'With names like that they have to be kind to plants,' Zafia whispered. 'They can't not be!'

'I wonder if they'll be as floppy as petunias or poppies!' I said.

They weren't. They were solidly built, very fair-skinned ladies, wearing lots of jangling jewelry, their crepe-paper faces heavily powdered and with weird greeny-blue stuff all around their eyes and bright pink lipstick. Petunia wore a striped purple and white dress and Poppy a yellow dress with purple polka dots. They walked majestically, like galleons in full sail.

'And these are the children,' Mom said. 'My son Vishwajit, my little girl Sameeha and that's their friend Zafia! Kids, these are Petunia and Poppy aunties who own Medley Gardens next door and live in Canada. Say hello.'

'Hello dears,' the ladies said together, in deep, rich, throaty voices. They didn't have fancy accents or anything like that. They spoke just like us. 'So nice to meet you, dears!'

We shook hands. Both of them had gorilla grips.

They looked around the farmhouse. 'It's so nice to know that decent people live next door,' Petunia said.

Tadpole gripped my arm. 'Bhaiyya, are they English?' she asked, looking puzzled.

'I think they're half and half,' I whispered back.

'At least the air is clean here and you can breathe properly,' Poppy said.

'Yes. And there's so much space here,' Mom said. 'The kids just love it. They're outdoors all day, running around, not stuck in front of a computer screen or the television.'

'So are you planning to shift next door?' Dad asked, as he brought them their drinks.

'No. We've lived in Canada virtually all our lives, ever since we left India in 1960. We've decided to sell the property.'

'I see, have you got any offers?'

'A couple, so far. But we'll be here for a fortnight and have appointed a broker.'

'It'll take more than a fortnight to seal a deal,' Dad warned.

'Yes. Well, we'll see. We're off on a cruise in January and will be traveling till March. We hope by then to have some serious offers. It should be ideal for a hotel or getaway resort or holiday home for a big multinational company. And now that you've moved in here, selling it might be easier,' Petunia said, smiling at us all. 'We can say decent people are already living in the area...it's not deserted.'

'It looks like such a beautiful property,' Mom said.

'It is but it is beginning to fall apart. The old Baba and his wife who have been looking after the palace have been doing their best, but it's only so much they can do.'

'Will you be living there during your stay?' Mom asked.

'We are thinking of shifting in a couple of days. We can supervise things better that way and need to check out what stuff we want and what we don't.'

After lunch we went to my room and stared over the wall at Medley Gardens.

'Tadpole spoke first in a small voice. 'Once they sell the place we won't be able to go over and meet our friends anymore! Why did this have to happen?'

'Maybe you could make friends with the new owners and they'd let you go over,' Zafia said.

'They'd think we're nuts if they catch us talking to Ustadji or the Princesses.'

Zafia smiled. 'I guess you'll have to be careful.'

Then Mom called us. 'Kids, would you like to come with us next door? Petunia and Poppy aunties want to show us around.'

'Sure, Mama!' Tadpole said, her eyes gleaming. 'We're coming!'

The two ladies had brought stout walking shoes with them, and changed into them. Their mood changed as we drove through the gates, which the poor old Baba somehow managed to push open. The sisters held each other's hands, became solemn, and occasionally one or the other would wipe a tear with a lacy handkerchief. We drove right up to the porch and tumbled out.

'Sometimes we feel we should just keep the place,' Petunia said with a sigh. 'It brings up so many happy memories of when we were little girls and then teenagers.'

'The trees have grown so much. It's a virtual forest behind the house.'

'And it was just scrub jungle full of partridges and peacocks and hares then.'

'But really, these old houses need so much upkeep. Everything just falls apart.'

We entered the huge ballroom. The wooden floor had been swept and even polished and the cover had been taken off the gleaming black grand piano.

'Our father used to play that piano!' Poppy said, walking up to it and raising the cover. She pressed a couple of keys and winced.

'Of course it needs tuning!'

They showed us around the bare, echoing rooms and then we went into the garden out in the front.

'This used to be a proper Mughal style garden,' Petunia said. 'It was divided into four quarters by water channels and fountains and had neat flower beds. But at least Babaji has managed to maintain a few of the flower beds beautifully.' She pointed at the rose and dahlia beds and some of the other flowers growing in pots.

They led us to the 'scared grove' where our friends stood. 'Babaji maintains that this is a sacred grove,' Petunia told Mom and Dad, 'and we respect his belief. His family has looked after the property for generations—and I think it was his great-great grandfather who declared it as such. No one dares cut a tree here, not even the British did after they snatched the property from the sultan who then owned it.'

'Tadpole, darling just look at the size of that banyan!' Mom exclaimed, 'It's like the banyan we saw at Rajbagh!'

'Yes, Mama,' Tadpole said innocently.

'We used to swing from the roots of this tree when we were little girls,' Poppy said, gently holding a prop-root in her hand.

'Why are you upset, Baby?' Ustadji whispered to Tadpole, who was now biting her lip as she looked at the big tree.

'Not upset,' she mouthed back. 'And shh…'

We walked down to the lake, where the Oleanders promptly began dropping their golden blooms left right and centre as if trying to impress the old ladies.

'You know, there's an old story about this lake,' Petunia said. 'Apparently before the British took over here, it was owned by a series of sultans. One of them—maybe he got his inspiration from Shah Jahan—filled the lake with enormous lily pads in which he piled heaps of jewels—diamonds, rubies, emeralds, sapphires and pearls and set them afloat to impress and woo his beloved.'

'Did he succeed, Aunty?' Zafia asked.

'I guess he did, my dear. She did marry him and they had fifteen children.'

Tadpole pinched me. 'See, that's what you'll have to do if you want Zafia to marry you and have fifteen children!' She grinned at Zafia. 'Right Zafia?'

We both went bright red.

'Tadpole, shut up!'

The Julies of course behaved abominably. They tried to trip up the old ladies, they tried to snag their clothes with their thorns and to us they hissed:

'Bring the old biddies over to us! We have something to show them, ha ha!'

We glared at them. Fortunately the Periwinkle aunties also appeared to remember them, for they steered well clear of them.

'That's *Prosopis juliflora*,' they commented. 'Look how it's virtually taken over this area. They're a real pest!'

'How can you get rid of them, Aunty?' I asked.

'I believe it's very difficult. You have to dig out their roots completely otherwise they come right back.'

We returned home after a while and the Periwinkle aunties went back to their hotel in Delhi. Then we dropped Zafia to her house. It had been really great having her over for these three or four days and I was going to miss her. Still, we had something good going between us and would meet at school.

'Check out those references and let me know,' I said, squeezing her hand as she said goodbye. 'We have to crack the mystery somehow.'

Our forays into Medley Gardens were limited after that. Petunia and Poppy aunty did shift two days later and they kept receiving potential buyers who they showed around, so we couldn't really roam around the gardens like we used to. After a few such days, Tadpole had had enough; she really missed our tree friends.

'Bhaiyya, come with me, I'm going next door to ask the Periwinkle aunties if we can play in Medley Gardens.'

So we went next door and rang the doorbell, the dogs milling around us, wagging their tails.

Mataji opened the door smiling; she petted the dogs and showed us in.

Petunia Periwinkle came down the stairs followed by her sister.

'Good morning, dears!' they chimed.

'Hello Aunty, we made some scones for you,' Tadpole said, proffering the tray which we had managed to keep out of the reach of the dogs.

'Dufus, Dorky...no! They're not for you! Genius, HighQ, behave yourselves!'

'Oh how sweet. Don't worry about the doggies, we had five when we lived here.'

Petunia took the tray and her sister picked up a scone. It was still warm, and very fresh.

'Now what can we do for you?' Poppy Aunty asked us through a mouthful of scone. Her eyes twinkled shrewdly; this lady was no spring chicken!

'Aunty, can we come here and play, please?' Tadpole asked, batting her eyelashes in a way that would have put Mom on a Code Red alert. 'We love the forest and the trees in the sacred grove. We won't scream and shout or anything.'

'Of course you can darling—as long as we still own the place you can come anytime you want. And bring your friends along too. It'll be lovely to have children playing in the grounds. It'll make this old mausoleum come alive again! Make as much noise as you want to. You can't imagine how quiet it is in Canada!'

'Thank you so much!' Tadpole said as Petunia Aunty came up and hugged her.

We scooted. Tadpole was beaming.

'Let's go and see the trees,' she said, grabbing my hand and pulling me along. 'At least we can play here until they sell the place!' Suddenly she stopped.

'Tadpole?' I knew the look on her face. She had just had an idea: a bad idea.

'What, Bhaiyya?' she asked innocently.

'You've just thought of something, I know the look on your face!'

'You're so suspicious, you're like the Government. Just chill, man! But...we should maybe ask them when they're expecting buyers so we are not around at that time.'

'Okay, so you can ask them...'

'Or we can ask Babaji and Mataji! They should know because

they'd be told when to make nimbu paani and snacks for the visitors.'

'What are you hatching Tads?' I asked. 'Out with it!'

She tried looking offended, but it didn't work. At last she broke into a wicked smile. 'I just thought if we could make noises like say, ghosts, when the visitors are being shown around the house, they'd get scared and won't want to buy it. You know, we can drop tins and things like that.'

'And run around covered in bed-sheets, yelling "bhoot"?'

'Bhaiyya you're making fun!' Her eyes filled with tears. 'I wish they wouldn't sell the place, that's all.'

'I know.'

'Let's ask Ustadji—maybe he'll have some ideas.'

But Ustadji was in one of his grumpy moods and not of much help and only complained about his aches and pains and creaking joints.

'Bring the visitors over here,' Princess Bo said, when Tadpole told her what she had thought of. 'At night! You see darling, we emit so much carbon dioxide at night that they'd get lightheaded and begin to hallucinate and actually think they're seeing ghosts! It's a time-honoured tradition and why no one sleeps under us at night. We'll ask Motia—the barn owl—to stage a couple of flypasts with his wife—he's a ghostly silvery-white and his screech is guaranteed to turn blood into water. The visitors will flee, never to return; pucca!'

'Thanks Bo,' Tadpole said. 'But aunty Petunia and Poppy make the appointments, not us, and they probably won't come here at night anyway.'

Over the next fortnight several potential buyers drove up to Medley Gardens in large fancy cars—or so Mom told us—as we were usually in school when they did. Every morning Tadpole would breathlessly ask Mom:

'Any news about Medley Gardens? Has it been sold?'

And Mom would smile at her and say, 'Not that I know of!'

Then we'd scoot across next door and accost Babaji and Mataji and ask them. To our immense relief, no buyer had been found at the end of the fortnight, when the Periwinkle aunties left on their cruise. At least till March, Medley Gardens was still ours to play and roam in as we liked.

As the winter progressed, the flowers bloomed in Medley Gardens. Galvanized into action by the appearance of his memsahibs, Babaji had redoubled his efforts with the flower beds—and he really did have a magic green thumb. There were dahlias and gladioli, nasturtiums and sweet peas, long beds of pansies which had faces like wise and ancient Chinamen, marigolds and roses, flocks and snapdragons (doggie flowers!) and of course poppies and petunias! The flowers talked and argued nineteen to the dozen.

'We're big, like multicoloured suns. You better bow down and worship us,' the dahlias crowed. They nodded their big shaggy heads as carpenter bees buzzed around them busily.

'Actually boss, we're sunflowers in case you've forgotten. We're the original sun-worshippers—we follow the sun around the sky!' the sunflowers said.

'I think the ma'ams are going to enter some of us in a Flower Show,' a gigantic deep ruby-coloured rose said. 'That's why the old Babaji is taking such good care of us!'

That in fact was the case—and there was more to it than just that. Petunia and Poppy aunty had called Mom from their cruise. They asked her to enter what *Tadpole* picked as the 'best roses and dahlias' in a flower show soon to be held at the Indira

Gandhi Centre for Arts, near India Gate.

'We've watched her interact with the plants and trees; there's something special about your little girl. And if the entries she selects, win, the trophy will be hers!'

The other flowers didn't take too kindly to the fact that only the roses and dahlias were to be entered.

'Pah!' snapped the marigolds. 'Flower shows are so elitist! They have nothing for the common bloom!'

'As if looks are everything!'

'Sweetheart, if you're a flower, looks and perfumes *are* everything!' one of the dahlias replied smugly.

'Yeah, we're not exactly known for our research in nuclear physics!'

'Just listen to them!' The marigolds shook their shaggy heads in disbelief.

'And to think people revere them and enter them in shows!'

The flower show was to be held on a Sunday. Poor Tadpole was in quite a state.

'I don't want to cut any of them,' she cried. 'They look so beautiful here.'

'Think of it like this,' Mom said. 'In a few days, a week perhaps, they'll wither and die. If they die here only you and Bhaiyya and Zafia and a few others will have seen them and appreciated their beauty. If you enter them in the show they'll be admired by thousands of people—they'll make so many people happy. And if they win a trophy, they'll have—or maybe you will have—a permanent reminder of how beautiful they were.'

'Mom, they have such swollen heads anyway,' Tadpole replied, tartly, 'you can't imagine how swollen it'll become if they win! You should just listen to them!'

'So what are you entering, darling?' Mom asked.

'Some roses and dahlias because that's what the Periwinkle aunties want. And some pots of poppies and petunias—we just have to enter those!' Tadpole grinned mischievously. 'Wonder what will happen if one of them wins!'

At school that week Zafia told us that a letter had come from the Forest Department granting permission to cut down the old Fish-Tail Palm in her garden, which was still leaning against the building wall. Her mom had instructed the gardener and Zafia wanted us to be there with her when the tree was brought down.

'I can't bear to watch it alone, and I can't bear not to be there at all,' she said.

So we went over on the following Saturday afternoon.

'Just look at this letter,' Zafia said, 'the permission is valid only for thirty days, they want us to inform them two days in advance of cutting the tree, we have to send a photograph of the site after the tree's been cut, we have to send the wood to a crematorium and send them a receipt and then we have to plant ten saplings. All this to pull down an already dead tree.'

'We have to cremate the tree?' Tadpole asked.

'Silly, they'll use the wood for other people's cremations, probably those who can't pay for it themselves.'

'As long as they don't expect us to get onto the pyre,' Zafia said.

'Don't give them ideas!' I grinned. 'They can think of anything!'

The mali brought a couple of helpers and they argued about how to bring down the tree. They would have to cut it and sling a rope around it and pull it down in such a way that it landed flat in the garden without damaging anything when it fell.

It was awful, hearing the dull 'thwack' of the axe as it bit deeply into the tree's trunk. We winced every time a blow landed, biting deep into the wood. I felt quite heroic holding the girls' hands until a shard of wood ricocheted off my forehead.

'Oww...we better go inside.'

'Yes,' Tadpole said, 'I can't bear to listen. How do lumberjacks bring down live trees that may be 500 years old and 200 feet tall, just because we need matchsticks? Don't they feel like murderers? They cut down whole forests; they're nothing but mass murderers.' Her hand crept into mine. 'Bhaiyya, do you think the new owners of Medley Gardens will cut down the trees there?'

'They shouldn't. At least not the ones in the sacred grove!'

'But what about the others?'

'Don't know, Tads, but I suppose they'd have to get permission and affidavits.'

The men had cut a wedge out of the trunk and had now gone up on the terrace to sling a rope around the top of the tree so they could pull it down. They stood well away and heaved. And with slow dignity, the tall tree came down, with a thud we could feel through our shoes even in the verandah. When the men started hacking up the trunk into smaller pieces we went inside.

'It's okay dear, the tree had died long ago, it wouldn't feel a thing,' Zaheeda Aunty said giving Tadpole a kiss.

'Aunty, how can we be sure?' Tadpole said.

'Well, darling the tree didn't have any leaves and it was just the trunk that remained...'

'Thanks for coming,' Zafia said, squeezing my hand. 'Tadpole, when is the flower show?'

'Next Saturday and Sunday.'

'Have you picked the entries?'

'Well, Babaji and I know which plants have the best roses and dahlias so we'll cut the blooms from those. The poppies and petunias are in pots, so we'll see which look best on Friday and decide!'

'Have you told the plants that they're taking part in the show?' Zafia asked.

'Yes, and they're hugely excited. They all want to have their Facebook pages and profiles updated and all of them want to be chosen. Really, they are so vain, you can't imagine!'

'As long as they don't try to kill each other!' Zafia said.

'Actually they did! One of the rose plants leaned close to its neighbour trying to spike it with its thorns! Can you imagine! And the other flowers, poor things, they're so jealous!' Tadpole shook her head. 'Actually it's a good thing they can't move around,' she said seriously. 'Otherwise they'd be murdering each other left and right.'

13

'Wonder which one of us she'll pick!'

'Me, me oh please let it be me!'

'Fat chance...'

Tadpole took my hand, biting her lips. Beside her, Babaji stood, with his seceteurs ready.

'Bhaiyya, we have to cut them now,' she whispered. 'Babaji— that one and that one...and that... Bhaiyya I hate this, some of them are just buds.'

'Tads they'd open tomorrow anyway and wither away in a couple of days, regardless of where they are.'

Deftly Babaji snipped off the roses and buds that Tadpole had chosen. Deep wine red ones, which glowed, orange-pink blooms that promised to be gigantic, pure ivory white ones and gorgeous yellow blooms, which made you feel happy just looking at them. The ones left behind looked sad but also a little relieved I think, and wished their compatriots well, old enmities forgotten.

'Bye and best of luck!'

'Bring back that trophy!'

'Make Medley Gardens proud!'

Then, we went to the dahlias...

It was pretty chaotic at the venue. Pickup trucks laden with plants of all kinds in pots and large containers were being unloaded. Flowers, in baskets, pots and vases of every possible description were being taken into the shamianas to be placed on display. We took our entry numbers and found our little enclosures—one for the roses, another for the dahlias and the third for the poppies and petunias. The judging would begin in an hour's time.

The buzz of conversation filled the big tent.

'We're from the Presidential Estate—the famous Mogul Gardens—why have they placed us here in the middle of all this riffraff! We'll catch some fungal infection—we'll have to be sprayed when we get back home. Just hope they don't have to quarantine us! Someone is going to pay!'

'Will someone please call the President on the hotline right now?'

A whole row of deep ruby roses just opposite us tossed their glorious heads angrily, and shouted at the same time like people do on television shows.

'Did you just listen to them?' Tadpole whispered, sticking her tongue out at them.

'We're from the Prime Minister's garden! But they haven't even given us SPG cover! We should be ringed by Black Cats, with their fingers on their triggers pointing their guns at everyone! It's a disgrace! Heads will roll, mark our words!'

This from the roses just next to us! Tadpole glared at them and made a very rude gesture.

'Tadpole!' Zafia hissed, horrified but hardly able to stifle a giggle. 'You'll get into trouble!'

'I've a good mind to pluck off some of their petals!'

'Hi kids, we're from the US Embassy, glad to meet you. Have a nice day!' another bunch of magnum sized roses called from across the aisle. They were so big-headed they could hardly hold themselves upright and the stems were supported by tissue covered wire. 'Howdy! Normally we live in California!' We stared at them in disbelief: they were gigantic, red and white striped and their calyxes were dark blue sprinkled with white stars—just like the American flag!

'Wow!' Zafia said. 'That's amazing!'

Mom and Dad had come along too and were wandering around the place, looking at the plants.

'Bhaiyya, you go and stand next to the petunias and poppies, with Babaji. Zafia you keep the dahlias company!' Tadpole instructed, taking charge.

'Okay!' It was her show, so we had to humour her. Luckily we were all in the same shamiana so could keep chatting, though it was more interesting to listen:

'We were born and brought up in Pusa,' some pansies were telling a group of silky pink and white mesembryanthemums. A whole bunch of others began introducing themselves—poppies, pansies, snapdragons, zinnias, gerberas, Swan river daisies (in baskets), carnations, cornflowers, cinerarias, tulips and others.

There was a stir at the entrance. The judges had arrived. Everyone stood up very straight and stiff next to their entries, some quickly sprayed their flowers with water. Each entry only had the bloom's common and botanical name and entry number written on a placard in front of it, so that the judging would be fair. The three judges would mark each bloom independently and the marks would be totaled and the winner decided. In case of a tie, a revaluation would be done and a final winner picked.

Two of the judges were ladies—one short dumpy comfortable looking, with scraggly hair and a kind smile in a gold and red sari; the other tall and thin-lipped, scowling and frowning in a purple and green sari. The gentleman, in a white bush shirt and grey trousers and white sandals, had silver grey hair, which was oily and needed to be cut and a big nose and sticking out ears. His watery grey eyes peered behind huge, thick spectacles. They knew a lot about flowers and gardening. They came around slowly, with their hardboards on which they wrote their comments and gave the marks. They murmured amongst each other and pointed at the blooms with their pens, examining them carefully and sometimes even sniffing them.

'Beautiful...'

'Exquisite!'

'What colour!'

'And size!'

They came to Tadpole's table and looked at her surprised.

'These are your entries, little girl?' Gold and Red sari asked her.

Tadpole nodded. 'Yes, ma'am.'

'You like flowers?' the gentleman asked. (A stupid question to ask someone at a flower show.)

'Yes sir, but I only wish we didn't have to cut them to bring them here.'

'And why is that?' Gold and Red sari asked.

'It's just not nice to cut something so beautiful.' Across the aisle I raised my eyebrows and winked at Zafia who was also listening avidly. My kid sister was laying it on thick again.

'My mother said they would die anyway and by cutting them and bringing them here we let many more people see them and be happy, but I wonder how happy *they* are! I mean how happy the flowers are,' Tadpole went on earnestly.

'What a perceptive and sensitive child you are!' Red and Gold, and even Purple and Green looked impressed. The gentleman looked puzzled.

'We don't mind being brought here at all!' the roses chimed and 'my' dahlias nodded their huge heads in agreement. 'We've met so many Very Important Flowers here and can see that we're as good as, if not better than any and most of them. Thank you!'

'Actually it's okay, they just told me they don't mind at all!' Tadpole told the judges. Then she bit her lip and smiled sheepishly.

'So sweet!' Red and Gold gushed, pinching Tadpole's cheeks. She went crimson.

'Very beautiful!' Even Purple and Green's mood seemed to be improving.

'Thank you, ma'am. Actually Babaji grew them—they're really his!'

'Very good! You must really love flowers!'

'I love trees too, ma'am,' Tadpole went on. 'They're very interesting.'

'So they are...'

Zafia too gave the judges the most charming smile imaginable.

'What magnificent dahlias!' the gentleman said, as Zafia dimpled. I thought he was looking more at her than at them, but maybe I was just getting jealous.

'Thank you, sir.'

'Excellent petal formation and colour shades.'

'Hey you!' one of the roses from the Prime Minister's garden shouted angrily at Tadpole. 'Tell them who we are and where we're from—at once. It'll be better for you—and him. Or tomorrow he'll find he's been transferred to Timbuktu and the Enforcement Directorate will land up on your doorstep!'

'Tell him yourself, you fat freaks!' Tadpole shot back while 'her' roses cheered her on. 'And what will the Enforcement Directorate—whoever they are—enforce? Let them come! I have four ferocious dogs that I'll set on them!'

'Did you hear that? She called us fat freaks and threatened us! Have her arrested for being rude and obstructionist and preventing a Government Flower from doing its duty!'

'Yah!' Tadpole sneered, 'which is? Sitting in a vase in a conference room listening to people talking till your petals fall off? Being jammed into a bouquet to be presented to some other greasy freak and be thrown away in the garbage two minutes later? At least my roses live and die free!'

'Little girl, we are Official Government of India Roses and your betters! Our ancestors graced the breast-pockets of Jawaharlal Nehru's achkans! Bouquets made of our relatives have been presented to Heads of State and First Ladies! Be respectful and apologize. Touch our feet!!'

'You be respectful first!'

'I'm telling you to tell the judges who we are!'

'Tell them yourselves!'

'They can't listen to us!'

'Yes,' Zafia chimed in suddenly from her spot. 'Maybe you should stop and think why a little girl and the two of us can understand what you say—even if it's mostly rubbish—and others can't.'

There was silence from the pompous roses. All the other flowers who had overheard all this were looking completely shell-shocked. Then suddenly they all cheered us. All three of us went a bit pink with embarrassment.

At last the judging was done and the judges retired to make their final decisions. Finally they were ready with their announcements. They went up to the dais and all the participants sat on the chairs arranged in front of the stage as the organizers ran helter-skelter checking the mikes and laying out bottles of mineral water. There were the usual speeches before the prizes were announced, though we were more interested in listening to what the flowers were muttering all the while.

'Will they get on with it and announce the winners?'

'Such tension!'

'My poor petals are already drooping!'

'We're sure to win! No problem! Relax!'

Even we were getting tense and wishing the judges would get on with it. At last they started announcing the winners—in a whole bunch of other categories: best winter vegetable, best creeper, best foliage plant and so on, till finally they came to the flowers.

Well, what do you know! 'My' poppies won second prize in their category and the petunias got the prize for the best 'massed flowers in a pot'!

'Well done, Petunia and Pansy aunties will be so pleased,' Mom said.

But neither the roses nor dahlias won in their categories.

'We come now to the biggest awards of the show,' Red and Gold sari announced. 'The "Best Bloom in the Show". I have to say we had a lot of difficulty in choosing the winner and have finally decided that it is a tie that...um...cannot be untied. So there are two winners:

'Entry No. 65, from Ms Sameeha of Medley Gardens for her lovely garnet rose; The Ravishing Ruby of Medley Gardens'. And also from Medley Gardens, Entry No. 453 from Ms Zafia, for her dahlia Lilac Sun.'

We tripped up on to the stage while our entries were brought up and huge rosettes affixed next to them announcing what prize they had been awarded. Before we could be awarded the trophies and have rosettes pinned on us, Tadpole and Zafia ran back down and went up to Babaji who was squatting in the aisle, smoking a bidi.

'Babaji, come on, they're your prizes; you grew them!' Tadpole said. They literally had to pull him on to the stage.

'Who's he?' Red and Gold sari asked.

'Ma'am, he's Babaji, he grew the flowers and looked after them, so he should receive the trophies,' Tadpole said.

So there was Babaji, beaming toothlessly, hugely embarrassed surrounded by three glittering trophies, his kurta resplendent with three gigantic rosettes.

We walked back to our enclosures and congratulated our winners. Tadpole was so happy she kissed all of them, beaming.

'Now that they've won so many prizes maybe Petunia and Poppy aunties won't sell Medley Gardens after all,' she said.

'Hey, will you listen to that?' Zafia said, cocking her head.

The angry words of the other blooms filled the scented air.

Tadpole made a rude face at them, 'Eat your hearts out,' she mocked, 'see what we got! Three trophies! Yah-yah-yah!' Then she delivered her coup-de-grace: 'What will you do? You'll be dead day-after-tomorrow, hah!'

'Tadpole!' I was shocked, but I knew what was really bothering her. In a couple of days, 'The Ravishing Ruby of Medley Gardens', 'Lilac Sun' and the poppies and petunias would also be dead, or dying.

Sure enough, a little later, she sprayed them with water and asked, 'How're you all feeling?'

'Oh we're great! A little droopy and tired but great! Will you tell the others at home that we won?'

'Of course we will! Well, we're going back home tomorrow evening so you can tell them yourselves!'

We spent the whole of Sunday at the show making sure no one touched or damaged our flowers. It's amazing how people want to touch and feel or sniff everything and they're not gentle.

'Looks plastic!' one stupid man in a grey pullover said, leaning over and feeling Ruby's petals none too gently.

'Kindly don't touch, Uncle!' Tadpole snapped, slapping his pudgy fingers off the petals. He looked surprised. Zafia spent the day with us too and would come home with us to spend the night, as her parents had gone out of town yet again. By Sunday evening, when the show ended, our prizewinners had started fading away; the petals were drooping and beginning to darken and crinkle around the edges. We took them home to Medley Gardens and arranged them in a crystal vase on the grand piano in the ballroom. Before doing that Tadpole insisted that we walk with them between the beds they had been grown in so they could meet their friends, even though it was dark by now.

'Mama, we have to let them meet their friends,' she said. 'After all they won!'

'Okay darling, but take Bhaiyya and the dogs along.' Mom dropped a kissed on Tadpole's head.

'Bhaiyya, you and Zafia bring the trophies—we have to show them to the others!'

So we paraded up and down between the flower beds. Both Ruby and Lilac Sun were looking quite exhausted, though the poppies and petunias were still holding their own pretty well.

'Goodnight and congratulations again!' Tadpole said softly and she gently stroked the velvety petals. 'We'll see you in the morning.'

'Maybe,' Ruby said hoarsely, 'I don't feel too good. But good night dear and thank you!'

Mataji, who had let us into the house, looked at the trophies beaming.

'Where's Babaji?' I asked.

'He ate his dinner and went to sleep.'

She saw us to the front door, giving the dogs a goodnight pat each. Tadpole flashed her torch at me.

'Bhaiyya let's go to the sacred grove and tell the trees!' she said excitedly. 'They'll be so happy!'

'Tads it's late, we better get back or Mom will get worried.'

'Nah, she knows we have the dogs with us! Please!'

There was a gigantic full moon up there, casting a bright silvery light on the landscape. We'd never been to Medley Gardens after dark—and well, Tadpole quickly came up to me and took my arm, as did Zafia my other arm. The dogs bustled around us, delighted with this after-dark adventure.

'What are you kids doing out so late?' the casuarinas whispered as we walked past them. We reached the sacred grove and put the trophies on the grass in front of Ustadji and the Peepli Princesses.

'Ustadji, wake up, see what we won at the flower show!' Tadpole cried as I put the trophies down on the grass. 'Three prizes!'

The Peepli Princesses shivered their leaves. 'Why do people only have shows and competitions for flowers and vegetables? Why is there no show for trees?' Princess Bo asked plaintively. 'They discriminate against trees!'

'And we give them oxygen and all...'

'Maybe it's because we take so long to grow and all people want is instant gratification. They want their wishes and desires to come true straightaway.'

'Good evening children, isn't it rather late for you all to be out?' Ustadji spoke gravely.

'Ustadji, we just wanted to show you these trophies that the flowers won!'

'Very nice!'

Zafia grabbed my arm and whispered in my ear: 'Vish, up

there—on Ustadji's branches—there's something moving there —and can't you hear that chittering sound?'

She was right. The leaves were rustling and there were creatures moving around amidst the branches chittering querulously.

'Ustadji, do you have guests? Up there on those branches?'

Suddenly four or five big bird-like creatures with ugly rat-like faces and leathery wings flew out of Ustadji's branches and flapped heavily across the silver medallion of the moon. Bats!

'Oh they're the fruit bats! My overnight couriers. They've had a dinner of figs and now will deposit my seeds faraway…They're VIP animals, so we treat them well!'

Then, the DDT Neems called out to us: 'Children you better go home quickly before you start seeing ghosts or faint!'

'Eh? What do you mean?'

'The Peepli Princesses are dangerous at night! It's well known they emit such huge amounts of carbon dioxide after dark that it can cause people to get light-headed and hallucinate if they stand under them; they see things and imagine the tree is haunted. If you stay too long you can also fall unconscious! Talk about carbon footprints!'

'Don't listen to them children. They're just jealous!' the Princesses chorused.

'Maybe if we sit under the Princesses, we will get enlightened like Buddha did!' Zafia said suddenly.

'More likely you'll faint and then one of Ustadji's precious couriers will drop a seed on your pretty head, which will take root and suck up your brains!' The Oleander Siblings had joined in the conversation.

'Better than eating your apples and getting a heart attack!' Zafia shot back.

'We do what we can, darling,' the Oleanders smirked.

But it really was ethereal out there: the slivery moonlight striped and dappled by the leaves and branches of the trees, quivering as though alive as the breeze rustled through the foliage.

'Hey you, idiot, aren't you going to kiss her?' Princess Bo suddenly hissed. 'It's a full moon night and you're in beautiful surroundings, what are you waiting for, dodo?'

I glanced around. Tadpole was walking through Ustadji's many prop-roots, giving him a blow-by-blow account of what all had happened at the flower show, the dogs milling around her.

'You know Ustadji it's so sad,' she said dolefully. 'Ruby and Lilac Sun—and the poppies and petunias won the prizes, but they'll soon be dead! Why does it have to be like that? Something good happens, but something bad happens soon too… Why do they have to die so quickly? They can't even enjoy their prize! It's just not fair!'

'Maybe it's not the fact of their life, or how long they live that's important,' Ustadji said, in a deep, grave voice (it's called a baritone) that was almost hypnotic. 'It's what they achieved in that time—no matter how long or short it was. These blooms have achieved fame—as no doubt I and the Princesses would have if only you organized shows for trees—they'll be remembered for a long, long time. Maybe that's why you have things like trophies—they're made of metal and they can't die but they will always remind you of the winners and achievers. Those flowers excelled and will be remembered for that. They made the people who looked at and admired them happy; they made them believe in beauty by being there for just two days. That's something!'

'Actually Ustadji—it's mostly Babaji's doing. He looked after them and pruned them and fed them and manicured them and whatnot. Without him they would have been nothing!'

'I suppose we all need someone to help us along,' Ustadji said.

'I mean I would be dead—and so would everyone else—without my tiny army of fig wasps!'

'Hey, will you stop standing there with your mouth open and kiss her?' Bo hissed and would have kicked me in the shins if she could have. I jerked out of the trance-like state I had gotten into and grabbed Zafia's hand and pulled her behind Princess Bo's ample trunk.

'Wha..?' she said, surprised.

I put my arms around her and kissed her clumsily; it sounded squelchy and not like a tender kiss but I didn't mind. Her mouth was warm and soft. We drew back.

She smiled, 'At last!'

'You mean?' I was feeling a little giddy, with what I had just done.

She nodded and planted her lips firmly on mine again.

'Bhaiyya, where are you?' Tadpole called plaintively. 'I'll tell Mama that you and Zafia left me alone in the dark and hid behind Bo so you could kiss!'

'Damn,' I said as we separated again, 'she knows where we are!'

Tadpole was standing a little distance away, grinning wickedly as we emerged sheepishly from behind Bo.

'Why don't you mind your own business?' I snapped.

'You shouldn't hide from me,' Tadpole said shrugging.

'You are a nosy little precocious grandmother, that's what!'

'Come on, we'd better get back—your mom will start worrying,' Zafia said, taking my and Tadpole's hands.

'Goodnight Ustadji, goodnight Princesses!' Tadpole called. She waved to the DDT Didis, 'sleep tight and don't let the bugs bite!' she sang cheekily. We picked up the trophies, whistled to the dogs and returned home.

Tadpole woke me at six-thirty the next morning, with Zafia standing beside her, yawning, all bundled up in her windcheater. Tadpole's cheeks were red.

'Bhaiyya get up, we have to see how Ruby and Lilac Sun and the poppies and petunias are before we go to school!' She yanked the blanket off me.

'Stop it! Oh…okay…damn cold…'

We sneaked out of the house, the dogs padding along with us as usual. Amma was fast asleep in Tadpole's bedroom and never knew a thing. It was cold and foggy and still quite dark. Our torch beams speared through the fog.

'This is fun!' Tadpole said swinging her torch around, her eyes glowing. But then she sobered up, when she remembered the reason for the trip. We slipped through the palace gate.

'How do we get inside?' Zafia asked her nose red with cold. 'The front door must be locked.'

'Babaji must have gotten up—or we'll wake him up!' Tadpole said. 'He or Mataji must be milking the buffalo by now!'

She was right. He was up, bright-eyed and freshly bathed, and had just finished milking the buffalo. (He supplied us with the milk as we hadn't got our own buffaloes or cows yet.) He took us inside and we stood before the prize blooms on the grand piano. Tadpole's cold hand clutched mine and I put my arm around her.

Ruby was drooping heavily. She had virtually exploded open and had dropped several petals. Lilac Sun too had shriveled and could barely hold his head up, his petals browning at the edges.

'Hello…' Tadpole said uncertainly.

'Baby! Good morning!'

'How're you feeling?'

'Not good,' Ruby croaked hoarsely. 'Not much time now. An hour probably less… So happy you came…'

Tadpole gulped and Zafia wiped a tear. I swallowed too.

'And what about you?' Tadpole hardly dared to ask Lilac Sun.

'My sun has set!' Lilac said, drama-king till the end. 'The fire has gone out; nothing but darkness now!'

'Does it hurt?'

'No,' they both said, 'it's more like a gradual fading away. You become less and less aware of things happening around you.'

'Look Tads, the petunias and poppies still seem to be quite okay,' I said. They were.

'We're good,' they said, but softly. 'We're just feeling a bit bad for them. Good you came, they were both waiting.'

Another two or three petals fell off Ruby.

'Thank you,' she said hoarsely again. 'Thank you for doing what you did for us, for entering us in the flower show. But…have to go now, have to go…goodbye and thank you…' She drooped some more, shedding yet more petals.

Tadpole put her face in my lap. 'Come on, let's sit down,' I said as Babaji looked on concerned and then went off to get tumblers of frothing hot milk for us. Zafia and I led Tadpole to the sofa and we sat down. She looked at us tearfully.

'She's died, hasn't she?'

'Yes, looks like it…'

'And Lilac?'

'Not much time I guess.'

'Can we stay?'

'We have to leave for school in a bit. Mom must be wondering where we are.'

'Look!' Zafia said suddenly, choking back a sob, 'I think he's gone too—his head just dropped down completely.'

And suddenly I had two sobbing girls to console—and try to keep my own tears at bay—all at the same time.

'Here, have some milk!'

Babaji and Mataji had brought us three steaming tumblers of milk on a stainless steel tray. They seemed to understand and never asked us why a couple of dying (and now dead) flowers upset us so much.

'We…we hardly knew them…just for a few days so why do I feel so sad?' Tadpole asked.

'Well, we got to know them pretty well in those few days,' Zafia said. 'They became like friends.'

'Like the trees of Medley Gardens,' Tadpole said, 'they're our friends too!'

'And they'll probably live much longer than we do,' I said, 'so we don't have to worry on that account.' I glanced at our two recently deceased prized blooms.

'Unless…' Tadpole said, her eyes huge and dark, 'unless something terrible happens to them. Then we will have to stop it happening on any account!'

'Nothing terrible will happen, Tads. Come on now, finish the milk and wipe your moustache—we'd better be going back.'

'If Medley Gardens is sold, something terrible might happen!' Tadpole said darkly as she put down her tumbler. 'I wish Poppy and Petunia aunties didn't have to sell it.'

Outside, the breeze had whisked away the fog and the sun was shining down brightly. It would be a beautiful day, crisp and cold, with warm blazing sunshine. It dispelled our somber mood quickly and Tadpole was skipping again by the time we got home.

'You know, if I were to buy Medley Gardens I'd make it a garden where everyone can come to admire the trees and flowers,' she said. 'Then all the plants here will feel special. Not only the ones that are entered in shows!'

14

Some days later, at school Zafia ran up to me during the lunch recess, looking excited.

'I've been looking for you all over,' she said and I went red with pleasure. She was in a different section and we rarely met up in school.

'What's up?'

'You'll have to come over. I found something in Ma's library last night that might be about Medley Gardens. I made a list of the chapter references and was checking if Mom had any of those documents or journals in her collection—and bingo! I found one.'

'Did you read it?'

'Nah, it was very late and Mom sent me off to bed.'

'Okay, I'll come over tomorrow morning. Promise me you won't look at it before I come!'

Her brown eyes twinkled. 'If you're good...' she teased. 'But bring Tadpole along too!'

'You think she'd let us research anything to do with Medley Gardens without her?'

We got dropped at Zafia's place next morning and she took us up to Zaheeda Aunty's library and study. It was an impressive room, not dimly lit and full of dark wood like most libraries are, but light and airy; one side was nearly all window and overlooked a park full of green trees. Bookshelves from floor to ceiling lined the other three walls. In the middle was her desk, piled high with manuscripts and journals and student assignments, presided over by a black goose-necked lamp and pencil stands. Along one side of the room was a long table with chairs arranged around it—what Zafia called the 'reference table'. There was a pile of fat, heavy old books and journals stacked on it.

'Come on, sit down,' Zafia said as we settled down beside her, one on either side. 'See this is what I found—it's a handwritten journal or diary.' Zafia opened a bound dark blue journal with gold rimmed pages. 'It seems to be an account of the taking and occupation of a palace called Dilkhush Kanwal Mahal, near Delhi in 1857 and what happened there later on.' She looked at me. 'Wasn't that what it was called before the name was changed to Medley Gardens?'

'Yes, yes!' I could feel my excitement rising.

'Who's written this?' I asked as Zafia leafed through the pages carefully. They were yellowing and brittle and had to be handled very carefully.

'Someone called Lt. Col. Henry Peter Featherstonehaugh!'

'Feather what?' We grinned.

'Okay, let's start from the first chapter...'

'You read!' I said, 'we'll listen!'

'Okay. Thank God he's got such lovely handwriting and the ink hasn't faded.'

The Taking of Dilkhush Mahal & Thereafter:
An Account by Lt. Col. Henry Peter Featherstonehaugh and
Robert Peter Featherstonehaugh.

15 October 1857 AD:

Our scouts, riding in the rocky countryside outside Delhi in search of insurgents and criminals who had taken part in the Mutiny spotted a large white building amidst the scrub jungles of the Ridge south of Delhi. We rode over and reached the place at dusk. It seemed like the perfect hideout for cutthroats and thugs and mutineers, so we quietly surrounded it and hunkered down. The building was guarded by high walls and had a strong gate—though there seemed to be no one at the guard-posts. There appeared to be a forest at the northern end of the grounds. Early next morning I led the men in a charge. We smashed open the gate with a battering ram and rode in, firing our muskets.

In front of the building was a Mogul style garden though the water channels had all run dry. There were however, beds of well-tended roses near the portico. We dismounted and entered the building, breaking down the front door. The men were excited.

'Sack the place, we take what we find!' I ordered as they thudded through the rooms. But it looked like the place had already been ransacked. There was nothing: the huge rooms were bare, there was not a painting on the walls: it was just the shell of a building.

'Search the place properly! Someone has been watering those roses outside!'

I set up camp in the main room and waited as the men set about searching the place. They returned with an old man in a wispy beard.

'We found him at the back, tending buffaloes. He says he's the caretaker, fakir-baba of the place. He looks after the roses.'

'Where are the owners?' I asked the doddering old man. He had shaggy white eyebrows guarding deep set eyes, which I didn't trust a bit.

They fled, sahib and took everything with them, he told me.

'What's this place called?' I barked.

'Dilkhush Kanwal Mahal!'

I couldn't believe my ears. We had found the notorious Dilkhush Kanwal Mahal; the Palace of Pleasure belonging to a line of cruel *sultans who had ravaged the country around for generations, looting and sacking after the Mogul Empire collapsed and the era of the Great Anarchy set in. They had accumulated a vast treasure—which according to legend they had hoarded in their palace. Now their descendants had obviously fled with this treasure, because we found absolutely nothing in the palace or the grounds.*

'How long has the palace been deserted? When did they go?'

'About a year ago!'

With a bodyguard of six men, I took the old man along for a thorough inspection of the grounds. East of the building, the land sloped downwards; it was a rocky scrubland full of thorny bushes and scrub and some scraggly trees. We flushed wild hare and a sounder of boar and partridge—it was good hunting ground. North, around a large lake stood what the fakir-baba insisted was a 'sacred grove' full of mature trees—banyans, peepal, other types of figs, and also a mango orchard. The largest tree was a huge banyan tree growing on a small hillock overlooking the lake. The large lake, surrounded by bulrushes, had an island with date palm trees growing in the middle.

This place would be perfect as a retreat. It was unlikely that the previous owners would ever dare come back and if they did, they would receive a welcome they would never forget.

I went up on to the terrace and raised the Featherstonehaugh Ensign alongside the Union Jack.

The Dilkhush Palace was mine.

A day later I got the happy news that I had had a son. We named the boy Robert Peter Featherstonehaugh.

Zafia stopped reading. 'I don't believe it! They just walked in and took the place!' she said, sounding outraged.

'He's actually mentioned Ustadji—that must be the big banyan he's written about.' Tadpole said. 'What happened next?'

We skimmed through the book—it wasn't too thick, thank God, just about 180 odd pages but we were too impatient to read it systematically from start to finish. Even so we got the gist of what happened: Lt. Col. Henry Peter Featherstonehaugh took possession of the Dilkhush Palace and promptly renamed it 'Medley Gardens' (on account of the 'salacious connotations' of its original name). He used it to spend his leisure times, riding out from Delhi during holidays and weekends with his friends. They went hunting and fishing and boating on the lake. Sometimes he would bring 'lady friends' over to 'escape the heat and dust of Delhi.' Then, when he was fifty-five years old—in 1882—he and his wife left to settle in England. Their son, Robert, then twenty-five, married a girl called Eileen Merriweather and they settled down 'like country gentry' in Medley Gardens. His father had left the journal for his son and Robert continued writing in it.

'Did this Robert fellow and his wife have any children?' Tadpole asked, fascinated that we were reading about actual people who had lived in a house and the gardens we were now so familiar with.

'No,' Zafia said frowning, looking back and forth through the pages, 'though it does say that this Eileen lady loved gardening and plants and got along very well with "the old fakir-baba".'

'He must have been our Babaji's father or grandfather...'

'I guess.'

'What else?'

'Well it looks like this Robert and his wife lived in Medley Gardens right until 1939 when the Second World War began. Then they left to settle in England.'

'Did he want to fight or something?' I asked.

'He was eighty-two at the time so I doubt it.'

Then Zafia's voice rose with excitement. 'Just listen to this!' she cried.

Departure:

02 January 1939: We sail back for Tipton, England. There's trouble brewing in Europe and it's time to go back home. With a heavy heart we sold Medley Gardens to a canny old Anglo-Indian soldier-of-fortune called Col. Justin Periwinkle whose wife is a native girl. Eileen is heartbroken. We have no children but she said that she knew and brought up every tree here as though it were her own child, even though most were much, much older than her! 'The trees here, they're something special,' she said. 'Each one has its own personality. We had such wonderful times here, we'll never forget.' She particularly mentioned three young peepal saplings that she and the fakir-baba had planted near the big old banyan, because according to the old man the 'banyan needs companionship or it will fret and die.'

Zafia looked up, her eyes shining. 'This must have been Petunia and Poopy's father. This is giving me goosepimples!'

'And those three peepals are the Princesses!' Tadpole was absolutely thrilled.

'The Periwinkle aunties must have been very small when they came to live there…' I said.

'Yes, listen, he writes on.'

Periwinkle seems to be quite a shrewd businessman—he has two five-year-old lovely twin daughters called Poppy and Petunia, who Eileen just fell all over.

It was a little eerie really. Zafia flipped back through the book and suddenly stopped at a page.

'Look, there's something about the fakir-baba here written by Robert's father,' she said, her voice rising with excitement. She read on:

We retained the services of the old fakir-baba of the palace. He was pretty old and bandy-legged but had started training his young son to look after the sacred grove, who he said would take over when he died as he had done when his own father had passed on. He was an excellent gardener and very protective of the 'sacred grove'. He would not allow anyone to even pick a fallen leaf from the place, which is so unlike what these natives normally do! Robert was fascinated by him and his wife, though we discouraged him from playing with his little son... They loved playing in the 'scared grove' running around and climbing the trees there—and the old man didn't mind that at all. He showed them how to look after the plants and flowers and trees, which they seemed to enjoy. Once they were so excited when they discovered a cobra near the banyan tree. We wanted to kill it, but none of the natives were willing to do that (and we certainly weren't going to flush it out ourselves from the depths of the tree). They said it was sacred and that if you killed any living thing in the sacred grove its spirit would haunt and kill your children. So we let it be and told Robert never to go there without adult company.

'So it was always a playground!' Tadpole cried, 'It was always meant to be a playground!'

It was more than just a playground at least according to what Lt. Col. Henry Peter Featherstonehaugh, wrote back in 1880:

Robert takes Eileen Merriweather—who he is ardently courting—for walks in and around the sacred grove, as well as for boat rides on the lake, when he comes down here for holidays. She says she just loves the tranquility of the place. She says the trees have a magical calming quality. I very much think she is going to become the next mistress of Medley Gardens for Robert has made it clear that he wants this to be his permanent home.

'Who's Robert?' Tadpole asked. 'I forgot!'

'He was that Feather fellow's son,' Zafia said. 'He mentioned him earlier too.'

'Bhaiyya, do you think this Eileen girl could also talk to the trees? She said they had personalities—maybe she talked to them like we do!'

'We could ask Ustadji,' I said. 'You know that's something we've never asked him—whether we've been the only human beings who have talked to them.'

Tadpole grinned mischievously. 'Yes we must. And then you can take Zafia for walks and boat rides and ardently court her, and she can become the next mistress of Medley Gardens.'

'Tadpole!'

Her face fell. 'I forgot—it's going to be sold!'

We flipped through some more pages, careful not to crease them. Again Zafia stopped suddenly. 'Look, there's something about the treasure mentioned here again,' she said.

It has always been a mystery as to what happened to the fabled treasures of the Dilkhush Palace. Tales of one of the sultans heaping 2,500 giant lily pads full of jewels and floating them on the lake to impress his beloved abound—every villager in the surrounding areas speaks of it—and yet that vast treasure has vanished. It's thought the sultan and his family took the treasure away in a huge caravan of elephants and camels while fleeing to Afghanistan, but no one really knows. We even had the lake dredged just to check—maybe the lily pads had sunk—but all we came up with was mud! There's certainly nothing at Medley Gardens. Still, we're filling up the rooms of the Palace with our own little collection of artifacts and sculptures.

'You mean they collected statues of naked people?' Tadpole asked. 'They decorated their whole garden with them!'

'We really ought to read this cover to cover,' Zafia said, 'and not just flip through it casually like this.'

'What does it say towards the end?' I asked.

'Just that they're due to leave for England...'

'I wonder why he didn't take this journal with him to England,' I said, frowning.

'Probably it got left behind by mistake, or might have got lost.'

'But how did your mom get hold of it?' I asked.

Zafia grinned. 'She must have picked it up from a roadside book stall in Daryagunj. Or she might have heard of some library closing down. They sell books by weight and she's bought hundreds of kilos of old, tattered books at times.'

'Pity there's no clue as to what happened to the treasure,' I mused. 'It just vanished into thin air.'

'The sultan's caravan must have got looted,' Zafia said. 'Mom said that in those days no one was safe. And people knew that the sultan was fleeing with all his treasures so they ambushed him.'

Zaheeda Aunty and Mom and Dad were hugely impressed when we told them all we had discovered.

'I'm amazed at your tenacity,' Zaheeda Aunty said, flipping through the blue journal. 'I didn't even know I had this in my collection!'

'Aunty, Zafia ferreted it out from your fabulous library,' I said. 'We just looked up the chapter references in the volume you gave us and found one of them here.'

'You should present this as a school project. You've actually done serious historical research and found out about an old, neglected palace that still exists. Well done kids! I'm proud of you!'

'My, my, you kids really are enamoured by Medley Gardens,

aren't you?' Dad said when Tadpole excitedly recounted our discoveries. 'That place is really worth preserving.'

'Yes,' Mom added, 'it would be perfect for an artists' or writers' retreat where they can come and paint and do sculpture or write in peace.'

'We love the trees there,' Tadpole said. 'Dad, is there any news about who's going to buy the place?'

'No, sweetheart. Petunia and Poppy aunties are still out of the country but they should be back shortly.'

'I just hope they sell it to someone sensible!' Tadpole said fiercely. 'Someone who likes trees! Not to some idiot five-star hotel fellow!'

'You know,' I said, slowly, once our parents had moved off to the other room. 'We can use the entries in the book to jog Ustadji's memory. I'm sure he would remember this Robert fellow and his wife. Then we can ask him details about what it was like when the Periwinkles came to stay.' I looked at Zafia. 'Come over tomorrow morning and we'll ask him.'

The next morning (which was Sunday) Tadpole lost no time in trying to find out. She walked up to Ustadji, looking very businesslike.

'Ustadji, many, many years ago did an English girl called Eileen ever talk to you?' she asked flat out. 'She used to walk around here with her boyfriend called Robert, holding hands I suppose. They got married and lived here for many years. You must remember them! After all she and the old baba planted your girlfriends the Peepli Princesses, so you wouldn't be alone!'

Ustadji's leaves rustled and trembled.

'Let me recall, this is something for the inner prop-roots. Yes, yes, they do remember faintly. She was a sweet lady.'

Princess Bo, who along with the other two, had been avidly

listening, butted in:

'Sweetie, sure he remembers. He was so jealous because that sweet lady and the baba used to fuss over us so much when we were small. He used to sulk and threaten us that he'd send his couriers to place his seeds on us to scare us!'

'Nonsense!' Ustadji said grumpily. 'Don't you listen to them little girl. But yes that girl did spoil them, fussing over them all the time—watering them and stuffing them with cowdung. All a self-respecting peepal seed needs is a crevice in a rock or a building and it manages fine on its own! No need for any TLC!'

'Ustadji *everyone* needs TLC!' Tadpole said solemnly, giving one of his prop-roots a quick hug. 'Even you!'

'Well I don't know about that but thank you nevertheless,' Ustadji said gruffly as the Princesses giggled.

'Ustadji, did that English girl Eileen, speak to you all like we do?' Tadpole asked.

'Not quite in the way you do sweetie, but we could let her know how we were feeling and she did pick up our moods. She was just a little bit off our wavelength and needed a little fine tuning that's all.'

'You know, Ustadji would have been a horrible old grouch of a tree if it hadn't been for us!' Princess Peepli said. 'As it is he used to threaten those poor Neems all the time, which is why they're so paranoid!'

'They're talking nonsense!' Ustadji said, 'don't you listen to them. Gossiping all the time—that's all they know!'

'Ustadji, do you remember the Periwinkle aunties who came to live here after the English people left?'

'Oh of course I do!' Ustadji chuckled. 'They were very mischievous and daring. As little girls they used to climb all over us!' He sighed, 'Then they too went away and we were left alone.'

'Yes, they left in 1960,' I said, 'they must have been around twenty-six years old.'

'But now they've come back!' Ustadji said. 'They were walking around here the other day.'

We looked at each other. They had come back, yes, but they were selling Medley Gardens. Dare we tell Ustadji and the others that?

'Tell us about them!' Zafia said. 'What were they like?'

'They were twins so like peas in a pod, what else! They did everything together; they really were a couple of tomboys!'

'And then...' Princess Ficki drawled melodramatically, 'they fell in love with the same boy!'

'Oh, wow, so what happened?' Zafia was agog.

'They fought bitterly over him.'

'Did he love them? One of them? Or both? Was he torn between them?'

'Neither!' Princess Bo snorted. 'He just wanted to have a good time with both of them! Oh yes, he enjoyed himself.'

'So what happened?'

'Well, the whole family packed up and left for Canada that's what happened. But I believe the sisters never forgave each other and continued to quarrel even after their father had died.'

And now they were selling Medley Gardens. It sucked.

We walked around the lake, talking softly.

'Should we tell them?' I asked Zafia and Tadpole. 'Shouldn't they know?'

'They'll be very upset,' Tadpole said. She shook her head. 'I hate that this has to happen! It's wrong!'

'They might be even more upset with us if they know that we knew and didn't tell them,' I said. 'We are their friends, after all.'

'Okay, so let's tell them,' Zafia said. 'We'll tell Ustadji and he can let the others know.'

We walked back to the big banyan.

'Ustadji, we have... some news...' I said hesitantly.

'Those Periwinkle aunties are planning to sell Medley Gardens!' Tadpole blurted out and then burst into tears. She hugged the big banyan. 'I hate them!'

'Easy there, don't cry sweetheart. Selling Medley Gardens? But it's been in their family for seventy-five years!'

'We don't know who the new owners will be,' I said. 'Or what they'll do to the place!'

'Well they won't dare touch us. No one can touch the trees in a sacred grove.' But even Ustadji's gravelly voice wavered slightly.

'It's those poor trees in the forest I'm worried about,' Princess Bo said shivering her glossy leaves. 'They've had it. They'll clear the place and put up a multiplex or shopping mall or some such monstrosity!'

'Well, we don't know anything as yet.'

'Mark my words that's what will happen!' Princess Peepli said. 'It's the nature of the beast. Give humans a pristine 1,000-year-old forest and you'll raze it to the ground and build some hideous cement and glass factory in its place and think that's progress!'

'But what can we do?' Tadpole cried.

'Maybe more than you realize,' Ustadji said gravely.

Little did we know how prophetic his words would be...

15

The Periwinkle aunties returned from their cruise by mid-February. Tadpole went over whenever she could. Zafia and I had major exams looming large so had to sit and swot at home: we could have taken our books to the sacred grove but there were too many distractions and the Peepli Princesses couldn't remain quiet for very long. Tadpole, however, had a plan, and she went right ahead to execute it.

'I'm going to try and make the Periwinkle aunties change their mind about selling Medley Gardens,' she said determinedly. She would walk around the gardens with them, chatting away and invariably take them off to the sacred grove.

'What do you talk to them about?' we asked her one day. She grinned.

'Oh about all the things that Ustadji and Naniji told us. I told them about the fig wasps and how such a tiny insect looked after such a giant of a tree and how Ustadji was at least 250 years old and was living history.'

'Were they impressed?' Zafia asked, smiling.

'Very! They didn't know anything! I don't think they talked to the trees or were able to, otherwise Ustadji would have surely lectured them too. They just fooled around—not like us!'

Tadpoles' eyes gleamed. 'They said I had some special affinity to trees and liked them very much… What's affinity?'

'A special relationship or attraction,' Zafia explained.

Then one Saturday in the middle of February she ran back home from Medley Gardens, bursting with excitement.

'Bhaiyya, Zafia you've got to come! Now! All the mangoes have burst into flower! There are about a zillion bees humming around them as well as other insects. They smell heavenly!'

We needed a break from our books and took off after her. She was right. The mangoes had burst into bloom—they had pale yellow-green flowers growing like sprays all over them, and the bees going berserk!

'Just look at you guys!' Zafia said, 'you look and smell heavenly!'

'Thank you dear! The bees are doing a great job. We're going to have a bumper crop! And yes, there'll be a basket of the best for you and the little girl!'

'What about me?'

'Have you got a catapult?'

'Um…no…yes…but…'

A loud cackling filled the air and suddenly Mithoorani swerved down and settled on Tadpole's shoulder.

'Baby, isn't it exciting! I'm having a Mangobloom party and you're invited. All my friends are coming. Here they are!'

We looked up. The sky was a-swirl with big green parakeets all shrieking at the tops of their voices. The flock—over a hundred—landed and disappeared into the mango trees. The cackling became somewhat muffled as the birds began stuffing their faces and a shower of half-eaten blooms descended.

Tadpole put her hands on her hips. 'Mithoorani, did the mangoes invite you? Or are you all just gate-crashing?'

'No formality darling!' Mithoorani drawled. 'It's a long-standing tradition and you don't need invites for that. We've been doing this for centuries.'

'That doesn't make it right!' Tadpole said severely. 'You need to ask if it's okay by the mangoes. It's their flowers you're hogging!'

'Oh it's okay darling,' the Mangoes said. 'There's plenty to go around.'

'It's just good manners to ask. You shouldn't just barge in and help yourselves. How would you like it if I stuffed my hand inside your nest hole and took out half your babies to train for a circus without asking permission?'

'Eh?' Mithoorani cocked her head to one side. 'You wouldn't do that...you're too sweet!' she drawled, nibbling Tadpole's ear affectionately. 'But you're welcome to take the brats!'

'Of course I wouldn't but you get the point?'

'Oh okay!' Mithoorani rolled her eyes and then looked at the trees. 'Dear Mangoes, can we help ourselves to some of your delicious, nectar-rich flowers, please, as we have been doing for the last 300 years or so?'

'Be our guests, dears. But don't interfere with the bees too much. You wouldn't want to annoy them and we don't want a fight, do we?'

Just then we heard the sound of voices and turned around. Through the trees we saw the Periwinkle aunties walking towards the sacred grove along with two men. The men were wearing dark trousers and jackets. One was chubby faced, with a bushy moustache and fair complexion and had curly black hair right over his ears. His close-set eyes flicked around. His pudgy fingers glittered with rings. The other had a narrow face and a greasy black fringe and had put too much gel in his hair. He was darker and shorter, but strutted like he was the boss, looking around as if he already owned the place. He was wearing white sandals with red and black striped socks.

'Quick!' Tadpole said, 'get up the trees!'

'But…'

'Up!' she said, shoving me in the back. 'Get up Bhaiyya—and you too Zafia!'

We scrambled up, trying not to disturb the bees too much. They weren't very bothered—they were too busy stuffing themselves with nectar and pollen and taking the loot back to their hive.

'And this is the "scared grove" that we told you about!' Poppy Aunty was saying to the men as they approached Ustadji. 'This old banyan has stood here for over 250 years. No one touches anything here. The old Baba doesn't allow it and our family has respected that ever since we had the property. It's been like that even when the British and the old sultans had the property.'

'Amazing!' the fair one said, eyeing Ustadji.

'It's become quite like a protected forest!' Petunia Aunty said. 'So in case you do buy the property we would appreciate that you respect that too. We could write that into the agreement.'

'But of course, madam. We understand. It will, however reduce the value of the property, you understand.' White Sandal said smoothly, 'Because we would not be able to use it for anything.'

'It would be as good as not owning so much of the land,' his partner added, 'therefore naturally the price would have to come down.'

The Periwinkle aunties looked at each other.

'Can we discuss this in private, please?' White Sandal said. 'It puts a whole new dimension on the deal.'

'Would you like to go back to the house?'

'No, if you stay here, we'll walk over to those trees there and have our discussion.'

'They're coming here!' Tadpole whispered peering down at them. Up in the branches of the mango tree we were well hidden.

The foliage was thick and dark. The two men walked over, even as the Julies tried snagging them.

They stood right beneath our tree. 'We'll beat them down to half price if not quarter,' said one.

'That's all very well, but they'll still want something in writing in the agreement, which will forbid us from using this part of the property.'

'We will agree not to touch the sacred grove. But say there is a devastating fire and the sacred grove burns down? Then what? Then we can do what we want.'

White Sandal frowned. 'When do we burn it down? After we buy the property?'

'But of course.'

White Sandal shook his head. 'It won't work. They'll get suspicious. It will become a court case.' His eyes gleamed. 'I have a better idea! We accept their offer. We say, we think that any place with a sacred grove in it has special value and meaning for us, that in fact for us a property with a sacred grove is far more valuable than one without one; that it is one of the main reasons we are so interested in buying it in the first place. Then we burn it down a day before we sign the deal. We tell them that since the sacred grove has been destroyed—and in fact all those trees burned down, the value of the property has come down drastically and that we're only going through with the deal because we made a commitment to two respected ladies! We'll get it at half the price! We can't break down the palace—it's a heritage building, but once this area is empty we can build here!'

Our eyes were like soup plates. Zafia put her hand to her mouth in horror and I had to put my fingers to my lips and warn Tadpole to keep shut. She was about to yell something rude to the men. They had started walking back to the Periwinkle aunties.

When they turned around they were both smiling widely.

'Forgive us, madams,' White Sandal said, bowing his head and doing a respectful namaste. 'We were hasty and have realized the error of our ways. While discussing we were suddenly enlightened!' He reverently looked at the Peepli Princesses. 'We realized that the real reason we were interested in this property was *because* of this beautiful sacred grove. How many properties have one? So good for the environment and so good spiritually for all who walk here! How many more people will be so enlightened? Humbly we would like to accept the offer you have made us.'

The Periwinkle aunties looked absolutely zapped. They exchanged glances and held each others' hands. Then Petunia Aunty turned to the men.

'Well, we hardly know what to say!' she said in a quavering sort of voice.

'We're so glad you've realized the value of the grove,' Poppy Aunty added. 'You know we never added a premium to the price because of it.'

'That would be like selling our souls!' Petunia Aunty said. 'You can't put a price on something that is sacred!'

'Maybe we can go back now and get our lawyers on the job to draft out the agreement,' White Sandals said. 'We'd like to take possession as soon as possible.'

'Certainly. But we will need a month at least to clear everything—and we're going out of Delhi again for three weeks. Say the middle of March? Around Holi?'

'Perfect. The lawyers will want time to draft the agreement.' 'Excellent!'

The two slime-balls shook hands with Petunia and Poppy aunties, right under Ustadji's wonderful canopy and they walked back to the house.

'Bhaiyya! Did you hear them?' There were tears in Tadpole's voice. 'They're going to burn down the sacred grove! We've got to stop them!'

'How?'

'We can tell the Periwinkle aunties what we heard. Come on, let's go. We'll wait for the men to go and tell them.'

'Tadpole they won't believe us. They'll think we made up stories because we don't want them to sell Medley Gardens.'

'But we can't not do anything!'

'Tadpole,' Zafia said frowning. The only way to stop them is to catch them actually setting fire to the place. Otherwise, they'll just say it started accidentally. And March is a very dry month with a lot of wind, so fires can start and spread rapidly.'

'I think we should still tell them,' I said frowning. 'Let's see what happens. They might hire extra security for those few days to ensure that no one sets fire.'

'But what if they set fire afterwards? After they buy the property? Which they will, even if they don't get it at half price!'

I shook my head. 'There's nothing we can do about that. It'll be their place.'

'Listen!' Tadpole suddenly said, cocking her head, 'listen to that!'

We did. We weren't the only ones to have overhead what those slime-balls had said. The buzzing of the bees rose to a crescendo and Mithoorani's friends were squawking hysterically.

'Did you hear? They're going to burn the grove down!'

'Where will we go for nectar?'

'This is our last Mangobloom Festival here!' a parakeet squawked dismally. And then both Mithoorani and Gingianus landed on Tadpole's shoulders, talking at the same time.

'Baby you have to do something,' Mithoorani gabbled. 'My

family has nested here for as long as time. We are historic residents! Where will we go?'

'Yo Chicklet,' Gingianus added, 'she's right. I may have had property disputes with parakeets but this is still our home. Where do we go? All the nesting holes in this area are occupied and do you know how expensive they are?'

Even the ants were panicking. The news had apparently reached the Queen and she had given her orders. A column of the First Folic Infantry Battalion marched out in search to 'seek and take by force if necessary' any other suitable and safe site for a nesting colony.

'General, tell the Queen there's no hurry!' Tadpole said, her nose inches away from the smart soldier ant gnashing his mandibles. 'We still have a month. We won't let them get away with this.'

'We have our orders!' the General said. 'Battalion, forward march! Huptwothree!'

We climbed down and as we walked towards Ustadji we heard the Neems and Peepli Princesses sobbing quietly. Even the Julies were too busy murmuring amongst themselves to catcall us.

Tadpole walked up to the Neems. 'Don't worry,' she said fiercely. 'We won't let them touch you!'

'Children,' Ustadji said hoarsely. 'Is it true? I couldn't quite hear what those men said; the wind was in the wrong direction. But is it true? Are they really going to burn us down and build something over here?'

'Yes,' Zafia said quietly. 'That's what they plan to do. But we're not going to let them!' She turned to me. 'Are we?'

'No!' I said vehemently, even though I hadn't the faintest idea of how we would be able to prevent them. 'Never!'

'Children! Listen,' Ustadji said in such a deep and grave voice we all paused. 'Those evil men must NEVER come here, let alone burn us down and try to build anything here. NEVER!'

'Come on,' Tadpole said grabbing our hands. 'Let's go and talk to Poppy and Petunia aunties right now!'

But we hesitated. A huge black Mercedes was parked in the portico. The men were still here, probably having lunch with the Periwinkle aunties. A chauffeur and a bodyguard who were the size of prizefighters sprawled asleep in the front seat of the car.

'Maybe we should come back later!' I said. 'They're still here.'

'Maybe we should meet them,' Zafia said. 'And get to know the enemy!'

'Look, there they are!' Tadpole suddenly said, pointing at the terrace. They were sitting under one of the 'chattris' having lunch there. Petunia Aunty suddenly spotted us and waved.

'Children!' she called gaily, 'Come up and say hello!'

We looked at each other and slowly went up the beautiful marble steps and out onto the terrace.

Petunia Aunty smiled at us. 'Come along dears, don't be shy!' She turned to the slime-balls. 'Gentlemen, these lovely children live next door—that's Vishwajit, Zafia and little Tadpole. They love playing in the sacred grove! Children, these gentlemen are the Rabbani brothers—that's Visnu and that's Siva. Say hello now!'

We did.

'Children, these kind gentlemen will probably be the new owners of Medley Gardens. Like you they love the sacred grove and have promised to look after it.'

'It doesn't need looking after! Tadpole blurted. 'It just needs to be left alone!'

'What a sweet little girlie!' Siva Rabbani (alias White Sandal) said, reaching forward to pinch Tadpole's cheek. She jerked away, looking ferocious.

'So shy!' the other creep added, smiling greasily, 'Ao sweet!'

'They're very empathetic to trees and plants. The little girl picked the roses and dahlias which won prizes at the recent flower show.'

'Wonderful!'

'Will you be living here?' I asked hesitantly, shuffling from one foot to another.

The slime-balls laughed. 'No, no—we are thinking of making this a seven-star heritage hotel and apa where only very sophisticated people will come. The building is historical and we will renovate it properly. It'll be a true palace again!'

'They say they'll restore the gardens to their old glory,' Petunia aunty said. 'Wouldn't that be wonderful?'

'Come on darlings, have some rabdi and jalebis!' Poppy Aunty insisted as Baba's wife hobbled up carrying a silver serving dish and bowls. We pulled up the wrought iron chairs and helped ourselves.

'That sacred grove is very sacred!' Tadpole suddenly said. 'It's said that very bad things happen to people who cut leaves or branches or trees there, or even if they just pluck a flower! It is not allowed.'

The slime-balls nodded benignly. 'But of course!'

'Baba's great great grandfather or whatever put a curse on it—anyone who touched it would die horribly, writhing and screaming in pain.' Tadpole rolled her eyes.

'She's right,' Petunia Aunty added mildly. 'The villagers only go there to pay homage—though Baba allows them to cut leaves and pick fallen branches from the forest behind the house.'

'How wonderful. We will of course worship its sacredness.'

Visnu Rabbani stood up. 'Madams, I'd like to go to the washroom.'

'Of course!' She made as if to stand up, when I shot to my feet.

'Aunty, I'll show Uncle where it is,' I said gallantly. The other brother had also got to his feet.

'I'll go along too,' he said.

I led them to the bedroom adjacent to the terrace and indicated the bathroom. They both went in together and shut the door, smiling at me—how gross was that! The bathroom was just enormous—a cavernous room with a mighty echo. Quietly, I positioned myself under the ventilator slit, high up on the wall. I could hear them clearly as their voices echoed hollowly around the huge room and right out of the ventilator down to my ears.

'We absolutely have to burn that jungle down. And even the one at the back of the house.'

'What about the building? If the building catches fire too it will have to be demolished. Then we can build anything we want.'

'Good idea, but we'll have to do it carefully. And burn it to the ground so there is no chance of rebuilding.'

'Absolutely!'

'Then we can really beat down the price. Burnt land, burnt building, out here in the wilderness...who will buy?'

'And they want to go back to Caneda quickly.'

'Have you seen that new farm next door? It's quite nice...'

One of them laughed hollowly. 'First let's get this!'

My jaw dropped. They had their greedy eyes on Circuit House too!

Out on the terrace, Zafia told me later, she and Tadpole sat in silence and fidgeted.

'Darling, we can request them to let you keep coming here even after they buy the property,' Poppy Aunty said kindly, sensing their distress and discomfort. 'We know you're upset by this whole thing. But you understand we can't guarantee anything. Once they are the owners, they call the shots.'

'Do you really have to sell the place?' Tadpole blurted, bursting into tears. 'We love it so much! It is so beautiful.'

The Periwinkle aunties looked at each other distressed.

'Yes dear, I'm afraid we have to. We don't really want to but...' She sighed. 'You see dear, we can't afford the upkeep, and the palace is simply falling down. It's better that it gets a new owner who can look after it in the way it deserves to be. Otherwise it'll just turn to rubble in a few years.'

'But those trees are our friends!' Tadpole sobbed. 'You can't sell our friends! They've stood there for hundreds of years!'

'They'll still be there—they are not going to be touched! The gentlemen have promised that. They said they're buying the place primarily because of the sacred grove.'

'Aunty they said that—but, but what if there's a fire and the sacred grove burns down? Then they can do what they like!'

'Darling, why should there be a fire? Of course there won't!'

At this point I came out onto the terrace with the slime-balls.

'Thank you very much for your kind hospitality, we must go. We've taken enough of your time,' Visnu said, smiling ingratiatingly. 'Our lawyer will be in touch with yours and draw up the agreement.'

They shook hands and drove off in their black Mercedes.

We, too, said goodbye to the Periwinkle aunties and wandered disconsolately back home.

16

'*Bhaiyya!*' Tadpole said suddenly a few days later, 'do you think Babaji knows that Medley Gardens is being sold?'

'I guess the Periwinkle aunties must have told him.'

'Will he stay on there? Where will he go? He's lived there all his life!'

'Let's ask him the next time we go there.'

So we did. He and Mataji were sitting in the backyard, sunning themselves. They smiled at us, but I thought looked a little sad too.

'Babaji, you know the memsahibs are selling this place?' Zafia asked them gently. She had been coming over every weekend so we could spend time at Medley Gardens before it got sold. (Even better, she would shortly be shifting here for the next three months because her parents were going abroad on a research project.)

They nodded.

'Where will you go?' Tadpole asked, squatting down next to them.

'We'll remain here. The memsahibs said the people who will buy the place agreed to that. As long as we're alive we will have our little cottage—and Budhoo!' Mataji looked fondly at the buffalo tethered nearby. Tadpole shook her head.

'Those are bad men. They're evil men. We heard them planning to burn down the sacred grove before they sign the deal. Then they'll reduce the price and get it practically free. They want to burn everything down—this forest and the palace too—so they can build whatever they want!'

Babaji's bidi fell out of his mouth and he flicked it off his dhoti. He looked shocked.

'Never!' he whispered. Mataji looked stunned.

'We heard them, Babaji,' Tadpole went on, 'You have to believe us!'

'They must never do that! It is forbidden!'

'But they will! They don't care!'

'We will have to stop them!'

'How?' Tadpole asked bluntly.

'We'll think of something. But this must never happen! They must not touch a leaf or twig in the sacred forest!' But we could see there was despair in Babaji's voice and his eyes. How could an old man and his wife stop such thugs? How could we? Besides, as Zafia had pointed out, we would have to catch them in the act, and that was pretty much impossible. The adults wouldn't believe us—who would? We sat with them for a while and then got to our feet.

'We'll think of something, I promise,' I said valiantly and Zafia and Tadpole nodded, knowing it was just to comfort the old couple.

'Come on,' Tadpole said, 'let's say hello to the trees. God knows how much longer we'll be allowed to.'

We wandered off to the sacred grove. It was pretty depressing. 'Hello children, do you have any news?' Ustadji asked. 'You know, this must never happen. They must not be allowed to touch us.'

'Never!' chorused the Peepli Princesses and the Neems and then all the rest of them. This was the first time that all of them agreed on something—and I could understand why. They'd all be burned to the ground.

'They can't do it!' Princess Bo wept. 'It doesn't belong to them!'

Even Kapok Maharaj was looking down and out. He'd dropped nearly all his leaves and his branches stuck out like the ribs of a broken umbrella. He greeted us somberly.

'Hello children. I'm thinking of canceling the party this year because of the recent developments. Gingi told us what the new owners are planning. Can you stop them?'

'We'll think of something,' Zafia said, 'we promise!'

The Mangoes were still in flower but said that they didn't want to work too hard at producing a bumper crop.

'If we're going to be burned down anyway what's the point?' they said. 'They'll burn us down and dig everything up and that'll be the end of Medley Gardens forever!'

We sat down at the edge of the lake—even the Oleander Siblings were quiet for a change—and looked hopelessly at each other.

'We never found out why this was a sacred grove in the first place,' Tadpole said. 'And why not the forest behind the palace? I mean they both have trees—but one is sacred and one is not! Why?'

'Maybe that's what the secret is all about,' I said slowly. 'That's what they're keeping from us—*why* it is a sacred grove!'

'We could ask Babaji!' Tadpole said. 'He should tell us!'

'He'd just say because it's always been like that,' Zafia said. 'Maybe because Ustadji was the first tree they found growing here...'

'And there were no other trees here at the time...' I said slowly.

'It was barren...' Zafia's eyes were thoughtful.

'A wasteland...with just rocks and shrubs....'

'So why plant a sacred grove?'

Tadpole looked at us like she was watching a tennis match. And then suddenly it struck us; rather like a thunderbolt.

We looked at each other our eyes widening, our mouths falling open. I think it struck all three of us at precisely the same moment. Everything suddenly slid into place: click, click, click!

Why was Babaji so insistent that the sacred grove must never be touched.

Why the trees were so scared and upset.

What Princess Bo had let slip when she had said: 'It doesn't belong to them!'

And most of all, Naniji's lecture on how forests should never be felled, no matter what they stood on, because they guarded the most precious treasure in the world—they held the very earth together....

Here in Medley Gardens they held much more than just that…

We looked at each other, our eyes shining.

'…the lost treasure of the Dilkhush Palace,' Zafia went on.

'It's buried under the sacred grove!' I breathed.

We stared at each other.

'*That's* what the secret of Medley Gardens is!' I said vehemently. 'They all know it but naturally they couldn't tell us! *That's* what Naniji hinted at! She was telling us and yet not telling us!'

'The sultan must have buried it here before fleeing, hoping he would return some day to retrieve it.'

'But he never did!'

'What happened to all the people who must have helped him bury it?' Tadpole asked. 'He couldn't have done it alone!'

'He must have killed them, what else. They did such things in the old days.'

'But this means…'

'Those men must NEVER burn down the sacred grove. Once they start digging…'

'And it's not theirs. It belongs to Babaji and Ustadji and the Peepli Princesses and all the rest of them. They've been guarding it for so long.'

'Do you think the villagers know?' Zafia said. Then she shook her head. 'I guess not. They would have dug it up if they had.'

'I guess they just believe it's sacred, that's all.'

'Should we tell Ustadji that we've guessed?'

I looked at the girls. 'What do you think?'

Zafia grinned mischievously. 'Let's just start digging somewhere near him!' she said, her eyes sparkling. 'And watch his reaction!'

'He'll freak!'

'Okay, we could do that, but we also really need to think of some way to stop those fellows from starting the fire!'

I have to admit that we got so caught up in the excitement of actually finding some treasure that we gave that top priority.

'So how do we go about it?' I said frowning. 'We have to start digging.'

'Not now or during the day!' Zafia said. 'Babaji and Mataji keep wandering around and will spot us.' Her eyes gleamed with excitement. 'At night! Tonight! After everyone's gone to sleep.'

'Yes, we'll bring a battery lantern and in any case there's a full moon these days,' I said.

'And we should bring the dogs too,' Tadpole added.

'There are shovels at home in the gardening shed, we can take those.'

We could hardly eat our dinner properly, we were so excited. Mom, Dad and Amma turned in at about 10 p.m. Zafia was sharing Tadpole's room because she hadn't wanted to sleep alone, so Amma had gone off to her quarter and was safely out of the way. The girls crept into my room at 10.15 their eyes bright with excitement.

'We'll set off at 10.30,' I said. 'Everyone should be asleep by then.'

With the dogs milling excitedly about us we snuck out, wrapped up in our hoodies and mufflers. We collected a couple of heavy shovels, a bucket and a rope, and shading our torches opened the gates.

We were lucky there was no thick fog—just a wispy mist that looked like tattered cobweb being blown around by the light breeze. The big silver moon shone down like a fluorescent coin, bathing Medley Gardens in its light. We slipped through the gate and set off for the sacred grove.

'Where should we start digging?' I whispered.

'Somewhere between Ustadji and Princess Bo,' Zafia suggested.

We flashed our torches around and selected a spot. 'Here,' I said, 'it's as good a place as any!'

'Eek!' Tadpole gave a small scream. 'Oh it's only you Gingi—you gave me such a fright!'

'What are you all doing here?' Gingianus asked sleepily. 'Do you know the time? You should be in bed! And what are you doing with those shovels?' His voice and little 'crest' rose in alarm.

'You can't use shovels here—it's not allowed!' Mithoorani squawked landing suddenly on Tadpole's other shoulder. 'This is an ancient sacred grove!'

'We just want to dig around a bit,' Tadpole said grinning. 'Don't worry!'

'But...but...'

'Let's start,' I thrust the shovel into the crusty earth with a grunt.

'Children! Children but what are you doing?' Ustadji asked in a hollow voice. 'You can't dig here. You'll damage my roots! Besides, it's forbidden!'

'Children, please stop!' Princess Bo squeaked, her leaves glimmering eerily. 'Please!'

'Put away those shovels!'

Tadpole went up to Ustadji and hugged one of his main prop-roots.

'We know,' she said softly, flashing her torch over him. 'We guessed. The treasure of Medley Gardens is buried under you all…right?'

The Peepli Princesses squeaked plaintively. There was a resigned sigh from the Neems. The Oleander Siblings remained quiet—for ten seconds.

'See, if you hadn't interfered right at the beginning we would have made them eat our apples right then and none of this would have happened!' they said. 'They would have been dead!'

'Oh shut up!' the Peepli Princesses said.

'How did you guess?' Ustadji asked.

We told him.

'Oh well,' he said philosophically. 'We did our best. We guarded it for more than 250 years. You know I was a very, very young sapling, and had just settled on this grizzled old neem when it happened. The rest of the area was pretty barren. There was a lot of turmoil amongst your species at the time and the sultan had to flee. Then one day the old Babaji came around here with the sultan and pointed towards me. He said I was sacred, and that if the treasure were buried here, he'd plant a sacred grove over the site and no one would touch it. The treasure would remain safe. So that's what they did. They dug all around me and buried the chests and sacks and then planted saplings all over them. And then over the years I saw the other trees grow—the Mangoes, and much later, the Peepli Princesses and the Neems. Now you know why they're so bitter—I started life on one of their ancestors. Now look at this place, so beautiful and green in spite of the Julies.'

'What happened to the people who actually buried the treasure?' Tadpole asked.

'They were killed. Their village was burned to the ground. There were no survivors.'

Ustadji sighed. 'Well now the treasure is yours,' he said. 'You've found it. I suppose it had to happen some day.'

'Not quite,' I said softly. 'But would you mind very much if we dug a bit?'

'Be my guest! It's all yours now!'

'Where would be a good spot to start?' I asked.

'Between prop-root 35 and Bo's main trunk. About 10 feet left of the prop-root where you've stuck in your shovel.'

I flashed my torch at the girls.

'Should we?'

They nodded. 'We have to. We have to be sure!'

We put down the battery lantern and picked up our shovels.

It was going to be hard work.

'Tadpole, you keep an eye out for Babaji, he musn't see us, or he'll have a heart attack! You keep looking towards the palace and tell us if you spot a light.'

'Okay!' The moonlight was bright enough for her to shin up one of Ustadji's thick prop-roots. 'Don't worry,' she told him. 'We're not going to let anyone harm you all.'

'When you find the treasure, you'll change your mind,' he said heavily.

Zafia and I dug solidly for an hour. It wasn't a very big hole, just deep—a shaft about two feet in diameter. Luckily, under the crusty top the soil was soft and moist, like a rich fruit cake, so we made good progress. We had to be careful about not hurting

Ustadji's myriad roots that crisscrossed all over, and bored deep into the earth: many were so tough and thick we just had to dig around them.

We had to cut through some of them though and occasionally Ustadji would grunt.

'Hey that tickles!'

'Sorry Ustadji.'

There were also rocks and stones that clunked against our shovels, which we had to dislodge. Some were pretty large, but thankfully none so big that we couldn't dig past them. We hung the battery lamp on one of the protruding roots we had unearthed: this way no light leaked out of the hole even though both of us looked like zombies, what with the mud and grime all over our faces, our teeth and eyes gleaming whitely. From time to time we paused to catch our breath.

'Hard work!' I grunted. 'There better be a treasure after all this!'

Soon we'd dug too deep for us to throw out the soil with our shovels.

'One of us will have to go up and haul up the bucket as the other fills it.'

Zafia climbed out first and I dug on, filling the bucket and hefting it up to her. She pulled it up with the rope, emptied it and handed it back down.

'You freak me out,' she giggled, looking down at me as she lowered the empty pail. 'Your eyes gleam like poached eggs!' A little later, she slithered down and I managed to clamber up and she started digging.

'And you are the lovely zombie princess of Medley Gardens!' I grinned.

'How long are you going to take?' Tadpole complained from

her perch. 'I'm getting bored and sleepy. Even the dogs are sleeping.'

'Okay, you can come down,' I called from the bottom of the hole, 'if anyone comes the dogs will warn us.'

'No thanks, I'm very comfy,' she said.

We must have dug about eight feet deep and were both pretty pooped and sweaty. It was well past midnight now. We'd taken off our windcheaters, our shirts stuck clammily to us. We were beginning to wonder if Ustadji had just sold us a pup. We were both absolutely filthy and our palms had begun to blister. To climb out of the hole we had had to gouge footholds into its sides and cling on to some of the strong roots. The person at the top had to lean over and grab the hands of the one climbing out and heave. We had to slither down into the hole carefully too, so we didn't fall or twist an ankle. It was tough, dirty work, especially in the dark.

'If they buried wooden chests, they must have rotted by now,' I said, looking up at Zafia peering down and thrusting my shovel in deep. 'And I'm beginning to get a bit fed up of this.'

All the surrounding trees were silent and the breeze had stopped. The mist was beginning to thicken.

'Found anything?' Tadpole asked from time to time, peering down at us from her lookout post. 'Hurry up, it's getting foggy.'

'Ustadji are you sure it's here?' I asked at last, wiping my brow and looking up at him, towering high and wide above me. The smell of rich, damp earth assailed my nostrils.

'Well, it's been so long, I can't really guarantee anything,' he replied. 'But that's as good a spot as any.'

'Thanks!' I said. 'I'm taking a break!'

Zafia caught my hand and helped me out of the hole and quickly slid down herself.

'Hand me the shovel, please,' she said. Her cheeks were pink under the grime, her eyes gleaming.

Fifteen minutes later, I went down again, without much hope. But finally, my shovel clunked against something. Was it yet another rock? I dumped it, buried under a pile of earth in the pail and hefted it up to Zafia. She emptied the pail and I heard her give a little squeal. And then:

'Vish…!'

'What?'

'This!' she said and slithered down the hole beside me, her face animated. 'Look at what you just threw out!' She unclenched her palm.

A gigantic sapphire-and-diamond ring nestled in her muddy palm. In the white light of the lantern it glittered brightly, despite the mud sticking to it. The central stone, the sapphire, glowed a deep cornflower blue, encircled with diamonds which shot rainbow lasers at us.

'My God!' I whispered. I took the ring from her, rubbed it against my shirt and gazed at it. How much more of this stuff lay buried beneath Ustadji and the others? Then I took Zafia's hand. She pursed her lips and spread out her fingers. I slipped the ring on her finger and smiled. She leaned forward and gave me a long gritty kiss. We stared at each other and then hugged tightly.

'You idiot, how are we going to get out?' I asked, moving back at last. The top of the hole was three feet above our heads.

'Oh shoot!' she giggled.

'Okay,' I said crouching down. 'You stand on my shoulders and I'll heft you up. Then you can pull me out!'

We did that.

'Let's show Tadpole now,' Zafia said, her eyes gleaming in her muddy face. 'She'll be thrilled!'

Tadpole was ecstatic. Then she looked at us mischievously.

'Imagine you got engaged in a muddy hole! I saw you smooch!'

'Tadpole!'

'So now we know!' Zafia said softly.

'Let's make sure!'

'I want to dig too!' Tadpole insisted. 'You've had all the fun so far!'

'Okay,' I grinned. 'I'll go down and you jump after me—I'll catch you!'

Zafia carefully lowered Tadpole down and I caught her. I handed her the shovel—which was almost as tall as her.

'There you go!'

'Uhh...it's so heavy!'

She dug valiantly for a bit, her face red with exertion.

Crrunch! Her shovel struck something.

'There's something in the way,' she said. I took the shovel and thrust it in hard.

'Shine your torch there!'

It was the splintered top of a wooden chest. I smashed the shovel on it, splitting the wood apart.

'Ooooh!' Tadpole's eyes were enormous. So must have been mine.

'Zafia,' I called hoarsely, 'get down here!' She slithered down in a trice.

Crammed together at the bottom of the shaft, the three of us gazed in awe at the glittering jewels still reposing in their rotting chest, now at our feet. Then the girls went nuts. One by one they picked up the ornaments and began adorning themselves. Necklaces, bracelets, rings, pendants, brooches, bangles, anklets, in gold and silver, studded with diamonds, rubies, emeralds, sapphires and pearls, pink, blue, black, grey and white the size of pigeon's eggs...

'You really do look like a pair of very muddy princesses,' I grinned.

'Look, here's a gold belt and a bejeweled dagger,' Zafia said, pulling it out. 'Now you can dress up like a rajkumar too! All you need is a pink turban with a ruby and a feather!'

For several minutes we just stared at the jewels. God knows how many hundreds of such chests lay buried all around the sacred grove.

Above us, the dogs were looking down anxiously and whining. Zafia took a deep breath.

'And now we must...'

'Hold on,' I said frowning. 'If we show this to the Periwinkle aunties they won't have to sell Medley Gardens after all.'

Zafia shook her head. 'We can't,' she whispered, 'We can't! Don't you see why?' And I suddenly realized why.

'It's like checkmate, isn't it?'

She nodded slowly. Tadpole's eyes were like grapefruit as she understood too.

I whispered, 'And we can't even take a picture!'

One by one the girls took off the ornaments and placed them carefully in the rotting remnants of the chest. At last only the great sapphire remained on Zafia's finger.

'But it looks so beautiful on your finger,' I went on wistfully as Zafia smiled, and quietly slipped the great ring off and handed it to Tadpole. She held the ring for a moment, and then gently dropped it in the chest.

'Bye,' she whispered. 'Bye!'

Her eyes glimmering, Zafia leaned forward and kissed me again.

'Let's cover up the hole and go home,' Tadpole said. 'I'm sleepy and cold and all muddy and want to have a bath!'

We all heard the collective sigh of relief from the Trees of Medley Gardens.

'Thank you,' Ustadji said softly. 'Thank you very much.'

'You know,' I said slowly as we walked back through the ghostly mist. 'But this is actually a no-win situation. If we tell the Periwinkle aunties about the treasure they would still have to dig it up and in doing so would destroy the sacred grove. And if we don't, those men will buy the place and do the same anyway. Either way, the grove would be destroyed and probably the whole of Medley Gardens.'

'Don't you see, there's only one way out,' Zafia said. 'We have to stop those men from buying Medley Gardens.'

Which was easier said than done. Now the threat of what those men could do loomed even larger. Once they unearthed the first bit of jewellery, they would go berserk with earthmoving equipments. No question about that.

How would we stop them?

Back home we discussed the problem. 'We have to find out everything we can,' I said. 'Especially when the agreement is to be signed. They said they'll set fire to the place a few days before. Maybe we can keep watch or something. Or Babaji can...' But I didn't quite like the idea of that. They could easily silence Babaji and Mataji.

'I'll go and pester the Periwinkle aunties,' Tadpole decided. 'You guys study for your exams. I'll find out everything.'

And so over the next few days, Tadpole spent more time in Medley Gardens than she did at home, and reported developments to Zafia and me.

'Petunia Aunty told me that the fellows want to move in just after Holi,' Tadpole reported. 'She said they made a special request that they be allowed to play Holi with the aunties at Medley

Gardens because their astrologer told them it was suspicious.'

'You mean auspicious!'

'Whatever! So they're coming on the day before Holi and will spend one night at Medley Gardens, play Holi the next day and then go back and wait for their lawyers after Holi to sign the deal.'

Zafia's eyes widened. 'That's it!' she whispered.

'What?' I asked.

'That's when they're going to set fire: the night before Holi. Everyone has a bonfire—to get rid of the Holika demoness—so that's what they'll do. Only their little bonfire will go out of control and burn down the sacred grove and everything else. That's what they're planning! And if they're with the Periwinkle aunties at the time, they can't be blamed for setting the fire. It will just be an unfortunate accident! They'll have the perfect alibi.' She raised her eyebrows. 'And setting fire to the demoness is supposed to signify the victory of good over evil!'

'Wouldn't it be easier for them just to get their men to sneak in and set fire to the place?' I asked. 'Why all the rigmarole? Surely they must have thugs who can do the job?'

'Yes, but then the Periwinkle aunties might suspect that something's funny and back out of the deal. But if the fire was to start while they're with their prospective buyers, celebrating Holi, well it will just be seen as an accident.'

It became even clearer with Tadpole's following report.

'They've told the Periwinkle aunties that their astrologer has said that they should have the Holi bonfire in the sacred grove. He said it'll make the grove even more sacred and it will be very suspicious, I mean auspicious, for them all and bring them good luck forever.'

'But the sacred grove is pretty big. How can they ensure the whole thing burns down?' I asked. 'I mean a bonfire is a bonfire.

It can't go far.'

'Well, imagine if Ustadji gets alight. The flames would then spread everywhere,' Zafia said, gloomily.

'Still there's no guarantee. There's plenty of space between some of the trees.'

'They might set other parts alight once the main fire is started. Who will know in the confusion? Flames are known to jump long distances. And as you know, it's windy in March.'

'So what should we do?'

Zafia leant forward. 'It's a long shot but it's our only hope. We have to catch them red-handed.'

We discussed the plan at length and then reluctantly returned to our books. Thankfully our last papers would get over just before Holi so we would be free.

'Tadpole, ask the Periwinkle aunties if we could spend Holi at Medley Gardens. It'll be for the last time, after all,' I said.

The Periwinkle aunties were getting more and more sentimental about Medley Gardens as Holi drew near.

'Of course you can come and play Holi here!' they agreed. 'We absolutely insist! In fact the Rabbani uncles will be celebrating here too. We'll have a traditional bonfire the night before and then play Holi here the next day and on the following day our lawyers will arrive and...' They lapsed into silence and took out tiny handkerchiefs.

'Don't worry, aunties,' Tadpole said, patting their hands like she was their grandmother. 'Everything will be all right!'

The trees certainly didn't seem to think so. A cold, blustery snap had pounced and the trees at Medley Gardens looked pretty depressed, shaken and stirred. Kapok Maharaji stood tall and gaunt, his bodyguards standing grimly to attention.

'Chicklet!' Ginigianus drawled in Tadpole's ear. 'HRH and

the princelings are especially nervous at this time. In many parts of the north, they're the trees that are singled out for the bonfire. They're the ones that get burned.'

'I didn't know that!' Tadpole said. (Neither did I.) Suddenly she ran to the great tree and flung her arms around it.

'Don't worry, Your Highness. We'll make sure nothing bad happens to you!'

'Thank you, little girl!' HRH RSC said heavily. 'But it's a deep-rooted tradition and if these men have planned to burn the grove down, they'll surely start with us. It'll be auspicious!'

The Peepli Princess sniffed tearfully and Ustadji looked like a tired old tree. Even the Neems stopped saying that their leaves were fire retardant. The Julies too didn't try and grab us anymore.

'Ustadji, don't worry. We've thought of a plan!' Tadpole told him, trying to cheer him up. 'We can't tell you what it is but we have thought of something. No one will set fire to any of you!'

'Baby, those are hard, cruel men who will stop at nothing to get what they want. I've seen their kind for over 250 years and I know what they're like. We're doomed!'

Zafia and I had exams, which did manage to distract us somewhat—poor Tadpole was most agitated as Holi approached. Of course we'd had to tell Babaji our plan because he was very much a part of it and would actually have to organize its implementation. He nodded, a steely, determined look suddenly entering his cloudy eyes.

'It is a very good plan and it will work. It will show those men. Now have some lassi!'

17

$\mathcal{T}$wo days before Holi, the villagers began streaming into Medley Gardens to collect dry twigs and branches from the forest behind the palace for their own Holika bonfire. Babaji had spoken to the headman and told him that they had to collect wood for the bonfire at Medley Gardens too, and they willingly agreed. They collected a huge mass of wood and stacked it up near Ustadji, much to his discomfiture. The pile was at least ten feet tall; it would be a mighty bonfire, indeed.

Straight after school on the bonfire evening we ran next door, the excitement and nervousness making our tummies rumble. Much to their annoyance, we left the dogs behind—they would probably spend the whole evening sulking and sighing, but they would have interfered with what we had planned.

'This is it!' I said, 'D-day! And H-Hour approaches!'

Chairs and tables had been arranged at a safe distance away from the bonfire site.

'It's going to be a very big fire!' Tadpole said worriedly, eyeing the tall pile of wood, arranged around a thick central limb. This had been cut from a solid semul tree (and a distant cousin of HRH Kapok Maharajji) growing in the forest section, so actually HRH Kapok Maharajji had been right to be so concerned. Apparently in some parts of the country a wholesale massacre of semul trees took place for this festival.

We walked around the sacred grove, looking worriedly at all

the dry leaf litter lying around. Our plan would just have to work.

'Well, we've done our best,' I said, 'now it's up to how the plan is executed.'

At around six that evening, the Rabbani brothers drove up in their Mercedes, with their bodyguard and chauffeur.

Another car, with five more hefty men followed the Mercedes.

'Oh shoot, they've brought backup!' I said.

Zafia looked worried. 'Those men will probably start the fires from different places, so the whole place goes up in flames properly. They're leaving nothing to chance.'

Despite our plan things were looking pretty grim.

'Come on,' I said heavily. 'Let's go and meet the enemy!'

We traipsed into the main living room where they were being served tea.

'Hello children, do join us!' Petunia Aunty said, as we walked in. 'Visnu and Siva uncles will be celebrating the bonfire with us this evening. They've even brought a huge bottle of champagne.'

But she sounded sad.

We said hello to the enemy and sat down.

The gorilla chauffeur and bodyguard were with the car outside, but the other liveried lackeys ran around helping a surly Babaji serve the tea.

'We'll wait till dusk and then go and start up the bonfire,' Visnu said smiling greasily at us. 'Aunty told us that you children would be joining us, so we've brought a whole lot of fireworks too.'

We exchanged glances. With what they had planned there would be plenty of fireworks even without any actual ones. And outside, we noticed, the wind had started picking up. It was becoming blustery. Not good.

At around seven, as dusk began to fall the Rabbanis got to their feet.

'Should we proceed to the site?' they said and began escorting the Periwinkle aunties out of the house—as if it was already theirs.

'Arrange the drinks and snacks and bring the fireworks!' Visnu snapped at the lackeys who hurried after us, carrying the champagne bottle and ice bucket and snacks.

'Bhaiyya, be ready to call the fire brigade,' Tadpole said as we followed.

'Hopefully we won't need them,' Zafia said, but she sounded doubtful.

We gathered around the bonfire site.

'Come on dears, let's set fire to this demon now!' Poppy Aunty said in a strained sort of voice. 'We'll just wait for some of the villagers to join us too—Babaji has invited them as this will be the last time...' She petered out and dabbed her eyes with her handkerchief. Soon, the villagers began trickling in, looking a little awkward and stared at the Rabbani brothers sullenly. They greeted the Periwinkle aunties respectfully and some of the women pinched Tadpole's cheeks and smiled at her. They were all very fond of her. Then they squatted on their haunches a little distance away. A little later, Mom and Dad joined the party.

The liveried lackeys ran to and fro carrying and serving snacks as Babaji hunkered down nearby and glowered at them. Mataji had joined a group of the village women a little distance away. The wind blustered through the trees, making them rustle agitatedly and dry leaves whirled around in crazy circles. A fire could race through the whole sacred grove with this kind of help.

'Don't worry!' Tadpole whispered to Ustadji, 'Everything will be all right!' She bit her lip and said softly, 'I hope...'

Visnu had taken the champagne bottle out of the ice bucket and had begun unraveling the wire from the cork. It opened with a muffled pop and he began filling the flutes. The Rabbani uncles had raised their glasses. Then Visnu beckoned Babaji.

'Please come,' he said smiling smoothly. 'You must start the fire because you have looked after this place so beautifully for all these years.' The bodyguard had lit a brand and handed it over to Babaji. Scowling ferociously, Babaji lit the fire.

Now there was no way that the Rabbani brothers or their men could be blamed for what they had planned to do—*they* had not actually lit the fire! The flames took immediately and began leaping and dancing hypnotically.

'To Medley Gardens!' they toasted, smiling with all their perfect teeth.

'To the victory of good over evil!'

The Periwinkle aunties looked at each other, forced smiles stretched across their faces. Mom and Dad looked a bit embarrassed too.

The flames leapt higher, fanned by the breeze. We stared at them for a while, as the dusk deepened and it became dark.

'Come on kids, what are you waiting for? Let's light the fireworks!' Siva said, getting to his feet. He summoned the chauffeur and bodyguard. They began lighting the firecrackers. The rockets shot up and burst into chrysanthemums of colour high up, green, blue, white, purple, and orange. The anars lit us up eerily, with their blinding white phosphorescent light before dying suddenly. We lit a few ourselves too, though frankly, our hearts were not in it.

'Thank god we left the dogs at home,' Tadpole said, 'they'd have freaked!' It really was a beautiful firework display—and then suddenly it was over and quiet descended, with just the flames of the bonfire still flickering and dancing. The villagers, squatting a little distance away near Ustadji seemed to melt away into the twilight evening. The chauffeur and bodyguard tossed the empty firework boxes into the fire and went off as did the lackeys—to help Babaji and Mataji prepare the dinner, they said.

'Should we go back indoors now?' Poppy Aunty said after a while. 'It's very warm near the fire!' The adults got to their feet and began making their way back to the house.

'We'll stay on for a bit,' I told Mom who was looking at us questioningly. 'It's fun watching the fire!'

'Don't go too close to it, kids,' Petunia Aunty said. 'And come to the house when you're hungry!'

We waited till the adults had gone and then moved towards Ustadji.

'This is it!' Zafia said. 'Crunch time!'

We climbed up Ustadji and settled ourselves, side by side on a convenient almost horizontal low branch.

'Now we wait!' I said, as we stared at the bonfire that had began reducing in size. A ghostly silver-white bird suddenly materialized on a branch in front of us. Motia, the barn owl. His face was like a mushroom coloured satellite dish and his slanting eyes looked at us reassuringly.

'Don't worry kids, I won't let anything happen to you,' he said. 'My wife and I will make sure you're safe.'

Their family had nested in one of Ustadji's hollows for aeons—it was their ancestral home as they put it.

'Mom and Dad will be wondering when we're going to get back,' Tadpole whispered, some time later as it became darker. Luckily the moon was riding high and bathed the sacred grove in its silver light. 'They're going to start yelling for us soon.'

We had anticipated this and had switched off our phones, so no one could call us back.

We sat up in Ustadji, waiting, watching. It seemed endless.

At eight-thirty, Zafia gripped my arm. 'Look!' she whispered pointing down the path, 'Someone's coming.'

It was the gorilla bodyguard and the chauffeur and one of the lackeys. They all carried large tin jerry cans and the lackey had a sports bag slung over his shoulder too. They approached the bonfire that was now dying down. One of them started kicking the embers towards Ustadji's prop-roots. The others went around emptying the contents of the can on the ground. The strong smell of petrol filled the night air. Then they stood back and picked up a flaming brand each and approached the petrol-doused area. Up on our branch, we suddenly felt Ustadji tremble violently, and nearby the Peepli Princesses too quivered their glossy heart shaped leaves, as if there had been an earthquake. A great restless rustle ran through the entire sacred grove. We switched our phones on video mode and then:

'What are you doing?' we screamed as we jumped out of the tree. 'You're setting fire here! Stop it!'

'Yaagh!' The men got the shock of their lives! They stopped in their tracks their mouths falling open.

'Don't you dare!' Zafia screamed.

The men exchanged glances and nodded grimly. They stuck the flaming brands into the ground, and leapt at us. Before I knew what was happening one had me in a chokehold and the other two had caught hold of Zafia and Tadpole, a brawny arm around each of their slender necks. They dragged us off behind Ustadji as we gurgled helplessly and struggled.

'Kill them,' the bodyguard grunted.

Then, just as we had hoped, the villagers, who had concealed themselves behind and up on the Peepli Princesses and Neems— and who had been vital to our plan—leapt from their hiding places shouting, 'Pakdo, maro! Catch them, beat them!' Our grand plan had worked just as we had thought!

Not quite!

Because suddenly there were guns in the hands of the goons, and their cold metallic muzzles were rammed against our heads, making us wince.

'Back!' the chauffeur snapped, 'Or we'll blow their heads off!'

The lackey unzipped his sports bag and my heart sunk as he lovingly withdrew what looked like an AK 47 from it and pointed it at the villagers, who were standing back stunned, all in a row.

'Don't move! And do not worry about the noise the gun makes. People will think it's just firecrackers!' He gestured for them to line up in front of Ustadji, with their hands up.

'Get a rope!'

They didn't have one, hah! But then they did a diabolical thing. The lackey reached up and cut long lengths of Ustadji's dangling aerial roots.

'Tie them with these!' he grunted and started on me. Tadpole and Zafia, their eyes bulging, were still struggling in the chokehold of the other two. Very soon all three of us were securely bound— by Ustadji's own roots. Then they gagged us with strips of cloth they cut from the tablecloth. All the while, the lackey pointed his AK 47 steadily at the villagers.

'Malik has said no witnesses,' the bodyguard said. 'We'll have to kill them all.'

'Get the petrol!'

They splattered petrol all around us as we exchanged horrified glances. Our plan had gone off the rails good and proper. These men were professional killers.

The lackey now reached into his bag again and took out more fireworks. My heart sank... I knew what they were going to do. They'd set off the fireworks and open fire at the same time, so no one at the house would suspect anything. And then set fire to the whole place. That AK 47 could decimate us and the villagers in about thirty seconds, tops. We were done for.

I was wrong. What they had planned was worse.

The chauffeur picked up the flaming brand again and leered at us. The lackey trained his gun steadily at the villagers. The bodyguard picked up another brand and bent over a long string of heavy duty firecrackers. We were surrounded by small pools of petrol that glimmered on the dry leaves and twigs around us.

They would set us on fire and then open up with the machine gun on the villagers, while in the background the firecrackers went off, dispelling suspicion. I looked around desperately and struggled frantically. Ustadji's roots dug into my flesh. I wanted to yell to the villagers to run—some might survive the hail of bullets from the AK 47—but they just stood there, their eyes stony and blank.

'Set them on fire!' the bodyguard said. He looked at me and grinned. 'You and your sisters will burn, but you will not even be able to scream!'

Right then, with blood-curdling shrieks Motia and Moti, his wife, swooped down with their talons extended.

'Whaa?' The men raised their flaming brands and struck out at the owls that dodged them easily, still shrieking.

Despairingly I looked at Tadpole and Zafia.

They looked back at me, their eyes huge and eloquent.

And then I saw Tadpole and Zafia's eyebrows rise in surprise. They both jerked their chins towards the bonfire and I twisted my head to see what they was looking at.

Racing down the path, behind the bonfire, in complete silence, were the four dogs—Dufus, Dorky, Genius and HighQ! Their ears were flattened back, their lips drawn back in silent snarls—they were in hunting pack mode! And they had chosen their prey!

When an angry, full-grown, 60 kg German Shepherd hurls

itself on you, you don't stand much of a chance. Dorky took down the chauffeur. The man was virtually flung off his feet and gave a startled yell, the flaming brand went flying and landed beyond the petrol soaked zone. Dufus took down the bodyguard and Genius and HighQ shared the lackey between them who fell spread-eagled on his chin smothering the firecrackers he had pulled out of his bag. The men had had their backs to the dogs and had been taken totally by surprise. There were yells and then stomach churning growls as the dogs held them by the throat, and shook them like rats. The chauffeur and bodyguards' guns had gone flying when they were hit by the dogs. The AK 47 let off a few rounds into the ground that set alight the petrol soaked leaves and twigs that surrounded us. Blue and gold flames flared up around us. There could still be a conflagration in seconds.

But the villagers were galvanized into action and they had come prepared for fire fighting. Some beat down the flames with sacks and blankets they had brought along while others threw mud over the flames. Anxious fingers cut away our binds and ushered us to safety.

Our plan may have backfired because we hadn't realized quite how dangerous these men were (though Ustadji had warned us), but in the end it had worked out well, thanks to the dogs. Babaji had told the villagers that there was likely to be trouble and they had agreed to hide in the Neem grove and behind the Peepli Princesses, and wait for the men to set fire to the place before catching them in the act and dousing the flames. They hadn't of course expected to have us taken hostage and have an AK 47 being aimed at them.

We called off the dogs and made a huge fuss over them as the villagers surrounded the goons and started beating them up.

'Take them to the house,' I said.

The men, sullen and stony faced—and quite frightened—were frog-marched towards the palace, the villagers beating them around the head as they pushed them. The village women—who had also stayed back—escorted us back. Behind us, the Holika bonfire had been stamped right out.

Tadpole looked back and waved to Ustadji. 'See you tomorrow, Ustadji! Hope you weren't too scared!'

'Thank you,' he said in an emotion-choked voice. 'I'm sorry that fellow used my roots to tie you with. You are very brave kids.' He sounded hugely embarrassed.

'Hey look,' Tadpole said, pointing, 'There are still some flames near that prop-root!' Even as she said it, Dorky ran over and raised his leg over the spot. With a hiss, the flames died down.

'Thank you,' Ustadji said, as Dorky wagged his big tail and looked pleased.

Tadpole took my hand. 'Bhaiyya, how did the dogs know we were in trouble?' she asked, petting Dufus who was trotting at her side. I shrugged.

'I guess we'll never know, Tads, but thank God they came when they did!'

'Yes,' she said thoughtfully, 'but we need to find out!'

'That's another mystery for you to solve,' Zafia said, tousling Tadpole's head. 'Whew, I've never been so terrified in my life!'

There was commotion inside the palace too. The other lackeys of the Rabbani brothers had been dragged in by more villagers as well as Babaji and Mataji. They too had been caught with petrol cans in their hands, trying to set fire to the forest behind the palace. As Mom and Dad and the Periwinkle aunties watched with open mouths, the men were lined up in a row, and their hands and legs were tied. The Rabbani brothers looked shell-shocked.

'What...what's going on here?' Petunia Aunty stuttered weakly.

'Aunty, these men were ordered to set fire to the sacred grove and the forest—and even the palace, so they could buy it cheaply,' Tadpole said. 'We knew, and they...they tried to set us on fire too!' She pointed to the Rabbani brothers. 'They gave the orders.'

The Rabbani brothers exchanged glances.

'M...madam, that's nonsense!' Siva huffed, trying to sound offended.

But the chauffeur, bodyguard and lackeys were not about to be betrayed like this. 'It's the truth,' they admitted quietly. 'They gave the orders to burn everything down and to make sure that there were to be no witnesses.'

'I think,' Dad said, taking out his phone, 'we should call the police.' He glared at Visnu. 'And the SHO is a very good friend of mine!'

Petunia and Poppy aunties stepped forward, their faces pink with anger.

'You tried to set fire to the sacred grove? You monsters!' Both of them raised their hands.

The sound of four slaps ricocheted about like pistol-shots. 'Get out of Medley Gardens,' they snapped. 'And don't ever show your faces here again. This place is not for sale!'

'Memsahib, they also tried to kill the children,' one of the village women who had kissed Tadpole went on. 'They tied them to the tree and were going to burn them alive! And they were going to shoot us all.'

'Are you all okay?' Mom asked, rushing up and hugging us.

'Yes Mom, we're good!' Tadpole said, 'Though it was pretty scary!'

'But...but what has been going on?' Poppy Aunty asked, bewildered.

'Aunty, we heard these men plot to set fire to the whole place,' Tadpole said nodding her head. 'Remember that day when you showed them around in the sacred grove? We were there too—up in the mango trees, and we heard them. They wanted to burn everything down so they could buy it cheaply from you and then build whatever they wanted to. That's why they wanted to play Holi here, and come here for the bonfire.'

'Oh my God! But how...' Petunia Aunty looked at the villagers questioningly.

'Aunty,' Zafia explained, 'we told Babaji what was going to happen and he got the villagers organized. We knew the only way to stop the men was to catch them red-handed. So the villagers went up and hid in and behind the trees after the bonfire party was over and waited. We did too. Then these fellows came along with their petrol cans...and we caught them.'

'Only they caught us before and were going to set fire to us,' Tadpole added.

The Rabbani brothers suddenly tried to make a break for it, but they were stupid. One: they didn't have the keys to the Mercedes, and two, the villagers were on them in a flash.

'Do you know who we are?' Visnu sputtered. 'Let us go this instant or you will be in very big trouble.' He took out his phone which one of the village youths snatched away, grinning.

'You're going nowhere except to jail,' Dad snapped. 'And nobody cares who you are. You tried to kill children.'

The cops finally arrived and we spent half the night explaining to them what had happened. The Rabbani brothers it turned out, had quite a dubious reputation (which the Periwinkle aunties had been unaware of) as so called 'developers'. We took the cops to the sacred grove, where the embers of the Holi fire still glowed. The petrol cans were still where they had been dropped, as were the men's guns, (nicely smeared with their fingerprints) and the sections of roots with which the men had bound us. And then there was the video evidence in our phones.

The Rabbani brothers and their gang were taken away.

We got back home at around two in the morning, tired but too excited to sleep.

Amma was all agog when she had heard what had happened.

'Amma, did you let the dogs out?' Tadpole asked her, determined as usual to get to the bottom of the mystery. 'You were the only one home with them.'

Amma nodded. 'They were all sleeping quietly on the terrace outside your bedroom, when suddenly they all got up at the same time and rushed down to the front door and began barking. So I let them out, thinking they wanted to relieve themselves, but they just ran off at top speed into the darkness, before I could do or say anything.'

'You know,' Zafia said slowly, 'I wouldn't be surprised if the trees of Medley Gardens warned them that we were in danger...'

'How?' Tadpole asked.

'We'll ask Ustadji tomorrow,' Zafia said. 'He might have sent some sort of message or SMS...'

'Really, I don't think you children should go next door anymore if this is the kind of danger you're going to get into,' Mom said next day.

'Mom! We only got into danger because of those men,' Tadpole said. 'The trees in Medley Gardens are our friends.'

'I'm sure they are. But we have to make sure nothing like this ever happens again!'

'How?' Tadpole asked. 'Now someone else will buy Medley Gardens and the same thing can happen all over again.'

I exchanged glances with Zafia. Even I hadn't thought of that. We'd won the battle but could still lose the war.

'Yes,' Mom said thoughtfully, 'that could happen, darling.'

But at least for the time being the trees of Medley Gardens were safe.

18

*I*n spite of our very late night, we were up early next morning, and rushed off to Medley Gardens to play Holi. Clouds of colour flew around, we doused each other with purple, green, silver, blue and red colours, smeared gulal all over Babaji and Mataji as well as the Periwinkle aunties and Mom and Dad. The villagers who had helped us the previous night also turned up to play.

Grinning like monkeys we set off for the sacred grove and approached Ustadji, with colours in our hands.

'No, no, you musn't!' he protested weakly as the Peepli Princesses giggled. Of course we scattered colour over his prop-roots and then went for the Princesses and Neems.

'I hope these colours are organic!' the Neems squealed. 'Otherwise our allergies will act up!'

I had a question I needed to ask. I went up to Ustadji.

'Ustadji, last night did you send some sort of alert to the dogs? Amma told us they'd been sleeping and suddenly jumped up and raced off.' I recalled how his massive frame had trembled when the goons were about to set fire to us.

'Not only me, beta. Every tree, every bush, every flowering plant, every leaf in the sacred grove and the forest—and that includes the Julies and Oleanders sent frantic SOS pheromonic SMS messages when you were in trouble. You won't believe the concentration of Mayday pheromones in the air last night! Of course the dogs picked them up and came hotfoot.'

'Thank you,' I said, 'I really thought we were done for!'

'You think we'd allow that to happen to you?'

We approached His Royal Highness Kapok Maharaj and were brought up short. Every branch was covered with huge red goblet like flowers from which a host of birds, squirrels, insects and god knows what else—were eating and drinking deeply and raucously. Kapok Maharajji's Grand Open House Party was in full swing. Mithoorani and her friends were shrieking at the top of their voices as was Gingianus and his gang. There were others too—flocks of bulbuls, babblers, crows, and little trilling yellow birds which we learnt were white-eyes. There was also a rather glamorous golden oriole couple and of course barbets and coppersmiths and drongoes.

Bees and wasps and hoverflies hummed and buzzed excitedly over the huge blooms, too drunk to realize that several of their kind were being snacked on by the partying birds. They were all stuffing their faces as fast as they could. Squirrels scooted from branch to branch, flicking their tails in a frenzy of excitement—and then of course the local gang of monkeys turned up. Heavy blooms thwacked down on the ground, they were so heavy they could hurt if they landed on your head.

'Welcome, children!' Kapok Maharajji greeted us in his rich baritone. 'Help yourselves! Every bloom contains 5 to 10 ml of the finest elixir, distilled with the utmost care and using techniques going back thousands of years!'

Gingianus and Mithoorani flew down somewhat erratically and perched on Tadpole's shoulders.

'Shuch a great rave, darling!' Mithoorani drawled and nearly fell off. 'Oopsh I think I'm a little shloshed!'

'Fabulous party!' Gingianus added, his crest rising and

subsiding excitedly. 'Just fabulous!'

Flocks of partying birds kept flying in and out. Suddenly a huge flock of pink and black myna like birds zoomed in, flying in tight formation.

'The rosy starlings have arrived!' Gingianus said, cocking his head.

'They're horrible! They want everything to themselves.'

'Ginganus they look a bit like you,' Tadpole remarked critically. 'Do you know them?'

'Yo Chicklet, I can't be responsible for all my relatives,' Gingianus said, raising his crest. 'They're cousins. Distant cousins. Very distant...'

The rosy starlings had started brawls with the other birds, and were driving them away. They chittered and chattered incessantly and belligerently and then began fighting amongst themselves. Suddenly the whole flock just took off together and whizzed across the sky like a skein of smoke being blown around.

'See you, kids! I have to be at the party at Teen Murti House in twenty minutes and then a reception at the President's Estate,' Mithoorani rolled her eyes.

'We heard what happened last night,' Kapok Maharajji suddenly said to us. 'And we would like to thank you. I got very worried when I saw the bonfire. You kids put your lives on the line for us—you were in the direct line of fire! We owe you big time.'

At last, tired and looking like complete baboons we returned home to bathe and change. Mom and Dad had invited the Periwinkle aunties over for Holi lunch and were busy in the kitchen, cooking.

At lunch, Tadpole tackled the Periwinkle aunties in her usual head-butt way.

'You know Aunty, I think you should declare Medley Gardens a Tree Sanctuary,' she said seriously. 'Then no one can harm the trees.'

Petunia Aunty smiled at her. 'That's a very good idea dear, but I don't know if we can actually do that.'

'Well part of it is a sacred grove,' Poppy Aunty reminded her sister.

'Aunties, please don't sell Medley Gardens. It's a special place—like the Taj Mahal. You can't sell such a place!' Tadpole pleaded.

'Tadpole, dear!' Mom said, 'I'm sure aunties will do what is best for them and Medley Gardens.'

'Come on Tads, let's go,' Zafia said, taking Tadpole's hand and getting up.

We spent the afternoon messing around in the sacred grove, not really enjoying ourselves though. Kapok Maharaji's Open House would go on for a couple of weeks now as more and more blooms blossomed every day. The Peepli Princesses too had begun putting out new leaves, which at first were a beautiful burnished coppery-bronze colour before they turned green. But what did it matter, if in the end all of it could be destroyed?

'Can you imagine what it must be like when they destroy an entire rainforest?' Zafia said softly. 'Thousands of giant trees, hundreds of years old—and everything that lives on them—killed. The earth itself destroyed forever…'

'Like committing mass murder.'

We looked at each other. We knew for a fact that gold and diamonds and gems lay buried beneath the sacred grove. If that knowledge ever got out it would be curtains, no questions asked. Only the three of us—and Babaji—and the trees of Medley Gardens knew about it. It would have to remain that way.

At around four that afternoon Mom rang me and said we should come back home. To our surprise, we found the Periwinkle aunties still there. They had spent the whole afternoon chatting with Mom and Dad.

'Sit down kids, and listen,' Dad said as the Periwinkle aunties smiled at us.

'We have something to tell you,' Poppy Aunty said. She looked at her sister. 'Since the events of last night we have been thinking.' She turned to Mom. 'Maybe you should fill them in, my dear.'

Mom nodded. 'Okay kids, it's like this. The aunties have decided not to sell Medley Gardens for the time being. Your Papa and I have agreed to look after the property and we'll be running it as a retreat for artists, writers, poets, playwrights and potters. Hopefully we'll be able to keep up its maintenance with the money we receive.' Mom smiled and added, 'Or we'll just have to take it from your pocket money! This way your precious trees are safe and you all can stop sulking!'

'You're not going to sell it?' Tadpole whispered, her eyes opening wide. 'Thank you, thank you, thank you!' She rushed up to the Periwinkles and hugged them and then hugged Mom and Dad.

'We know the trees make you so happy,' Petunia Aunty said. 'So how could we take that away from you?'

And we knew what lay beneath those trees. It was a very precious secret but one we would keep forever. As Naniji had told us, there are some things far more valuable than gold and silver and diamonds and pearls and precious stones. And they would have to be protected forever.

Acknouledgement

Huge thanks to Sudeshna for giving the manuscript a jolly good shakedown and getting rid of a whole lot of deadwood!

www.ingramcontent.com/pod-product-compliance
Lightning Source LLC
Chambersburg PA
CBHW061519020726
47502CB00006B/2149